Prey for the Wolf

An Olivia Darrow Mystery, Book 6

S.L. Waters

Published by AB Books, 2022

Table of Contents

One

Things have been pretty quiet for the last two weeks. When I implemented Sam West's spyware into the CSB's, Civic Security Bureau's, home office databases, I expected immediate fallout, but nothing so far. Hayden Mitchell, the lead technician for forensics, and Asher Lewis, assistant to daytime coroner, Tress Conner, have been keeping an eye on the software's activity using an old gaming console that Asher reconfigured for this specific job. For the moment, all they've found is the manipulated program sitting there, waiting for some specific keystroke, word, or phrase to be inputted before setting sail around the entire network, grabbing whatever Sam's after without being noticed.

His hitman, Jake Stewart, has been summoned elsewhere, so my temporary babysitter is not currently available. I'm grateful for the neglect because I hate being treated like someone who can't take care of herself, no matter the rightful concern behind it. Sam believes I might be a target in the striker killings, which is why he's had Jake keep an eye on me wherever I go. In his absence, I always have my CSB service weapon with me. I'm convinced the bomb that was rigged to detonate in one of the conference rooms at the home office in Whitebridge was meant for me, But Internal Affairs hasn't been able to determine who placed it and why. Or even how the security systems in the main building were temporarily disengaged, knocking out the locks to the room, allowing anyone to waltz in. Let alone get through the main gate, which isn't heavily guarded on the weekends.

In my opinion, it has everything to do with the Red Rover Case I was a part of. There were three of us trying to determine who was responsible for a string of murders using illegal, armor-piercing rounds called strikers. One of the victims, Luke Cobb, was killed by Jake, but I'm the only person who knows that, and I'm not disclosing it to anyone since the bastard deserved it. We were able to link a smattering of victims together—including my deceased boss—as well as two shell companies, one possibly laundering money for the Vilks Cartel, drug runners out of the country Navital. There was a fourth in our group. However, he disappeared shortly after his car was found burning along the side of the road and a bullet with his blood pulled from a nearby tree. At first, I was optimistic that Matt Walker (Weber when he's on assignment) would be found, but it's been weeks now without any sign.

I'm slowly losing hope.

The detonation at the home office killed my colleague, Parker Haynes, along with three other detectives. While conducting our investigation, we were kept to the Delta conference room on the third floor of the main building, and I was always the first one in every morning. Except that day I overslept, and Parker was the one who opened the door, triggering the explosion. The other person in our group, Candace King, is still coping with his death since the two were somewhat of an item away from the office. I check in with her occasionally, but her drinking has worsened, and Director Cruz is threatening to place her on leave if she doesn't get help. I've managed to curtail my alcoholic vice for the time being, but it could rear its ugly head at any moment if given the appropriate stressor.

Right now, I'm heading into my second job as a bartender for the strip club Verdigris in Nok Sector, the entertainment district for the state where nearly everything is legal, including prostitution, drug and smoke dens, and anything X-rated. Of course, it's also home to every hotel, theater, casino, and recreational venue for families and singles. Each sector has a CSB station dedicated to patrolling the streets, except in Nok. Drones are used since the roads can become too crowded during certain nights, preventing vehicles from getting through during non-emergencies.

The primary car I drive is called a Nimbus. The body is black with lighted, blue neon cords accentuating every curve. It's streamlined to where the front of the vehicle comes almost to a point while the rear sits a little higher. The tires are thick, heavy rubber that grip the road with ease. The interior is a soft, dark material with small, blue and silver flecks. And the doors swing up not out. It's February, so I'm not able to ride my motorcycle called a Rune, which is my preferred mode of transportation. The other vehicle I own is a

Halo, a very expensive electric car that Sam gave me the morning my boss was gunned down. It has trackers stashed somewhere on the undercarriage or axels, so I don't drive it unless I want Sam to know where I'm going.

I take the highway around the outer ridge of the sectors that make up the state of Asmor, exiting onto Chestnut, then after a few blocks turn right, followed by a quick left, and proceed down the alley where I park behind the club. It doesn't open until ten p.m., but I like to get here early and prepare for the onslaught. Being a Thursday, we shouldn't be too crowded. After shutting off the engine, I grab my purse and work bag off the passenger seat, lock the car, and using a code to gain access, I enter through the back door. The hallway lights are ablaze, though they're not bright, and when I reach the end I veer left, heading for the changing room where everyone gets dressed and stores their personal items into designated lockers.

A few of the girls are already undressing when I enter, their uniforms hanging off the corner of the locker openings. What you do in the club determines the lovely outfit our boss, Joe Ambrose, has you wear. If you're a bartender, attendant, or waitress, you don a mini dress made of fishnet with the sides cut out from just under the armpits to the tops of the thighs, thin leather bands crisscrossing over the exposed skin. A thong is the only undergarment since nothing else is to adorn the outfit, so your tits are in full view of the world. The colors range from black, to white, to blue, in that order. The lap dancers and escorts have it far worse. Theirs is a leather bikini with mesh cups for the bra, thin, leather straps holding the top around the neck and connecting it to the bottom, which is simply a thong with snaps. Color options are green and red. The strippers wear whatever the hell they want since they're not in their clothes for very long.

After opening the locker, I shove my things inside, undress, and don the garish outfit. The only thing I leave on is a teardrop pendant Matt gave me right before New Year's. It was removed once, but that was by someone else. We had decided to become a couple those final days of a very tumultuous year, then he vanished. Sam completely denies having a hand in it, to which I genuinely believe him, considering Matt was working for the billionaire businessman like I was, and still am … I think.

Before leaving the dressing room, I run my fingers through my shoulder-length, dark blonde hair with its maroon and light blonde highlights, then add a bit more deodorant. The heels I have on enhance my five foot eight height by a few inches. I try to maintain my athletic build by spending time at the pool and fitness center at CSB headquarters in Hunnat Sector, which is in the center of the state. When I reach the floor, the main lights for the club are currently on while everyone prepares for the evening, so they accentuate every flaw and blemish in the building, which Joe will need to fix someday soon. Once the doors open, those go off as neon and twinkle lights take over. The bar sits in the middle of the floor between the DJ booth and the tables just outside of the pods where the escorts perform their tricks. The stripper poles are on the stage to the other side of the DJ, with their own sets of tables and darkened booths.

"Hey, Liv," Alice says, joining me while I take stock of what we need. She's a little shorter than I am, is super skinny, and has bright red hair. Even though she's in her mid-twenties, she's dating Hayden, who's in his forties. The pair are odd in their own right and complement each other tremendously. "How's Matt?"

I haven't told her what happened, so I lie. "He's good. Busy working."

I grab one of the bouncers, and he follows me into the storage room where we gather the items needed. Then Alice fills the coolers while I make the premixes, dumping the cold concoctions into the machines.

"I wish Nikki hadn't left so abruptly," she comments from her spot on the floor. "The party was all set and she just up and quits, even though she had already given notice."

Nikki Burris was one of the escorts here at the club, and a friend. We spent New Year's Eve together down at the private island of rapper, Dallas. A few weeks later she announced she was moving since she'd been offered a new job. Alice was planning to throw her a going away party, but Nikki called Joe and left before her schedule ended. He's been scrambling to replace her ever since.

"She was offered a lot of money to go work at Pure Bliss in Prescott when it opens. I don't blame her for getting out early."

"I suppose," Alice replies, disappointment etched on her face.

As we're finishing, Joe enters with his best friend, Henry, attached to his arm. I'm not sure how the two know each other, but it's been for decades. My boss is a man in his sixties with a firm body and graying, sandy hair. Henry is at least ten years older with soft features and white hair. They're both roughly the same height, six feet two inches. Joe makes sure Henry, who's a widower, is here as often as possible so he's not left alone, doddering around his desolate apartment. All the girls view him as a grandfather-like figure, and he's one of the nicest men you'll ever meet.

"My lovelies," he says, sitting on his reserved stool at the bar by the partition. He gives Alice a peck on the cheek as she sets down his club soda, and one to me when I wander by.

"How are you doing, Henry?" I inquire, wiping the countertop.

"Ah, about the same … depressed."

"Which is why you're here," Joe chides. "Now, behave yourself."

"Never." Henry laughs as my boss walks away.

At the stroke of ten, the lights switch and the music starts. It takes a good hour for the club to be at half-capacity, which doesn't bode well for a Thursday night. Typically, men and the occasional woman start their weekends early. There's just something about February that keeps them home. It can't be the weather since we don't get snow, with the exception of an occasional flake or two, or the deep freezes that effect those north of us. This month is a constant disappointment.

Out of sheer boredom, I lean back against the counter and watch the women perform on stage. I'm always jealous of their muscle control when hanging upside down with only their calves to keep them from sliding and hitting the floor. Their cores alone have to be tight. Of course, a few use drugs to get them through the routines, and even maintain their thin figures. That's not uncommon in this industry.

Turning around, I startle at the man sitting behind me. "Shit, Sam, don't scare me like that," I reprimand, my hand plastered against my rapidly beating heart.

He laughs. The smile that creases his face makes his chestnut-hued eyes sparkle. He's in his late thirties, stands at six foot four, has a firm body, champagne-colored hair, and the profile of a wolf tattooed on his right bicep. He's charming, charismatic, and women fawn over him like he's a meal. For now, though, he claims to want me permanently in his life, but the feeling isn't exactly mutual.

"Why are you here?"

"I have a meeting tomorrow morning with a land developer about some properties for sale," he replies, still grinning. "Seeing as the hotel I'm staying in is just across the street, I thought I'd stop by for a drink and see if you were working."

"What do you want?"

"Anything on tap."

After selecting a pilsner glass, I turn and fill it, then place the drink in front of him, but don't add it to the pay screen assigned to his seat.

"Somehow I never imagined you wearing an outfit like that." He gestures to the garment, his hand stroking the air as if he owns it. There's a subtle hint of disapproval in his voice.

"I have been for the last eight years, ever since I was twenty and started working here. How else can I buy the toys I like to have? CSB doesn't pay enough for me to own the Nimbus, let alone a Rune on top of that."

He furrows his brow. "You didn't purchase those after moving to Waterside?"

I shake my head, then rest my arms on the bar top and lean forward. "This girl has expensive taste when it comes to certain things."

"At least food and flowers aren't one of them," he teases.

"Thanks for the weekly carnation delivery, but my house is starting to smell like a funeral parlor. Why are you sending them anyway?"

"So you know I'm thinking about you. When do you get off?"

"We close at two, but normally we don't leave until nearly three with all the cleanup and receipts that have to be handled."

He frowns. "I need to be up early. Are you free tomorrow night?"

I straighten up, collect a tray filled with dirty glasses, and start washing them in the sink. "One of the homicide detectives is retiring and his party is tomorrow, but it should be over by ten or so."

As he lifts his glass, I notice that neither of the backs of his hands are stamped with the traditional 'x', the color of which indicates what sort of entertainment you've purchased. I'm about to comment when Joe comes over, requesting an introduction.

"What brings you to Nok?" my boss inquires, sitting beside Sam.

"I want to expand my casino and thought this would be a good place to start." He stares at me. "The sector comes highly recommended." Then he winks.

Not once have I ever seen Joe become flustered with excitement, except tonight. "I'd be happy to assist with any questions."

Sam moves his attention fully to the older man, since it was mainly focused on me. "My dinner date is standing me up tomorrow evening. Would you care to meet at my hotel, say around six? I'm staying at The Concordia."

"That would be wonderful." The pair shake hands, and Joe nearly prances away.

"People just fawn all over you wherever you go, don't they?" I quip, wiping my wet hands on a dish towel.

"Not all of them. There is one person who's awfully hard to get. Maybe you can help me with that."

I roll my eyes, which causes him to laugh.

Finishing his beer, he reaches into his pocket, removes a solid gold money clip, and extracts twenty dollars, setting it on the bar. "Let me know what time you'll be over so I can inform the front desk. Oh, and maybe bring the outfit."

I go to swat him with the towel, but he moves out of reach and scampers to the exit without collecting his change. Ringing up his drink, I pay the tab with the money he left and put the rest in the tip jar for Alice and I to split later.

"Who was that?" she asks, having kept her distance during the entire exchange.

"Just a friend."

She blushes. "Right, Olivia. Friend. Man, you're going to have to start beating them away with a stick if any more try to get into your pants."

Ignoring her, I go back to filling drinks and washing glasses. At the end of the night, there really isn't much cleanup left to do, so Alice and I take the cash and receipts to Joe's office, change, and head home. I pull into the garage a few minutes before three, make sure the alarm is set, brush my teeth, then strip and get into bed.

Much of the following day proceeds like normal with reviewing outstanding case notes and tracking down leads on a death that I was assigned last week. For the moment it still reads as a suicide, but every avenue must be pursued before stamping it officially. After lunch, the five of us meet in the conference room for the homicide department. Our boss, Supervisory Detective Frank Corro, leading the way by making sure Gabe Foster, who's retiring today, doles out his open cases appropriately. Thankfully, there aren't a lot. The bulk are assigned to his replacement, Ben Walsh, who's in his mid-thirties, my height with tight muscles, hazel eyes, an oval face, a small nose, and short, brown hair. His physique is made more prominent by the form-fitting clothes he insists on wearing, leaving nothing to the imagination. I swear there's a one-eyed snake coiling down his pants leg.

"Liv, you're getting back the Leslie Marsh investigation," Frank says, handing me the skimpy file.

I've known the man since I was a child. He was assigned my mother's murder case. He's six foot, stout with short, graying, auburn hair, and a ruddy complexion. Also, he's nearing sixty and is currently dating a pleasant woman by the name of Jane Crawford, mother to my deceased half-sister. They're surrogate parents to me, while I play daughter to them. Today, he's dressed in his traditional blue suit with a gray checkered tie. He wears them so much I think it makes up a good portion of his wardrobe.

The case he's referring to is a homicide from last year. When it was given to me, I wasn't aware of my father's connection to the dead woman, finding out during her autopsy that she was carrying his child. He was the prime suspect, but had an alibi. The only person he ever confessed to killing was my mother, right before he put a bullet in his brain. It's obvious nothing further has been done with the investigation after it was handed to Gabe, leaving plenty of work for me to do. However, it's going to be much harder to find leads and gather information with so much time having lapsed. I might as well pass it along to the cold case squad and let them have a crack at it.

"The party for Gabe will start around five. Food is being catered from Slingers, and a huge sheet cake was also ordered. Unfortunately, drinking isn't permitted to those still on duty, but there will be provisions for those who aren't," Frank announces from the doorway. "Take this time to review his notes and bombard him with questions while you still can." He nods to the overweight man sitting in the back corner, whose greasy, brown hair clings to the top of his head and the patchy facial pubes on his face could use a good shave.

My workstation is next to Gabe's, but Ben has chosen an empty desk toward the entrance where our waiting area is, hopefully allowing me to spread out. There are only four full-time homicide detectives—including my boss—though our section of the sixth floor can hold three times that. Frank is very picky about who he allows in his ranks, so if you make the cut, it's because he trusts you implicitly … and you work hard at your job. I'm not saying the other detectives don't, but their case loads are a lot heavier, so more are needed.

Stephen Jeffries slides his chair next to mine since two of his cases—one from Gabe and the other he was assigned to originally—mirror Leslie's, causing Frank to believe we might have a serial killer on our hands, but that hasn't been verified. Just a few years older than me, Stephen has sandy-colored hair, soft features, and a ruddy complexion like Frank, only not as severe. We compare notes, evidence that was collected, and photos taken at the scenes where the bodies were discovered. With both of our CSB issued tablets propped on the table, we jot down additional items to check, including how the perpetrator has been able to knock out the entire Hub system in the state for several hours, which shouldn't even be possible.

In our country, when you turn thirteen each person has a microchip implanted just under the skin on their right wrist. It houses names, residential addresses, age, and work locations. A full history of the owner from the time the small cylinder is tucked under the epidermis until it's removed, usually after death. The Hub is responsible for maintaining and tracking the citizens, each state with their own offices.

For the cases Stephen and I have, the monitoring system was rendered useless from the time our victims went missing, up until an hour before their bodies were discovered. The three women—Eve Barrett, Dawn Nielsen, and Leslie Marsh—were found naked with their throats slit from ear to ear, completely drained of blood, ligature marks around both wrists and ankles, and their bodies oddly posed. Nothing else has been found near or on the bodies to give any hint as to who the killer might be. Checking for similarities with age, where the women worked, where they lived, who they dated, and what they did behind closed doors, there aren't any. Not even in looks. If there's a pattern, Stephen and I can't find it.

Just before five we pack up, store the files in our desk drawers, and head up to the ninth floor where the breakrooms are located. The elevator core with its four lifts rises out of the center of the tile-covered floor, depositing us around groupings of tables and chairs that are smartly decorated in grays and blues, CSB colors. Streamers, balloons, and banners cover nearly every square inch of the vast room, adding to its otherwise bland décor ... even expanding into the corner where the vending machines are kept. A long, plump sheet cake topped with yellow buttercream frosting sits on a table of its very own, small packages and cards littered around it. Large, plasma screens are adhered to the walls displaying a hockey game being played out of state, but the sound has been muted so as not to interfere with conversations.

I can smell the food, the tantalizing aroma of beef wafting through the open doorways leading into the various food stations where we can purchase our meals during normal business hours. It's not being served yet, so the four of us venture over to the table with the drinks, pouring ourselves glasses of spiked punch into tiny, plastic party cups, the word 'Retirement' stenciled just under the rim. There are only a handful of additional partygoers, but more will arrive, especially with the premise of free food and booze. The man of the hour begins wandering around the room while Stephen, Ben, and I sit at one of the far tables.

A few minutes later, Tress and Hayden wander in, making a beeline for our area. Tress is always smartly dressed, even when she's dissecting people. She's in her mid-forties, has dark skin, a pleasant smile, and short, black hair. She must have just gotten off shift since the scent of death lingers on her clothes, contradicting her purple, chenille blouse and dark, tweed slacks. Hayden isn't as well put together. I think the only time I've ever seen his unruly, brown hair combed has been for court. He's tall and his clothes always appear disheveled no matter what he's wearing, which today consists of jeans and a plain gray T-shirt.

"I so need this," Tress says, chugging the punch after pouring herself a cup.

"Hard day?" I ask, sipping at mine.

She snarls. "My boss is an arrogant prick."

I nearly spit out the liquid but catch it before splashing the table. Not once has she ever spoken ill of her supervisor, so the outburst shocks me. "What did Lloyd do now?"

"Fucker has an ego the size of the Standene Ocean, and it's only gotten worse now that he's dating some model. Always has to show off, even when she's not there to kowtow at his feet. I'm seriously thinking of quitting."

"Dear God, don't," I utter, seizing her arm. "If you go, Taylor won't be too far behind, leaving Asher and those poor interns defenseless."

Taylor Strum is Lloyd Rhemick's assistant during his night shifts at the coroner's office. She's the only other female, besides Tress, who can tolerate the bastard. It wasn't long ago he and I were an item, but that quickly fizzled, which I'm grateful for given some odd behavior on his part the last several months. Such as breaking into my house and dousing it with roses while I was away, even after he told me our relationship was over. He went ballistic upon learning I had moved on. Slammed my front door so hard it shattered the pane of glass inlayed into the wood. Now, we're barely on speaking terms.

"The academy has an opening for an instructor in their medical examiner program. I'm thinking of applying for it," she continues, finishing her drink. "More pay, better hours, and no Lloyd."

"I can't stop you, but it's going to be hard for them to hire a replacement."

"Maybe Lloyd can use little miss perfect. Apparently, she's in her final year of medical school." Tress nods toward a group I hadn't seen enter.

Following her gaze, I first stare at my former lover in his freshly pressed, pale blue linen dress shirt, black slacks, and polished loafers. Tonight, he's wearing contact lenses, but he bounces between them and glasses depending upon his mood. He's in his early forties, tall, with short, black hair, chiseled features, and growing biceps, which is something he started at the end of last year. The thing wrapped around his arm is somewhere close to my height, maybe around my age or a little younger, with long, straight, blonde hair that cascades down her back without much effort. She has a fit build, a pear-shaped face, and delicate nose. She's also nothing but legs, according to the short hem of her cream-colored sheath dress with its short sleeves. Gold bangles cling to her porcelain skin, and her sharp blue eyes sparkle with each smile and laugh.

"What's her name?" I ask, after refilling our tiny cups.

"Clarissa Reed. She comes from money like he does. I guess their families used to go way back, but after Lloyd's parents died, they lost touch. When she decided to attend medical school, her father refused to pay for it, so she went into modeling to cover the costs. A career more suited to her talents, in my opinion."

Leaning back in the plastic form chair, I examine what I'm wearing and feel extremely inferior, causing me to wonder why Lloyd took the time to start anything with me in the first place if that was always in the background. Being a Friday, I decided to wear jeans, sneakers, and a thin, red, wool sweater. My hair is now long enough that I can pull it back into a small ponytail, which it is currently in. The only jewelry I wear is the silver teardrop pendant on a matching chain. Glancing at Clarissa, I notice her fingernails are professionally manicured in a deep azure, where mine are too short to polish.

I nudge Tress in the side. "Let's eat."

The five of us get in line, Stephen introducing Ben to Tress since the pair have never met before while Hayden and I chat quietly. As they're making small talk, I sense a hostile gaze boring into the back of my head. Turning, I spot Lloyd scowling, daggers jutting out of his irises in my direction. Clarissa is too busy talking with Chief Daven to notice. I roll my eyes as he squeezes her waist, then plants a kiss on her lips while she's in the middle of a sentence. I return to my conversation, pretending I didn't notice. After filling my plate with salad and an Italian beef sandwich, I return to the table and try to block him out. I'm nearly successful until the pair decide to join us without being invited.

Lloyd introduces his darling to everyone, leaving me last. "How's the boyfriend?" he asks, disdain dripping from his lips like poison.

"Missing, in case you hadn't heard. Thanks for asking."

"What?" Clarissa utters, appearing genuinely shocked. Her voice is soft and warm, but firm. "That's horrible."

"Knowing Liv, she's already moved on from the loss."

Stephen places a firm hand on my arm—a move he must have learned from Frank—preventing me from hitting the asshole.

"At least I have a grieving period, Lloyd. Unlike you. How long after I told you to get lost did you start dating that one?" I point a finger at Clarissa. "A day? Maybe less?"

His face reddens, then he snatches his girlfriend's wrist, stands, and drags her away.

Tress places a hand on my back. "Is he really missing, Liv?"

I nod. "It's been almost a month since his car was found burning on the side of Interstate 47. There aren't any leads, at least that I know of. Frank, the chief, and Director Cruz are handling the case. No one will tell me anything."

"I'm sorry, honey." Tress pulls me into a side hug, then we return to eating.

Going back for seconds, I try to not overeat, but I need something to offset the alcohol-filled punch, considering I still have to drive to Sam's hotel. Gradually, the others go mingle while I continue to sit, enjoying the solitude, which is again interrupted by Lloyd, but he's alone this time. Clarissa nowhere in sight.

"Is it past the princess' bedtime?" I chide as he sits.

"Hey, I came over to offer an apology. Frank told me what happened."

"He didn't need to do that," I grumble, crossing my arms over my chest.

"I know. The man is simply worried about you, like I am."

Cocking my head to the side, I say, "Don't do that. You don't need to pretend to care or even be my friend."

"Fuck, Liv, I'm not pretending." Running his fingers through his hair, he lets out a deep sigh. "I miss you. I miss us."

I don't respond.

"Are you driving a new car? I thought I saw one pulling out of your driveway earlier."

"Yes. A friend of mine gave it to me."

He raises his eyebrows. "Halos are expensive. Who is he?"

"No one you know." Which is a lie.

Everyone in the world of the wealthy knows who Sam West is, but I don't advertise our relationship. Particularly when all of his dealings aren't necessarily legal ones.

I'd like to remain alive.

"Is it serious?" Lloyd asks, pushing the subject.

"I really don't want to talk about it. Especially with you."

The corner of his mouth curls and he appears to be stuck between wanting to be mad and sympathetic. "I should get back to work."

"Don't forget to bring Taylor food," I say as he stands. "I'm sure she's starving."

Grumbling under his breath, he leaves after a trip to the food stations. I check the time on the wall clock, noticing it's getting close to nine. After cleaning up my plate and cup, I join Frank and his group, trying to distance myself from the unsettling feeling Lloyd left me with. Shortly, the cake is cut and doled out. The majority of people head home right after they've stuffed themselves with sugar. I linger a few more minutes, then finally head down to my workstation, making sure to use the bathroom first. Removing my purse from the bottom desk drawer, I retrieve the phone Sam gave me in January and send a text letting him know I'm leaving and should arrive at the hotel in about a half hour. As I'm slipping my holstered 9mm and badge into the bag, he replies for me to use the valet service when I arrive.

After donning my gray, quilted parka, I take the elevator to the lobby, then exit the building and hurry across the street to the parking garage, trying to dodge the bitter cold wind as it kicks up between the two structures. I finally had the license plate for the Halo registered with security so I can access the employee side of the garage. After the arm at the bottom of the ramp rises, I turn right onto Lange and take it all the way into Nok Sector. It dead ends at Chestnut where I go left, the hotel on my right a few blocks later. The Concordia isn't as elegant as the resort Sam owns in Prescott in the state of Aberdeen, but it's stylish to those who aren't used to the finer things in life.

It's a twenty-story structure constructed from cement, metal, and green-tinted glass. Lights flicker down the sides and around the marquee that stretches over the circle drive. I barely have the car stopped when the valet, in his stunning canary yellow tuxedo, comes to open the door. Grabbing my purse, he hands me a yellow chip with a black number stamped into the plastic, then drives toward the garage. The turnstile doors continue to slowly rotate without prompting, allowing ease of entry into the two-story lobby, its high ceiling covered in dimpled copper plating. The walls are papered in khaki with a Greek key pattern along the edges. The floor is a white marble. Columns reach from floor to ceiling, cutting off segments of the lobby between the reception desk, a café, the elevators, and a vast seating area.

An older man with salt and pepper hair trots over to me wearing a tailored gray suit, a gold name tag pinned to his lapel indicating he's the manager of the fine establishment. "Ms. Darrow," he says, almost out of breath, "this is for you." He hands me a plastic key card. "Mr. West is in suite 2002."

I thank him, then head toward the elevator, pressing the button for the twentieth floor. It rises swiftly, not an ounce of noise coming from the gears overhead. When the doors open, the hallway is identical to the lobby in décor, but on a much smaller scale. Sam's room is right across the way, so I tap the card against the reader and wait for the tiny indicator to change from red to green before trying the handle. Inside is a large sitting room overlooking 22nd Street, affording a view of Verdigris down the way on Chestnut. Like most hotels I've been in, the style for the room matches the rest of the establishment. One way to keep costs down. After the door is closed, I bolt it and go in search of the bedroom, which is off to the left. Another panel of windows covers the one wall, an elongated, ornate dresser sits by the door, a large, plasma screen hangs above it, and a king-sized bed rests against the far wall, Sam sitting on top of its fluffy covers completely dressed, with a rose between his teeth.

"Are you serious?" I chuckle, setting my purse onto a chair by the windows, the heavy drapes wide open. I place my parka on top of the bag and stand at the foot of the bed.

"What?" he asks, smiling as best he can. "Why are you laughing?" He spits out the rose. "That's not as pleasant as it looks." After swinging his legs over the side, he stands and approaches me. "How was the party?"

"Boring, but there isn't much you can do at headquarters to liven things up."

Wrapping his arms around my waist, he lowers his head, his soft lips pressing hard against mine.

"Did you find any properties?" I ask while he coaxes me toward one side of the bed.

"A couple." His hands run under my sweater, stretching up to unhook my bra. "There's one behind the arena that looks promising." As his mouth moves to my neck, I can't help but let out a contented sigh. "Dinner with Joe went well." Sam takes off my top and starts unzipping my pants while I work on removing his clothes. "He speaks very highly of you."

Stepping out of my sneakers, the cell phone in my back pocket starts to chime, but I let it fall to the floor with the rest of my garments. Sam's warm mouth slides down to my chest, a breast slips into it, and he sucks on the nipple until it's hard. His hands cup my bare ass while my fingers tug on his hair. Closing my eyes, I groan softly. We lie down on the bed, my head prominently on the pillow. Our lips devour each other, the heat between us intense, almost combustible. Spreading my legs, I bend my knees and Sam penetrates me. Our rhythm is steady and hot.

"Something tells me you've got a kinky side," he whispers, nibbling my ear. "When do I get to see it?"

"I haven't decided yet," I gasp, arching my back.

A slow rumble of my phone vibrating floats under the currents of the mattress squeaking from our lovemaking. I'm enjoying myself too much to dare answer it.

"Tell me." His lips take to the breast he neglected, suckling as if to draw milk. It's intense and very satisfying. "I want to know what you've done. What I get to look forward to."

"Fuck, Sam," I moan, his thrusting increasing.

My muscles seize him, grasping him in a firm hold while the rest of me trembles from the orgasm. His body shudders, his yelp of satisfaction loud. Resting his head on my sweat-soaked chest, we both work on catching our breath.

He slides onto his side, then places a hand on my stomach, which gradually wanders down between my legs, teasing my overly sensitive clitoris, causing me to come hard, soaking the sheet. "Well, there's one thing," he says, smiling. "You've been holding out on me, Olivia."

"I didn't want to spring it all on you at once," I reply, giggling like a schoolgirl. "Some guys can't handle a strong woman."

Taking my hand, he wraps his fingers through mine. "Marry me."

"Sam—"

He covers my mouth with his, cutting off my protest. "I won't have you sign a prenup."

"I don't care about the money, and I'd want to sign one just to protect you … and me."

He grins. "Is that a yes?"

"I didn't say that."

"But it's not a no."

Taking a deep breath, I let it out slowly. "Let me think it over."

He kisses me fervently, climbs back on top, and we fuck well into the night.

Two

The incessant ringing brings me out of a pleasant slumber, but I momentarily forget where I am due to the darkness of the room while bright lights from outside cast odd shadows across the ceiling. Bending over the side of the bed, I rummage through the pile of clothes, finding my phone, Frank's name scrolling across the top. Checking the time, I notice it's a few minutes after one. I haven't been asleep long, but a call at this hour of the night is never good.

"Hello?" I ask, my voice hoarse.

"We've got a fire in Nok Sector," he practically screams to be heard over the sirens wailing in the background. "Meet me in front of the Requiem. There are casualties." He abruptly hangs up.

As I'm staring at the screen, Sam stirs beside me.

"Who was that?" he mumbles, draping an arm over my waist.

"Frank. I have to go."

Hearing the alarm in my voice, Sam reaches over and flips the switch beside the bed, igniting the lights. "What's wrong?"

"There's a fire down the street," I reply, quickly dressing. "Casualties, but I don't know how many."

"Shit. Call me later so I know you're all right."

I lean over, kiss him hard, then stand after securing my sneakers. At the chair, I remove my weapon and badge, attaching both to the waistband of my jeans. Glancing out the window, since the drapes were never closed, as I'm putting on my outer jacket I notice orange in the distance, but I can't see the smoke because of the night. Dozens of red and white lights flicker off surrounding buildings.

With the valet chip in hand, I head down to the lobby. It takes the young man a few minutes to retrieve the car. I tip him, then lock the purse in the trunk, and get behind the wheel. Turning right onto 22nd Street, I take that down to Highland, hang a left, then a right onto 23rd, which is blocked off by emergency vehicles. Parking in a vacant lot, I shove the keys into my front pocket after locking the car and rush toward the scene, showing my badge to those trying to stop me. When I finally locate Frank across the street from the blazing club, he's busy talking to the fire chief. The heat is so intense it's curling the paint on a few of the closer vehicles. A makeshift morgue has been setup in the middle of the parking lot down the way under an enclosed tent, keeping prying eyes and media from photographing the deceased.

"Olivia, you arrived here fast," my boss comments.

"I was just a few blocks away. What have we got?"

"So far, ten confirmed fatalities, but they're pulling more out every minute. Stephen and Ben are on their way to help with the interviews."

"Where do you want me to start?"

"Grab the first ambulance that isn't hauling a critically injured person." He reaches into the inside pocket of his coat, removing a pad of paper and pencil. "Here, you're going to need this."

I start with the first rig I see, delicately asking questions to those whose lives narrowly came to an end. Many are in shock and unable to articulate what they saw; others are fretting over friends still trapped inside. I do manage to ascertain that the fire started maybe an hour or so ago, according to one of the bouncers, who was ushering people out of the front door. The club was at capacity, if not over it. The music was blaring, everyone was having a great time, then suddenly the power went out, throwing the entire establishment into utter darkness. Smoke filtered out from one of the lounges in the back of the club and panic ensued. People who weren't trapped by the flames became trampled in the desperation to escape. Returning to Frank with my findings, I can't help but stare at the disaster.

The entrance into Requiem is a single door with a flashing neon sign cascading down the glass, changing colors every few seconds. It's now smashed on the concrete. The club is underground, no windows, and no emergency exits. There's only one way in and out: the main entrance. I've been inside of the place just once, but it was enough for me never to return. The décor was cheap, thick coats of lacquer protected the wood for the bars and dance floor, the furnishings were over stuffed, and decorative paneling covered the walls. The interior was designed for esthetics, not safety. There are sprinklers littered throughout, but knowing the fire load as I do, they would've been quickly overrun by the intense flames, rendering them useless.

Ben and Stephen join us with their interviews, which they hand to me since Frank has made me lead on the investigation. Over the course of the next hour more bodies are pulled, some charred beyond recognition. Those will require dental records for identification. I follow them into the tent, which reeks of burnt flesh and smoke, nearly choking any clean air trying to filter in. Lloyd and Taylor have the daunting task of identifying the remains, each rushing down the rows with an intern trailing after them carrying toe tags and a marker, trying to keep up with the onslaught. Using a scanner, the young woman goes from one body to another, exposing only their right arms from under white sheets being placed on top of them by the rescuers from the fire department. Tears stain her face, her burgundy hair is hastily tied up behind her head, and her fingers tremble with each new victim.

"How many so far?" I ask, kneeling beside her.

"Um, seventeen I believe. They just keep coming."

"Do you need help?"

Taylor shakes her head. "We have a couple of more interns on their way to help move the bodies to the morgue."

Stepping over to Lloyd, a distressed expression deeply creasing his face, I check in and let him know I'll be handling the investigation. He nods and continues to work. Outside, I wish I could inhale a good amount of fresh air, but there just isn't any. The dark smoke has turned lighter due to the flames dying out, but there's no telling when this will actually end. The four of us continue to watch the operation, clicking off numbers in our heads as victims continue to mount.

"Detective Corro," the fire chief calls, waving us to join him in front of the abandoned club next door. "You need to see this."

Following him into what was once Temptation, a strip club that closed several years ago for hiring minors, we're forced to step over broken glass and warped floorboards at the entrance. It's been boarded up, so a crowbar would've been needed to break into the building. Flashlights swing back and forth inside of the pitch black by firefighters in full gear. Dust and grime covers every surface with spiderwebs hanging from a few of the overturned tables and chairs. Dark, torn paper peels down from the sagging walls while the thin carpet is ripped and shredding in a few spots.

"Since parts of this structure sit over Requiem, I had my men come in here to check for hotspots. You're never going to guess what they found."

He directs us deeper inside and to the far right where the stage should be, its four tarnished brass poles still standing equal distance from each other. Old posters cling to the backdrop, exposing former ladies in all their glory. The chief picks up a chunkier flashlight off the floor and shines the bright beam onto four lengths of rope dangling beside each of the poles. Following the light upward, we notice they're tied to the crossbeams above the stage, a catwalk allowing easy access.

My wrists begin to itch, the sensation of rough cords wrapping around my tender flesh, splaying my body apart. An errant memory frantically tries to resurface. Biting my lip, I work on hiding the rising panic attack. Sweat covers my brow, and the stale, pungent air swirls around my throat, choking me. Flashbacks from my past seize control of my thoughts, so I force myself to concentrate on the here and now, not wanting to alert the others to my sudden distress.

The thick, nylon ropes are a dull white, their ends woven into slipknots. Without gloves, we don't dare touch anything, but it's tempting. The chief continues to swing his flashlight down to the stage floor, exposing warped wood doused in large red, almost brown, stains. It splashes onto the carpeting under our feet, spreading outward as if still seeping from an invisible source. I catch the waft of death desperately clinging to the air.

"Collins should be here soon," Frank says, taking the flashlight from the chief. "I'll have her team work in here. Stephen, this will be your scene. Ben, you'll assist Olivia. Hayden's group will be assigned to your investigation."

"James is on his way as well," the chief adds.

Professor James Holloway is the fire investigator for the state, and also teaches fire science at the CSB academy. According to him, I'm his favorite student, and he's had thousands since every officer is required to attend his classes.

Frank turns to me. "Don't be surprised if he has you run the fire scene as well."

"You remember who owns the Requiem?"

He nods. "Yup. Let's discuss that outside. Stephen, stay here. I'll send Collins to you."

The chief remains behind as well while the three of us retreat. Frank gives Ben a brief rundown on the series of fires that have cropped up in Nok over the past month, all Centurion owned properties. The company had once been the brainchild of Kane Cassidy, a millionaire, convicted felon, and ex-lover of mine. He was killed last month in a series of professional hits that have yet to be solved—the Red Rover Case. It's the same one Matt was working undercover on when he disappeared. After the explosion at the CSB home office occurred, the investigation was reallocated to Frank, Chief Daven, and Director Cruz—though he was already the head of it.

I shiver and grow despondent still thinking about what could've happened if I had been early that morning. A thought I quickly shove away.

The first two fires set in January were attributed to a short in the electrical boxes, which are outside most of these rundown buildings along the outskirts of the sector instead of inside like they are for newer construction. When I bet Frank that a third one would happen, it was finally slotted into the arson category. This is the fourth Centurion building to burn, but the only one with fatalities. The others had either minor injuries to those inside when the fires started, or the structures were completely empty.

"This one feels different," I comment when Frank finishes his explanation. "And not because of the victims."

"It's underground, which is unlike the others," my boss responds.

"It's not that. Something else." The cell phone in my back pocket chimes, Lloyd calling.

"I need you down at the tent immediately," he says, sounding strained. "Someone we know was just pulled from the building."

Shoving the phone back into my pocket, I bolt down the street, ignoring Frank's bellowing, and try my best not to trip on the hoses crisscrossing the pavement. Pushing back the tent flap, I gasp at the sight. There have to be over thirty bodies, if not more. I spot Lloyd over to my left, a grim expression on his face. He's kneeling on the soaked asphalt, his pants covered in dirt, sweat, and ash. A smoke-stained arm sticks out from under the sheet. Without lifting his gaze from the body, Lloyd hands me the scanner clutched in his shaking fingers. Taking it from him, I have to read the name on the display a couple of times to make sure I'm seeing it correctly.

"Nikki?" I croak. "It can't be. She moved a couple of weeks ago. The reader has to be wrong."

"I thought so to," Lloyd says, the tiredness in his voice apparent. "Then I pulled back the sheet to double check. It's her."

Setting down the device, I kneel opposite him, grip the top of the sheet with cold, quaking fingers, then slowly remove the covering, exposing her ash-caked face. Her once bleach blonde hair is charred, flaking away from the scalp in places. The satin of her blouse is badly burned, the skin shedding underneath. Her lip is cut and there's a deep laceration on the side of her head. Retracting the sheet more, I notice blood soaking her torso, several bullet wounds penetrating just below her breastbone. I show Lloyd.

"She was probably dead before the fire was set," he comments, taking the cover from my hand and draping it back over her body.

"Where was she found?"

"In the back room, isolated from the rest of the club. The door was closed, which is why she didn't burn like the others close to her general area."

"I need you to make her autopsy a priority. Give the bullets to Hayden if you find them."

Lloyd nods, picks up the scanner, and gets back to work while I step out of the tent, Frank pacing on the other side.

"What's going on?" he demands.

"Is Hayden here?"

My boss points to a pair of men conversing around the yawning doors of a forensics van. "He's with James." I move to step away when Frank stops me. "Liv."

"It's Nikki Burris."

Releasing me, he asks, "Are you going to tell Joe?"

"I will later."

Making my way over to the van, I try not to let my emotions get the better of me. The scene, the victims, and the investigation come first, my feelings a distant second if not third. Professor Holloway shakes my hand, his thick, calloused flesh grating against my tired skin. He's in his sixties, is gruff, mostly surly, with shaggy, gray hair, a square face, and raspy voice. His heavy denim jeans add to his bulky frame, as does the black sweater and matching overcoat.

"We have to wait until the chief gives the all-clear before we can head inside," the older man says, adjusting a thick, metal folder with attached clipboard under his arm. "That won't be for hours since he has to ensure the structure is safe for us to enter. It's going to be a long day."

"I'll buy the coffee," Frank says, joining us.

Turning to Hayden, I ask, "Does Alice have keys to Nikki's old house?"

"She should. Why?"

"Have her give them to you later tonight."

He tilts his head. "Liv, what is it?"

"I have to tell Joe before you say anything to Alice, but Nikki is one of the victims."

His eyes widen. "How the hell is that possible? She moved."

"That's why I need the keys so I can search her house. I want you with me when I do it. We'll collect anything that might have been left behind. Hopefully it'll give us a clue as to why she didn't go."

"Just let me know when."

Someone comes over to collect Frank since a staging area has finally been setup for the media to gather. He states he'll bring coffee and donuts when he's done giving his briefing. James and Hayden start sorting out the gear we'll need, making sure we have enough tin cans to contain pieces of evidence in case an accelerant was used—it'll prevent the vapors from escaping—as well has paper bags for larger items. Stepping off to the side, I remove the phone from my pocket and check the time, which is slowly approaching four. Highlighted on the screen are two missed calls and one voicemail message, all from Nikki. The first one was at 11:35 p.m. and the last at 11:42. Covering one ear with my hand, I press the phone to the other and listen.

"Liv, I need you to come down to the Requiem. It's urgent. I can't tell you over the phone, so please hurry." She sounded terrified and desperate. Playing the message again, I listen for background noises, picking up the muffled sound of a thumping bass, but nothing else.

Knowing Joe is probably still at the club working on the receipts from the night, I decide to call him and break the news.

"I'm watching Frank give a press conference on the fire at the Requiem. Are you there, too?" he inquires, a few seconds after answering.

"Unfortunately. It's bad, Joe." My voice catches in my throat, tears well in my eyes. "Uh, Nikki, she … she was inside."

Silence.

"Joe?"

"Are you sure?" he asks weakly.

"Yes. I confirmed the ID. I'm so sorry."

"Can you do me a favor and call Tanner to come pick me up at the club? I'm not feeling too well."

"I'll do that right now. Do you need me to send an ambulance?"

"No, just my husband."

Thankfully, Tanner is a light sleeper when Joe isn't home. He answers on the first ring. I explain the situation and ask him to keep me informed. Tucking the phone into my back pocket, I find an isolated niche by an abandoned fire engine, squat down, and bawl, not able to suppress the stress anymore.

By the time the sun rises, all of the ambulances have left and only a few firetrucks remain. Frank kept his promise of donuts and coffee, which the five of us eat while we wait for the structure to be deemed safe enough to enter. Collins, her team, and Stephen left hours ago. As did the last of the vans carrying the remains of those who were trapped inside of the inferno. The death toll reached fifty-six, with more bodies discovered when the firemen began doing their overhaul, checking for hotspots and chucking out items onto the sidewalk if they were in the way. The fire moved so rapidly, just a little over a thirty made it out. I'm surprised the structure is still standing. Climbing into the van, Hayden starts doling out hazmat suits with heavy boots to wear over our clothing. I remove my parka, placing it in the van to claim later.

"We're not going to wait?" Ben asks, holding the outfit by its collar.

"The building will need to be torn down as soon as possible to keep people out," James comments, taking off his shoes. "It's now or never."

Once suited, we each shove a fistful of gloves into our pockets, strap masks over our mouths, and goggles to protect the eyes. Hayden gathers his team around so they can hear the instructions on what to focus on, how to properly collect and document evidence, and who will be handling sketching and photographing the scene.

"We need to be meticulous and thorough," Professor Holloway instructs. "If you have a question, ask either me or Detective

Darrow, who's in charge. Nothing should go unnoticed or overlooked. The littlest detail can make or break a case. Most of you are familiar with this procedure. It's the same one we used when investigating the fire on the ship *The Chelsea* back in September, except that was on a much larger scale. Any questions?"

No one raises their hand.

Paper bags, cans, boxes of gloves, labels, markers, and evidence tags are gathered while I hand off my notebook to Frank so it doesn't get lost. He wishes us luck, then leaves for headquarters. James advises he'll be writing down our findings in his metal folder while Ben and I root around for a cause and reason behind the destructive flames. After several long minutes, the fire chief gives us the go-ahead. His men remain inside in case things start to get dicey with the structure's integrity.

Passing by the shattered glass door, the horrid stench of melted plastic, singed flesh, and seared wood permeates the air. The masks we're wearing simply make our breathing easier, not filter out smells. Nothing but absolute darkness awaits us. Floodlights with extensions stretching up toward the street hook into portable generators, then turn on, allowing us to see inside of the din. As the teams split off, each taking a pre-designated section, I stand in the center of what was the dance floor, the overhead gel lights melted, dripping onto the burned floor in some macabre artform. The DJ booth is a mass of wire, charred wood, and scorched fabric over toppled speakers. The bathroom doors in the wall to the right of the entrance hang off their hinges. Their signs are now mere silhouettes of the images that once adorned them.

James hovers behind me, pencil at the ready. I'm sure he's probably noticed a couple of details, but is waiting for me to pick up on them before mentioning anything. Visually searching the ceiling, I spot the sprinkler heads dangling precariously from the cork-style panels. Holes have been poked through for ventilation, exposing metal trusses. Following the pattern of the sprinklers, I notice there's one missing by the entryway leading toward the first bar in the adjoining room. Looking down, I spot the head among bits of insulation. I don a pair of gloves and pick it up to examine it closer.

"Well, this was useless," I comment. Handing the device to Ben after he's gloved up, I request a pike poll from one of the firefighters, then clear sections of the ceiling where the sprinkler should've been, raining dust and debris on top of me. "Look, no piping. There never was a suppression system in here."

"It's not unheard of for owners to simply shove sprinkler heads into the ceiling to pass inspection and give the illusion of safety when in actuality they're contributing to the spread of the flames." James calls for a tin can. The item is placed inside after being photographed and tagged. The lid is sealed and taped; my initials scrawled across the top to maintain the chain of evidence. "That explains why the fire wasn't extinguished, but not the cause behind the accelerated growth."

Slowly, we continue our trek toward the rear of the club, requesting evidence collection when its warranted. In the first bar toward the back, Ben points out a possible pour pattern down the walls, but since I've been inside of the club, I tell him it's more than likely residue from the decorative paneling that was used, which is no longer present. I have Hayden take samples anyway just to be sure. Hours pass as we search inch by inch for the origin. The majority of the victims were recovered from the two lounges at the very back and the smoke den situated in the center of the maze. In the narrow hallway between the den and lounge number two, there's an unusual char pattern coming down from the ceiling. Almost like an inverted 'v'.

"What's above us?" I ask, pointing skyward.

"Empty apartments," Hayden replies. "The entrance to them is behind the structure along the alley."

"You come with me. Ben, stay with the rest of the team. We'll be right back."

The three of us, including Professor Holloway, retreat up the main stairs, then traverse the alleyway between the Requiem and the venue next door, which received some water damage like Temptation did on the other side. The alley behind the edifices butts up against the Brimher River, which surrounds the sector. It's clear from how the structure is built that the club expands beyond the two-story apartment building nestled on top. We wait for the fire chief to join us since his men need to determine whether or not the floors will support our weight due to the damage they received from the blaze.

"I can only let two of you go at a time," he states upon his return. "One of you and one of mine. Who's first?"

"Me," I volunteer. "Then Hayden to collect whatever I find."

Following the firefighter, I step where she does, carefully maneuvering around scorched planks and gaps in the floorboards. The hallway we enter is narrow like the alleyway, two doors on either side for the four apartments on this floor. I guesstimate the corridor between the smoke den and lounge two is somewhere in the rear dwelling on our left. Smoke, fire, and water damage infiltrate the surroundings. It's a tiny, one-bedroom abode complete with galley kitchen and closet-sized bathroom. Between the living room and slim pantry is a heavily charred door, unlike the rest of the place where the conflagration wasn't as severe. Inside of the petite room is a water heater, furnace, and electrical box.

"Let me see your flashlight."

After unhooking it from her utility belt, the young woman hands it to me. Carefully, I kneel and crawl my way inside, focusing on the exposed wires dangling under the box and leading down into the floor joists, which are shared with the ceiling for the club below. Removing the mask, I inhale deeply, getting a whiff of gasoline and sulfur. I retreat, return the flashlight, and we head back outside.

"It's like the others," I comment, coughing from the toxic air I briefly inhaled. "Hayden, collect the floorboards and the electrical box. You're going to need to run chemical analysis on both."

"Let me get the right containers from the van. The ones I have with me won't be big enough." He leaves, the chief going with him while the firefighter who escorted me remains behind to take Hayden inside when he returns.

"What are your preliminary findings?" Holloway asks once I have my breathing under control.

"The fire was started in the utility closet for the back apartment and deliberately directed down into the club. Since it was in the walls, it would've burned through the wiring, knocking out the power for the club. Without a fire suppression system, there wasn't anything to combat the flames. Add on top of that all the combustible materials that filled the spaces and adorned the walls, the back rooms would've reached flashover in just a matter of minutes. The heavy, toxic smoke is what would've killed most of the victims before the flames consumed them."

He scowls. "I hate places like this. Choosing profit over people. Maybe now some of these owners will wise up and follow the codes designed to protect their properties and patrons."

"Only if there are people willing to enforce the rules. You might want to find out from the chief who the inspector is, or was. Get him or her fired for not doing their job. Depending upon their negligence, I can add them as accessories to the murders."

"'I'll handle that since you're going to have your hands full informing all of those families."

When Hayden returns, I go back down into the club and check on Ben. Hours later, as the sun starts its early winter set, we pack it in and I make sure to collect my parka. The forensics team returns to headquarters to process the evidence collected while I head home, overly exhausted. I park the Halo in the detached garage, close that door, and open the main one to gain access to the house after disarming the alarm. Setting my purse down on the desk in the study, I place my gun and badge next to it, along with my cell phone, then remove Sam's and give him a call after noticing a dozen messages from him.

Sitting on the edge of the bed, I strip, taking my clothes directly to the laundry room so they don't stink up the rest of the house. "I'm going to take a soak in the tub, eat, and go to bed."

"I've been watching the reports all day. They're not releasing much information on the victims," he says, a television on low in the background.

"They won't until Frank or I sign off on it. The families have to be notified first. He'll more than likely be the one since he left the scene this morning and I just now got home."

"You probably don't want company tonight." The disappointment in Sam's voice is undeniable.

"I'll fall asleep on you. When do you leave?"

"Tomorrow. Even if I was staying, you're going to be busy. Call me if you need anything."

We hang up, then I head into the bathroom and turn on the faucet, filling the tub with warm water and adding lavender-scented bath salts. My muscles ache as I wash thoroughly, scrubbing my hair and skin until raw with body wash. After drying, I wrap myself in a fluffy robe and make a peanut butter and jelly sandwich, then go around checking the locks and turning on the security system before shutting off the lights. I forego brushing my teeth since I don't think I can lift my arms that high, drop the robe, and crawl under the covers, grateful to be in my soft bed, even if it is alone.

Three

Frank picks me up close to nine the following morning. He pulled a few detectives from SVU to help notify the families of those who've so far been identified. We spend a good part of the day finishing the list, consoling those who had already determined their loved ones perished. It's grueling work, but also part of the job. Next, we head over to the coroner's office, which is across the street from headquarters between Cassidy and Chestnut. Parking in the lot that runs along Streman, we enter through the main door and punch in a code to gain access to the rest of the building since it's a Sunday, and there isn't a receptionist on duty during the weekends. We find Tress and her assistant in exam room one just to the left of the hallway where it crosses into a T-section. Asher—who's in his late twenties, skinny, wears glasses, and is a gaming nerd—sits at the computer console at the far end of the room entering information as Tress rattles it off.

"It's going to take weeks to get through all these bodies," she laments, stepping away from the metallic examining table a charred corpse currently occupies. "We've had to store quite a few of them at the morgue in the basement of Grove Hospital. We just don't have enough refrigerator space."

"How many left to be identified?" I ask, leaning against the white, sterile wall, keeping my distance since the smell of burnt flesh is forever seared into my nostrils.

"Twenty-four. We're collecting missing persons reports that were filed yesterday, then subpoenaing their dental records to confirm identity. I have some of our interns doing the grunt work since they need the practice at performing autopsies. Lloyd and Taylor were at it all night. I don't think either of them slept yesterday. Currently, I'm running on caffeine and fumes."

"Did he handle Nikki's first like I requested?"

Tress gestures for me to join her at the computer with Asher, where he pulls up the report. "She was killed sometime between 11:30 and midnight. He found three bullet wounds, but no slugs. They probably were through and throughs. There was also trauma to the head caused by a blunt object, strangulation marks around her neck—which wasn't noticed until she was washed—and heavy bruising near the genital area. He tried to run a rape kit, but it came back clean. The guy must've used a condom."

"I'll see who from Hayden's team searched the back room. Hopefully they found the bullets. I can narrow down the time of death for you. Nikki called me at 11:35, then again at 11:42, leaving a message."

"What did she say?" Frank inquires.

"That it was urgent I get to the Requiem, but she didn't specify why. I missed her call because I wasn't near my phone." *If I hadn't, would I be among the casualties?*

Asher augments the time with the new information, adding a note as to why he changed it.

After jotting down a few pieces into the notebook I used yesterday, I ask, "When will you start releasing bodies?"

"As soon as I can."

We thank her, return to the car, park in the employee section of the garage, and step into headquarters. Since it's non-office hours, we have to use the biometric scanners to get to the elevator core. Needing something to drink, I press the button for nine. Frank buys us each a bottle of Coke from the vending machine, then we sit at one of the tables.

He cracks open the cap and takes a swig. "Do you mind if I hear the message?"

I pull the phone out of the pocket of my dress pants, since I had to look professional today, rest the device on the table, unlock it, and play the recording using the speaker option.

"She sounds terrified," he comments. "Was it because of the fire?"

After swallowing a mouthful of soda, I shake my head. "No. I think she was killed before it was set. The room she was in is the same one I found Kane's sister, Brooke, being kept. The firefighters had to break down the door because it was locked from the outside. Hayden was able to recover the computer from the manager's office, but it was in pretty bad shape. He's hoping to extract the security recordings once the necessary repairs have been made to the drive." I drink some more. "What I can't figure out is why she was there? First, she gives Joe her two weeks' notice stating that she's been offered a job at a new club opening in Prescott. Then, with only a few days left, she up and quits out of the blue. Now she's beaten, raped, shot, and killed here in Nok."

"Was Hayden able to get the keys to her house?"

"I'm checking with him on that today."

Frank's face turns ashen while he stares at his bottle. "Joe took the news pretty hard. Tanner had to take him to the emergency room shortly after picking him up from the club. They think he had a mild heart attack."

"What?" My jaw drops. "Why didn't you tell me earlier?"

"Because he asked me not to. Chloe is managing Verdigris in Joe's absence." He reaches across the table, taking hold of my hand. "He's going to be all right, Liv."

Tears well in my eyes. "I did that to him. I should've waited."

"No. Don't you dare think that. He was already watching the news as it was unfolding. Eventually, Nikki's name would've come out, along with the others. There's nothing you could've done. Besides, he'd rather hear it from you than some stranger on the television."

"How long will they keep him?"

"At least a few more days. Visiting hours will be over by the time we're done, but we can use our badges and security will let us in. I'll go with you."

Looking around for the clock, I notice it's a few minutes past three. "I saw Hayden's name on the rollcall board beside the elevator in the lobby. Let's go see what he has."

We finish our drinks, tossing the bottles into the recycling bin since we can't carry them onto the forensics floor, the labs of which are on level nineteen, along with Hayden's office. Normally when I step off the elevator for that section, I'm inundated with the aroma of chemical solvents. Today, however, the smell from the fire is still affecting my senses, blocking that nasty odor from penetrating.

Making our way through the rows of stations with their highly expensive and innovative machines, we enter the small room in the far back corner, Hayden staring blankly at a couple of pieces of paper strewn across his desk. Frank closes the door before we sit.

"Gasoline," he says without formally acknowledging our presence. "Just like the other fires. But it wasn't just on the electrical box for the apartment, it was splashed all over the walls. This just doesn't make any sense. Someone would've noticed."

"Can you pull up old interior photos of the club that might be on their website?" I ask, moving my chair alongside his. It takes him a few minutes to locate the appropriate ones. "Focus on the walls for the lounges. What do you see?"

He scrolls between the various images, each showing a synthetic covering in various hues and textures. It's not wallpaper. "Is that polyester?"

"When it burns, the material leaves a gasoline-like residue behind. It's what Ben thought was a pour pattern."

"And that's why the fire grew so rapidly."

Frank chuckles. "James was right, Liv. You do have a knack for arson investigation."

"That should make my teams' lives a little easier." Hayden reclines in his chair, looking satisfied with the finding.

Moving mine back, I ask, "Who handled collecting evidence in the back room?"

"Let me look." Spinning around, he pulls a packet of papers off the file cabinet behind him and flips through an assortment of pages. "Dalia. She was in there all day."

"Do you know if she recovered any slugs?"

Going back to the computer, he types for a few moments. "According to the report she filed, three rounds were pulled from the back wall. She sent them to ballistics. Let me give them a quick call." After picking up the phone on the edge of his desk, he dials an internal extension, mumbles a few words to whomever answers, then promptly hangs up. "They were strikers."

No, that can't be.

"Are you sure?" I ask, hoping I heard him incorrectly.

"That's what the man said."

I turn to Frank, whose eyes are wide like mine. "This can't be a coincidence."

"But she doesn't fit with the other victims," he retorts.

"She's connected to at least one of them. She knew Luke."

Besides being my boss, I was placed on an undercover assignment by CSB to spy on him. Having been murdered by Sam's hitman, Jake is still out of town and Nikki wasn't involved with anything that would've placed her life in such danger.

At least, I don't think she was.

"Hayden, did you get the keys from Alice?" I ask, changing my focus to him.

"I have them right here." He opens the top drawer of his desk and tosses them to me. Two silver keys dangle on a ring attached to a plastic mold of an elephant.

"Meet me at her house in Range Sector around ten tomorrow. Don't bring anyone else from your team. Just you."

"All right."

Frank and I take our leave, heading down to my workstation. He turns on the computer where Gabe once sat while I get mine up and running, then work on adding notes into the case file. I'll be glad when they relocate his computer equipment so I can rearrange mine.

"When someone was killed with a striker, it happened after money was stolen from TITAN Industries' holdings and transferred into an account out of the country," Frank utters, thinking out loud while he works. "We're still going under the assumption that the Vilks Cartel owns, or at least is laundering money, through that entity."

"Nikki didn't have connections to either of them."

"Not that you know of."

"Frank, I knew her. We worked together. Even partied together on a few occasions. She has absolutely nothing in common with the other victims." I go on to tell him about New Year's Eve down on the private island, Everlast. How Nikki had stayed there for close to two weeks, flew to Prescott for a few days, then came home. "I even had Aleese pull her Hub recordings, which verified her story. It was after that she gave her notice to Joe."

"Do you know why she went to Prescott?"

"To see Dallas' new club. The one he hired her to work at. And before you say anything, I plan on calling his record label tomorrow to find out who his agent is so I can talk to him."

"You don't have his direct number? But you partied with him," Frank teases.

"Luke brought me down to the island, remember? He would've had it. Not me." I could ask Sam for it, but I want to do this through proper channels. "Was her family notified?"

"I did that yesterday afternoon by phone since her sister, Tabitha, lives out of state. Nikki had her listed as an emergency contact on her employment records at Verdigris. Tanner let me have a look at them since he has a key to the club. She's a piece of work. Couldn't care less that her sister is dead and wants nothing to do with claiming the body. I tried to see if there was anyone else in the family, but there isn't."

"I'll handle the funeral arrangements if she won't."

"Joe will probably help you with that also."

I nod and go back to adding notes to the files. Frank hums while he works, which I never knew before. Typically, he's up in his office on the seventh floor, so it's odd that he's sitting beside me.

"Hmm," he says, rubbing his chin. "Nothing was moved from TITAN's accounts recently."

"You have access?" I ask, sliding next to him.

"Director Cruz sent a drive that allows me to search the home office's databases since they're more thorough. I used a remote login from this terminal to mine. Weren't you given one?"

"Yes, but it was confiscated by Internal Affairs when they took my laptop."

In actuality, the device is in a manila envelope tucked into a secret compartment in the floor of the walk-in closet for a home I own in Range Sector. I had planned on moving back into it after the charges against me for the deaths of my husband, Robert Dean Morgan, and his lover were dropped. There are pieces of furniture already in the home to give the illusion that it's occupied, but for the moment I'm stuck living in the house on the posh island of Waterside. Sam doesn't know about the other place, to the best of my knowledge, and I plan on keeping it that way.

Going back to my desk, I ask, "How's the Red Rover Case coming along?"

"We're having to rebuild it since nearly all the evidence was destroyed when the home office was bombed. The only thing we have is what you took before the attack. There haven't been any new sightings of Carlos Montoya. There's a new undercover detective working at Calhoun Steel to monitor Wallace Shaw's dealings now that Matt is gone. We're convinced that they're the ones making the strikers, only we can't yet prove it. Not sure if it's a companywide endeavor, or just Wallace's, as a way to make money he's lacking from not being on the board of directors. I have a call set up with Sam West tomorrow. He's the chairman for the organization."

Biting my lip, I try not to react to Sam's name, and the fact that he never mentioned the meeting to me, but I did know about him being on the board. "Who did you and Joe hire to handle my dad's funeral?"

"Evers and Summers. They're on 29th Street in Range."

I jot the name on a pad of paper beside my keyboard, finish my notes, and shut everything down. "Can we get something to eat before swinging by the hospital?"

"Of course."

After he's done, I grab my purse off of the floor and we head out, stopping to pick up a quick bite from one of the many fast food places in Vale Sector, where all state government and medical buildings are located. Since the gift shop in the hospital is more than likely closed for the day, I have Frank pull into the closest florist so I can purchase a bouquet of lilies, which are Joe's favorite. Entering the parking structure on 11th, we find a spot on the third level, then take the connecting walkway that bridges the two structures together over the road so we don't have to worry about traffic. We leave our weapons locked in the car, so only our badges are clipped to our waistbands. Security waves us through without any problems. Frank already has the room number, so we bypass patient information and take the elevator to the tenth floor, room 1057. The nurses at the station inform us that visiting hours are over, but my boss explains the situation and we're allowed into the room.

It's a single occupancy, the mechanical bed resting against the wall on the right. Joe looks frail under the bright, white sheets. An IV drips into his left arm, while a nasal cannula sits just above his lip, poking into his nose providing oxygen from a valve in the wall. He's pale, appears thinner than normal, and is staring out the window looking lost. I try not to burst into tears at the sight. Tanner, who's always impeccably dressed—today is no exception with brown loafers, pressed, camel-colored dress slacks, crimson sweater with a paisley pattern, and a matching silk scarf draped around his neck—is sitting in the corner reading, then looks up when he notices us.

"Darling," he says, standing and gliding over to me, wrapping me in a warm embrace.

He and Joe have been together for over thirty years. He's tall, thin, with short, white hair, and is slightly hunched over due to crippling arthritis. Before the debilitating illness struck, he was a world-famous painter. Now, he owns a gallery and occasionally picks up a brush if he's not having a flare up.

Joe slowly moves his head and smiles. "Those are my favorite," he says, spying the flowers.

Tanner takes them from me and adds them to an existing bouquet since there aren't any empty vases. The sterile room is heavily perfumed with the dozens of flowers scattered on the table and windowsill. I step up to the bed, taking Joe's hand without the IV.

"I'm sorry."

He squeezes my fingers. "Don't be. I hadn't been feeling well for a few days."

"The stubborn ass refused to go to the doctor," Tanner scolds, folding his arms over his chest.

"Well, I'm here now."

The older man grumbles, then goes to adjust the pillows behind his lover's head. "You should've accepted Olivia's offer to send an ambulance. What if traffic had been bad?"

Joe swats the air as if there's a fly buzzing around his head. "Stop your bitching. It was after four in the morning. Who the hell is out that late?"

"Besides you?"

Tanner and Joe are my relationship goal, if I ever decide to settle down again. Sam's proposal sits in the back of my mind, but I doubt he's serious. Besides, he's using me to gain intel from CSB's databases and systems. I'm sure when he has whatever it is he's searching for, I'll be tossed aside.

That's what I have to keep reminding myself so I don't get caught up in his web.

"When are you heading home?" I ask, squeezing his hand.

"Wednesday, but they want me on bed rest for at least a week, if not longer. Chloe says she can handle the club in my absence." He looks at me hopefully. "There isn't any chance you'd be able to help out, is there? I know you're busy with the investigation, so don't worry about it if you can't."

"I'll have to see day by day how things are going."

"You should promote that woman to assistant manager, then you wouldn't have to work so many long hours every damn day," Tanner fumes. "She and Olivia are the only ones you trust in that position anyway."

Joe grins at me. "Want to own the club?"

I laugh. "How many pain killers are you on?"

"I'm serious, Liv. Tanner's right. I need to get out of the business while I'm still young."

"Now you're being drastic," his husband chides. "You love that place. Besides, Olivia has a career."

"A dangerous one."

"And dealing with other club owners isn't? There's practically a turf war going on down there."

My ears perk up. "What do you mean?"

"Nothing," Joe replies. "He's exaggerating."

"To hell I am." Huffing, Tanner moves around to the other side of the bed, standing next to me. "You think all those fires are random? Do you honestly believe they're going to stop even if the one from Friday was catastrophic?"

"Is it just the arsons that have you concerned, or is there more going on?" Frank asks, moving closer to the bed.

The couple look at each other. After a few uncomfortable seconds, Tanner responds, "Last week Joe received a letter at the club. He mentioned it to a few other owners we're friends with, and they had gotten one as well."

"Who sent it?"

"There wasn't a postmark on the envelope, just an address typed on cream-colored paper. An expensive brand given the thickness of the fibers and the card stock used for the general communication." Tanner wrings his hands. "It wasn't signed. The sender advised it would be wise if we sold Verdigris to them, or face the possibility of it burning down. They're supposed to send another letter in a couple of weeks with an offer on the property."

I narrow my gaze at Joe, steaming under my collar. "Why didn't you say anything when you received it?"

"Because shit like this happens all the time. It's no big deal."

"Liar," Tanner croaks. "You've never had a letter like this before."

"That you know of."

Tossing his hands up, Tanner storms out of the room, muttering under his breath.

"Joe, I'm going to need that letter," Frank states.

He shrugs. "What's the big deal? Everyone is overreacting."

Now I'm the one throwing my hands into the air. "Are you kidding me? Joe, please, take this shit seriously. Shut down the club for a couple of weeks until we find out who's setting these fires. The building needs upgrades and repairs anyway. Now would be the perfect time to do that."

"What will the girls do for work?" he protests. "They'll move to other venues, and I'll never get them back."

"Have them help with the renovations. I'm sure they have suggestions to improve business and increase revenue."

"That's not a bad idea," Frank adds.

"I'm going to lose money."

"Joe, February and the beginning of March are always slow. This is the perfect time."

"Fine," he growls. "The club will temporarily shut down starting tomorrow. I'll call Chloe tonight and tell her. Tanner can give you the letter. It's at the house."

"Nikki's sister isn't coming to get her, so I plan on handling the arrangements," I comment.

Joe smiles. "Tell me the final cost and I'll pay for it."

I kiss him on the cheek just as Tanner returns.

"And I'm serious, Liv. Consider buying the club. The girls love you, and you already run it better than I do. Make Chloe your manager."

"Let me think about it."

The three of us walk out together so Joe can get some rest. Frank decides to pick up the letter after dropping me off since he'll be on the island where the couple also lives. It's not long until I'm home, ditching the dress apparel and putting on sweatpants and a T-shirt. It's close to eight, so I make myself a small dinner, then sit on the couch in the family room to eat and watch movies. Sam's phone is sitting on the coffee table where I left it this morning. Reaching for it, I call him.

"Hey, beautiful," he says in his traditional greeting. "How did it go today?"

"Brutal. Frank and I spent most of our time consoling families, and we're still not done. Do you remember Nikki from Dallas' New Year's Eve party?"

He chuckles. "It's kind of hard not to. She was flirting with everyone there. Including me."

At the remark, my paranoia kicks into overdrive and I have to work hard not to let it slip into my tone. "She was one of the victims."

"I'm so sorry. That had to have been tough to deal with."

"It is. Her sister doesn't want anything to do with handling funeral arrangements, so I'm going to, and Joe said he'll pay for it."

"That's awfully nice of him, and you."

After taking the last bite of pasta, I set the bowl onto the coffee table. "The thing is, she wasn't supposed to be in Asmor. She quit Verdigris and supposedly moved to Prescott for a new job."

"When did she tell you this?"

"Toward the end of January. Nobody had heard from her, so I contacted the Hub and obtained her microchip recordings. It showed she was at Everlast for an additional two weeks, flew to Prescott for a few days, then came home. She wasn't answering her phone or text messages, so I had Frank send a couple of officers to her house just to make sure she was all right. Then she phoned me." Pause. "She said Dallas offered her a job."

"That's quite possible. He's been in the recording studio for the last month, which is in Prescott. Do you want me to give him a call?"

"No, since it's for an investigation. I'll try getting ahold of his manager to see when he's available."

"Olivia, I can give you Dallas' number."

It would save me a lot of time. "Fine. Text it to me. Joe wants me to buy the club."

"Really? Are you going to?" Sam asks excitedly.

"I have a job. Besides, he loves that place. It keeps him busy."

"Is there a reason behind his request?"

Against my better judgement, I tell Sam about the letter, hoping he can provide some insight from a business perspective.

"Typically, if you're trying to force someone to sell, you steal their employees or smear their reputation, not destroy the venue. It's counterproductive. Burning down a business would be seen as a net loss because not only will the current owner cash in on the insurance policy, but then add on top of that top dollar for the prime, now vacant, real estate, and he walks away better than the person doing the threatening. Verdigris is in a great spot being close to so many hotels and down the street from the arena. It does need a bit of work, but that's simply cosmetic."

I cross my legs and lean back against the cushions. "Then why is someone going to all the trouble of harassing a few of the other clubs as well if it's completely pointless?"

"Was the fire you went to Friday the only one in the area?"

"No. It's the fourth in the last month and a half. All owned by Centurion. Kane Cassidy's former company."

There's hasty scribbling in the background. "In what part of Nok were the structures?"

"On the outskirts along the river where the seedier places are located." I reach for the tumbler of water on the coffee table and take a drink.

"Excluding the one from Friday, were the others occupied?"

"Just two, but only minor injuries. No fatalities."

Sam doesn't say anything for a few lengthy seconds. "Let me think about your situation, but if Joe really wants you to take over the club, I'm more than willing to finance the endeavor. It would be great for the casino I'll be constructing. An easy shuttle ride between the two places. You'd make a killing."

"There isn't a way for me to run Verdigris *and* remain a CSB detective."

"Would he be willing to sell to me?"

I let out an exacerbated sigh. "I won't let Joe get rid of the club. He's put too much time, energy, and money into that place. It's not like him to give it up so readily. Tanner, his husband, isn't having any of it either. He knows what it's like to lose something you love to do. This would break him."

Of course having a heart attack, even a mild one, has a tendency to change people's perspectives.

"Well, if he is serious, let me know. I wouldn't change anything he doesn't want me to, if that helps."

I wait a few seconds before asking my next question. "Why didn't you tell me you have a call with Frank tomorrow?"

"There wasn't a need." His tone is flat, emotionless, which happens when he's hiding something.

Wanting to push the topic further, I decide not to since it'll be easier to get the information out of Frank after the meeting than it will be Sam. "When will you be in town again?"

I sense him smiling. "Miss me already?" He chuckles. "The next few weeks are loaded with meetings for the casino and Calhoun Steel. I'm also flying out to go over the construction plans for Monarch Landing with the crew I've hired. They just broke ground on the main building this past Wednesday. So, it might be a while. You can always come here.”

“This case is going to take all of my time. Plus, we’re still training the new guy. Currently, he’s shadowing me, so I can’t fuck this up.”

“We’ll find time, Olivia. I promise.”

After ending the call, I take my dirty dishes into the kitchen, then return to the family room and continue watching the movie.

Four

The skies are overcast, threatening rain. It's also cooler today than yesterday, so I make sure to don my parka on top of the navy-colored sweater I'm wearing. I decided to put on jeans and sneakers because I want to be comfortable while rummaging through Nikki's house, though there probably isn't much left inside. But you never know. Driving the Nimbus, I take the highway, getting off on Tremont, and only have to travel a few blocks until I come upon her upscale neighborhood. Hayden's van sits in the driveway of the white stucco villa with its three-car garage. I park on the wide brick beside him, get out, and lock the car. With the house key in hand, I approach the front door, but Hayden stops me to dust the doorknob for prints. While he's doing that, I snag a pair of gloves from his tool kit and slip them on.

"Nothing," he comments when done. "It looks to have been wiped clean."

On a hunch, I turn the knob and the door swings open.

"Nikki never leaves her doors unlocked. Someone's been here." I shove the keys into my pocket.

We enter into a two-story foyer where a crystal chandelier dangles, the walls brightly colored. The first thing I notice is that all the furniture is still there, along with dozens of boxes stacked three high in the dining room off to the left. Additional containers sit on the granite countertops in the kitchen with its scullery, pantry, and laundry room tucked behind it. Each room packed; their boxes labeled in heavy, black marker. Hayden remains in the foyer while I continue the walkthrough, returning to the dining room, then taking the hallway to the right where I enter a small nook that houses three of the five bedrooms. To the right of that is a home theater with leather seats and a floor-to-ceiling screen. More boxes line the walls, presumably from the bedrooms, since that's what's written on the corrugated cardboard. Going back to the front of the house and beside the mudroom next to the garage is a guest suite. The master bedroom is to the right of the foyer, with a walk-in closet the size of my living room, a reading room, and bathroom with a shower stall and sunken tub the size of a hot tub. More containers, some of them plastic, sit on the floor close to the vanity.

"I don't get it," Hayden says when I return to the foyer. "I thought Nikki moved."

"It looks like she was still in the process."

"How do you want to do this?"

Taking one of the kits and an extra camera from around his neck, I say, "You handle everything left of the foyer, including the garage. I'll take the bedrooms and bathrooms, then we'll meet in the home theater area. Collect anything that looks out of place, broken, or smudged with something organic. Dust for prints if you feel it's warranted. Just use your judgement. When we leave, I'll place a 'Do Not Enter' sticker along the door and its frame. Shout if you have questions."

He nods, enters the dining room, sets his kit on the table, and gets to work opening boxes while I check the master suite. Placing the large toolbox onto the floor, I notice the mattress has been stripped of its sheets, so I photograph it. Searching under and around the bed, everything looks to have been vacuumed, not even a single hair can be found stuck to the fibers. Next, I turn to the dresser and start searching through the drawers, finding them still full of clothes. I check everywhere, including under and behind each piece of furniture. Nothing. The hamper only has a few garments and the cabinets under the vanity in the bathroom have all been emptied, including the garbage can. After peeling off the plastic lids, I rummage through the containers' contents, finding a partially used bottle of lotion labeled 'Pure Bliss'. The same name Nikki said Dallas was going to call his club.

Could she have made up the story? Why?

Methodically, I move from room to room, not leaving anything to chance, but nothing appears out of place. They're not as tidy as the master bedroom, leaving me to believe Nikki may have been raped in her own bed. Hayden hasn't made a sound, so I assume he's having the same amount of luck that I am. In the home theater, I do find a plane ticket laying on one of the end tables, so I photograph it before picking it up. It's a one-way flight to Granada, our neighbor to the north, for Friday, February 27th. The name on the ticket isn't Nikki's, but Helene Donovan. Opening the kit, I remove a plastic evidence bag, slip the ticket inside, seal and label it, then go back to searching. I'm nearly done with the room when Hayden joins me carrying what looks to be a passport.

"You need to see this." He hands it to me.

Turning the hard, brown cover the image on the identification page is Nikki's, but the name is the same one on the ticket. "Where did you find this?"

"Inside of her car, which is still in the garage. She must have taken a cab to the club Friday."

"Or she was dragged there." I show him the plane ticket. "She was definitely not moving to Prescott. Nikki was leaving the country."

"It doesn't make any sense," he comments, taking back the passport to bag and label it as evidence. "Oh," reaching into a paper bag, he removes three legal-sized documents and hands them to me, "I found these insurance policies tucked in a kitchen drawer."

"Take the passport and plane ticket back to headquarters. I'll hold onto the policies. There's an errand I have to run before going into the office. I took a few pictures since the bedding is missing from the master suite, the carpet looks to have been vacuumed, and the garbage is missing."

"I didn't see a vacuum anywhere in the house. Whoever did the cleaning must have taken it with them." He claims the items, and leaves with the other kit and camera in hand after giving me a sticker to place on the door.

Finding a marker in the kitchen, I fill in the case number, my name, and contact information in the section designated for these details. I leave the marker behind and tuck the policies into my purse, making sure the front door is locked before slapping the sticker in place.

My other home is just down the street, so after backing out of the driveway I travel for a few blocks, then turn right onto Clover. I've owned the ranch for almost seven years and miss it terribly. It's the first dwelling at the entrance for my subdivision, right where the road bends around to the back of the property becoming Trier. It gives me two driveways and no backyard neighbors. Using the panel on the dashboard for the Nimbus, I disarm the alarm and raise the garage door. Exiting the car, I enter through the door off to the right and step into the tiny hallway leading into the living room, the dinette and kitchen to the left, and the utility room to the right.

The interior still smells of fresh paint and new carpet from the repairs done after a bomb exploded just outside of the front door. Thankfully, I was in the kitchen when it happened, so the walls and appliances protected me from the blast, though I was hit in the leg by a ball bearing. The scar it left is minimal. The furniture consists of items I no longer needed in the house on Waterside—such as the dinette table, the couches from the living room, and the bed and dresser from the spare bedroom. I still have to replace the curtains that had adorned the window beside the front door. At the moment, everyone can easily see inside.

Crossing the living room, I enter the bedroom where I have the same lack of window décor, then go left into the bathroom at the far end of the room. The walk-in closet is straight across, so once I'm inside I close the door, keeping my little secret from prying eyes. This was converted into a panic room back in September. A place I could safely hide from an abusive husband. There's a steel pocket door housed behind the vanity that is supposed to slide into place when I activate the sensor on the panel embedded into the wall. It also has a direct link to CSB station three, allowing me to communicate with them.

Carpeting used to cover the floor, but that was replaced with hardwood, which makes removing the cover for the hidden compartment much simpler. This space has its own electrical line from the street, separate from the rest of the house in case something was to happen. The cavity is treated by a cooling unit so the true computer for my security system doesn't get overheated from being inside such a cramped space. Those familiar with the house, except

Frank and Hayden, assume the system is routed through a panel in the garage, which is actually camouflage. There are a dozen cameras positioned around the exterior of the house, snagging every angle and recording it. Setting the cover aside, I reach into the cool chamber and remove a manila envelope and five-subject notebook.

When I was temporarily living in one of the apartment buildings at the home office in Whitebridge, I kept private notes, separate from the ones stored on my work laptop and those on the whiteboards we were using to keep track of our findings for the Red Rover Case. No one knows about my prizes, and I plan on keeping it that way for as long as possible. Searching for a pen in my purse, I turn to the page I had created for Nikki when she was initially missing and add notes from what was discovered today, in addition to the fire and her autopsy. Along with a few theories as to why she lied about where she was going, and a possible reason she was at the club. I'm wondering if she stumbled upon something either when she was still with Dallas on Everlast, or when he took her to Prescott. I won't know until I ask him.

After a quick review of the notebook, I place it and the envelope back into the compartment, seal the chamber, then leave, making sure the garage door closes and the alarm is set. By the time I park in the garage at headquarters it's past lunchtime, so I head up to the ninth floor and purchase a hot, roast beef sandwich with a side of fries and a bottle of water. Sitting at the same table I did for Gabe's retirement party, I take my time eating, working through my head what I'm going to say not only to Dallas, but Nikki's sister. I prefer to have telephone conversations rehearsed before actually calling anyone. It takes the anxiety out of the situation. At least for me, anyway.

After tossing out my garbage, I take the half-drunk water bottle and go down to my workstation. Sam texted Dallas' number to me last night, so I wrote it down before leaving the house since I don't normally bring his phone with me to the office. Once the computer is up and running, I open a blank document to transcribe the conversation while I'm having it. I should have Ben join me, but since Dallas and I know each other, adding a third party might make things awkward. Using the phone on my desk, I dial. It rings several times before I'm sent to voicemail where I leave my name and office number, not daring to give him my cell or a reason for the call. A minute later, he phones back.

"Olivia, how are you doing, sweetheart?" he asks, sounding excited to be hearing from me. "Hey, I'm sorry about Luke. If you still need a job, I'd love for you to join my entourage. It pays great money."

"Thanks, Dallas, but I'm all right for the moment. Listen, I wanted to ask you about Nikki Burris."

He whistles. "That babe is hot, let me tell ya."

"She mentioned you had hired her to work at a club you plan on opening in Prescott."

"Huh?" he asks, seemingly confused. "I have no clue where she got that idea. She did accompany me to my label's recording studio in that sector for a few days. Everything was going really well, then she suddenly up and left one night. Didn't leave a note or anything. Just vanished."

"Can you think of why she would've done that?" I ask, typing away.

"Nah. There was a killer party my manager threw at a massive house owned by Lamar Records. They produce my music," he replies, boasting. "Anyway, Nikki was having a blast, getting to know a few of the celebrities who love to come hangout. She was really making some high-class friends. Sometime around midnight, or maybe it was earlier, I don't really know, she disappeared. One of the security guards said she called a cab and went back to our hotel, but when I got there, all of her things were gone. The person working the front desk at the time said she took off for the airport. I've been trying to get in touch with her, but she's not answering."

"Dallas, Nikki was killed Friday in a fire."

He gasps. "Are you serious? Damn, that's horrible. Fuck. Give her family my condolences."

"I will. Thanks."

"Come down whenever you're free, sweetheart. We'll have a blast."

"Let me check my schedule and I'll get back to you."

He chuckles, then hangs up.

My next call is to Frank.

"Do you have a minute?" I ask, finishing up the notes, adding them to the case file.

"Sure."

Delving into my conversation with Dallas, I leave out the fact that Sam gave me the number and claimed the rapper's manager passed along my message. "Nikki either saw someone or heard something she wasn't supposed to at that party." I go into detail about what we found at her house.

"It affirms she was targeted and fleeing. Requiem might have been burned down to cover up the murder."

Scratching my head, I say, "But who did it? That's what's stumping me."

"The audio/visual guys up in forensics say they'll have the recordings from the club ready tomorrow. Hopefully, those will give us a clue. Have you spoken to the sister yet? Maybe she'll be nicer to you than she was to me when I broke the news."

"She's my next call. How was your meeting this morning?"

"It went well. Mr. West is going to have the company's sales and production records pulled and examined by an outside source. He's to let me know what they find."

"Can you do me a favor and see if Lamar Records is listed on those financial reports I handed to the chief for TITAN Industries? I'm going to research who they're owned by. They're the ones producing Dallas' music and held the party."

"Do you think he's connected?"

"I don't know."

Setting down the receiver, I turn to my computer and start looking for incorporation documents listing Lamar Records, since that'll identify who's handling the financial side of the business. If I still had the drive for the home office's databases, this search would probably go a lot faster. An hour later, and in need of a break from the computer, I remove Nikki's insurance policies from my purse to look them over. All three of them have a different beneficiary and are worth one million dollars apiece. Eyeing the names typed on the recipient lines, I decide now's the time to phone Nikki's sister, Tabitha.

"Hello?" she asks, picking up on the second ring, a dog barking in the background.

"Tabitha, my name is Olivia Darrow. I worked with your sister, Nikki."

She lets out an aggravated sigh. "Are you a whore too?"

"No, ma'am. I'm a homicide detective, but I also bartend at the club where she worked."

"What do you want?" Her tone is hostile.

"Since you're not going to claim her body, I was wondering if you wouldn't mind telling me if your family buries or cremates."

"Why?" she huffs.

"I'd like to follow with what her last wishes would've been, but she didn't leave a will. Her boss and I are planning her funeral, and we want to do it properly."

"Oh." A bit of the anger seems to have subsided. "We cremate."

"Then I'll arrange for that. Also, she had three insurance policies. One has you as a beneficiary and the others are for Travis Sterling and Devon Sterling. Are they related to you?"

"They're … they're my sons. Travis is five and Devon is three. Nikki … Nikki left them money?"

"Yes, ma'am."

"She never even met the boys," Tabitha says, her voice cracking. "My husband insisted on sending her announcements when they were born, but I was against the idea. Can you tell me what they're worth?"

"It's a substantial amount of money, Mrs. Sterling."

The sound of wood scraping along tile overtakes the barking. "How much?" Her voice quivers, all animosity disappearing.

"One million dollars each."

"She didn't know them," the sister whispers.

"Nikki would've wanted to make sure you were all taken care of. She had a very big, caring heart."

"I never sent her pictures, and now she's ... she's gone."

"I'm sorry, Mrs. Sterling."

"Please, call me Tabitha." I can tell her spirit is broken. The sister she had painted as deplorable and not worthwhile, isn't who Nikki was at all. It's a shame her realization didn't happen sooner. "And you're making the arrangements?"

"Yes, I am."

"Let me know when the service is. I'd like to be there."

"I will definitely do that. Would you mind if I ask you another question?"

She chokes back sobs. "No, go ahead."

"Do you know someone named Helene Donovan?"

"Is this related to what happened to my sister?"

"I'm not sure yet. We came across it in our investigation."

"Um, let me think." Her breathing is labored and forced, probably from both guilt and grief. "The only thing coming to mind is Helene was our grandmother's name and Donovan was our mother's maiden name. But I don't see how that could be relevant."

"I'm sure it's just a coincidence. Thank you for speaking with me."

After hanging up, I place the policies into one of the drawers for my desk. Next, I call Tress to see when Nikki's body will be released, which can be today. I phone Evers and Summers Funeral Home, making arrangements to meet with the director tonight at five. Needing a breather, I head up one floor where the captains and supervisors have their offices. It's a labyrinth of walls and doors, each labeled with the division and officer's name. Frank's in one of the corners, affording him a view of the sector. He's typing slowly at his keyboard, then waves me in and instructs me to close the door.

The beige walls need a fresh coat of paint, the stained, gray, Berber carpet should be replaced, the fabric on the couch resting against the wall to the right is starting to fray, and the coffee table in front of that is badly scuffed. His desk is metal, like my workstation, the chairs a pre-form plastic with thin cushions, and there's a dead plant along the windowsill.

"Lamar Records was a client of Larrel Kindreth," he says while I sit. "I've not been able to tie them directly to TITAN, but it can't be a coincidence that they had the same accountant."

"I haven't come across anything listing the owners. Maybe you'll have better luck."

He nods. "Chief Daven has been updated on your findings and requested that I travel to Prescott to do some digging into Dallas, his manager, and the record label in person. He wants me to interview those at the party. Perhaps they have insight as to why Nikki took off. He doesn't want the detectives out there handling it and fucking up our case."

"When do you leave?"

Leaning back in his chair, he clasps his hands in his lap. "Wednesday, but I don't know when I'll be back."

"I have an appointment with the funeral director today, so I was thinking of having the service Sunday. It gives Tabitha time to get here."

He smiles. "I'm glad she's changed her mind. God only knows what you'll do when I go. Hopefully you don't stick me in a pauper's field."

"Why the hell would you say something like that?" I retort. "Don't make jokes."

"I'm not, Liv. You're the person I have listed on all my documents, including my will. There's no one else. It's just you."

"Well, you'd better not be going anywhere for a long time, or I'll kick your ass."

He laughs. "That goes for you, too."

Taking my leave, I return to my desk, finish up a few things, then head out to the car after stowing both my holstered weapon and badge into my purse. No need to scare the funeral director. Turning left onto Lange, I take that all the way into Range Sector where it bends so it's no longer parallel to 29th Street, but perpendicular to it. Going left, the one-story, white brick, and mortar business is a few blocks down on the left. The parking lot is empty, with the exception of two hearses and a lone dull-red sedan in the back. After locking the car, I traverse up the sloped concrete walkway and knock on the wooden door with its glass panels blanketed in thick curtains. The older man who answers is sharply dressed in a tailored charcoal suit and polished oxfords.

"Ms. Darrow? Please come in," he says, shaking my hand with a firm grip.

The quietness of the inside rattles my nerves. I haven't been in a structure like this since my mother's wake, which I barely remember. The walls are paneled in white wainscotting, and the floors are covered in deep pine-colored carpet. A walnut reception desk sits off to the left while a small seating area near a dormant fireplace is to the right. Straight ahead is a hallway separating the viewing rooms, two on each side. I'm led to a smaller corridor to the left, then into an office where miniature urns and coffins adorn one wall, along with sample vault material a casket is normally kept in while underground. Taking a seat on the wood-back chair, I nervously lower my purse to the floor and cross my legs, suddenly feeling very underdressed for this occasion.

"How did you hear about our home?" the older man inquires, sitting across from me and fumbling with a leather portfolio.

"You handled my father's arrangements last year."

He grins. "Ah, yes, I thought the last name sounded familiar. What can I help you with today?" His manner is pleasant and calming, his tone even but kind.

I explain about Nikki and the reason I'm dealing with the service, which is because her sister is out of state—no need to reveal the truth when it's not relevant—in addition to what I'm looking for service wise.

"I'd be more than happy to assist with your needs. There's a splendid mausoleum crypt at Parkholm Cemetery which caters to those who've been cremated. It's a lovely indoor structure made from pristine white marble with Greek columns and a glass entryway."

"That sounds perfect." Never having done this before, and being alone, I feel overwhelmed by this endeavor, but I try my hardest not to let it show. "What about urns?"

Standing, he brings me over to a section with shelves holding various styles. "These are easily customizable if you should so desire."

I select a teakwood grain marble one, then we return to the desk and start filling out the paperwork. The service will be held this Sunday at 11 a.m. right outside of the mausoleum since I'm sure there will be many attending, and not everyone will fit into the cramped aisles. I thank the man for his time, collect my copies of the papers, and head home. While making dinner, I call Joe at the hospital with the details, and he's adamant about having a gathering at the club afterwards.

"The girls are eager to get going on fixing up the place," he says, chuckling. "They've got so many ideas it's ridiculous."

"That's good to hear. I'll let Chloe and Alice know about the arrangements. They can inform everyone else."

"Tanner will handle the catering. He'll insist on it."

After hanging up, I take my bowl of soup over to the stools for the kitchen island to sit and eat while making the calls. Tabitha doesn't answer, so I leave the information on her voicemail, along with my number in case she wants to phone me back. The rest of the evening is spent cleaning and doing laundry, tasks I hate.

Five

Entering the office the following morning, I find Hayden pacing back and forth in front of my desk. "It's happened," he murmurs, keeping his voice low so Ben doesn't hear, since he's the only other person in the room.

"What has?" I ask, sitting, shoving my purse into the bottom drawer.

"The spyware. Asher called last night to tell me it's hit the Hub systems, financial databases, and business directories all linked to the home office. It must have launched while he was at work."

"Does he know what keyword or phrase was used to start it?"

Hayden pulls over a chair, sits, then leans far forward, his hands clutched together tightly. "TITAN."

"As in industries?"

He shakes his head. "No. It was typed in as an acronym with a period between each capitalized letter."

"Can he tell where it was initiated from?"

"Somewhere in Whitebridge, or a sector close to it, but that's the extent. He wasn't able to get an IP address. The gaming console is recording the data being pulled. It's going to take a few days to get the complete readouts of what was pirated."

"Do you have access to the Red Rover Case I was working on?"

He shakes his head. "That's being handled by Collins. I won't be able to get near it without her noticing."

I let out a long, deep sigh. "All right. Have Asher continue to monitor things, and we'll regroup when he has the information. Did Alice tell you about Nikki's funeral?"

"Yes. She plans on ordering a large bouquet to have at the service. I think some of the other girls are doing the same thing.

Whatever we can't leave there, we'll bring to the club for the gathering."

He takes his leave just as Stephen comes in, setting his things down on his workstation before turning to me.

"Collins was able to match the DNA of our three serial victims to the blood found in Temptation," he says, leaning against my desk.

"With his killing grounds shut down, the perpetrator will move elsewhere."

"There hasn't been a death matching the others since November. Maybe he's stopped altogether."

I glare at him. "People like that don't quit until they're caught. How about we have a psychiatrist take a look at the cases? Maybe he or she can work up a profile. Give us some insight we're not seeing."

He smiles. "That's a great idea, and I know the perfect person." Returning to his desk, he turns on this computer, then starts making calls.

Ben joins me, and we review the notes and additional findings—though not many—that the forensics team located when processing the evidence we took from the fire. The tedious part of this job is all the reports that have to be completed for every damn thing we do. Notes and logs are duplicated for each case, adding to the hours of typing. Just before lunch, Frank calls to tell us the video recordings are ready and to meet him on the eighteenth floor.

The audio/visual section of the forensics department is far more sophisticated than any of the other areas. Each technician is given a pod—a nearly encapsulated desk with five screens and the latest computer equipment—that reach from floor to ceiling. They're round, resembling something you might find in a science fiction movie, and completely soundproof, though the workers wear noise-canceling headphones to make sure they're not disturbed. There are twenty such sections scattered across the large, carpeted space. A viewing room is housed next to the elevator core, so it's away from the windows and any glare that might come through.

Hayden and Frank are seated in theater-like chairs surrounding an extended terminal. Across from that is a full-length screen, which takes up much of the far wall. Ben and I sit beside them while one of Hayden's techs queues up the video.

"There isn't any sound," the young man says when the recording appears, but doesn't play, "so we won't know what was said. I've put together a compilation to make viewing easier since there were a lot of camera angles we had to work from."

"This is solely focused on Nikki," Hayden adds.

The technician hits play, and the viewing starts with her coming down the stairs for the club, a bulky man behind her, gripping her by the elbow. She appears nervous, shaking a bit while her companion keeps his head down, the black baseball cap on his head low enough to block most of his face.

"Can you pause it?" I request.

The video is stopped so I can study the man. He's tall, muscular, and is wearing a long-sleeved shirt, jeans, and gloves, all in black.

"He's the same person who killed Kane. I recognize the cap. He wore it in the recording the security cameras for the prison van captured."

Ben leans forward, resting his arms on his thighs. "Her lip is cut, but I don't see the laceration on her head."

Frank instructs that the video continue.

Nikki banters a bit with the bouncer, a strained smile creasing her painted lips. They're let in without paying a cover, which is how she and I got in last time. The man guides her toward the hallway left of the DJ booth, which empties into the second bar. The space is so crowded, Nikki is practically pressed against her assailant's body, his arm firm around her waist to prevent her from slipping away. No one seems to notice the pair enter the hallway at the far back where the door for the secret room is kept. After turning on the lights, he shoves her inside, then closes the door, drawing a weapon from his waistband.

"Stop it," I order. "What make of gun is that?"

Hayden moves his chair beside the tech and runs a scan of the image through a firearms database. "It's a CS .40 with a silencer."

I look at Frank. "Calhoun Steel."

"They do manufacture most of the guns bought and used in this country. Including ours. So that's not really a surprise."

The video plays. Nikki has her hands up, but without audio there's no way to tell what's being said. She seems to be pleading, which only makes the man angrier. He keeps his head lowered enough that we can't see his face, making me believe he knows where each of the cameras in Requiem are located. Reaching into the back pocket of her tight fitting, white pants, she removes her phone, unlocks the screen, and selects a contact. I glance at the timestamp for the recording: 11:35 p.m.

"She's calling me," I state.

When I don't answer, the pair begin to argue. Her captor switches his handling of the gun to the barrel, then hits her across the side of the head with the grip, cutting her and knocking her to the floor. She doesn't get up right away. It takes her several minutes to regain her bearings, using the bedframe beside her to help her stand. He waves the gun at her again, this time the barrel pointed at her chest. Nikki's shaking worsens and it's obvious she's crying. Again, she tries calling while her companion steps closer, practically breathing into her ear. She holds the phone in such a way he can hear my voicemail pick up. This time she leaves a message. The two start to argue again, and he shoots her three times. She falls backward, moves for a brief moment, then goes still. He opens the door, turns off the lights, and leaves. The video ends.

My thirst for alcohol surges realizing Nikki wasn't calling to tell me something important, but to lure me down to the club. He used her to get to me. She's dead because of our friendship.

"Olivia?" Frank says, placing a hand on my arm while I continue to stare at the blank screen.

"It's my fault," I mumble.

"No, it's not. This probably stems from whatever she saw or heard at that party."

"Then why call me if not to bring me down there to die? Who wants me dead so badly that they'd blow up the home office and murder a friend of mine after she couldn't get me on the phone?" Anger and terror battle for dominance, turmoil seizes my every muscle and nerve, and all I can do is simply sit there and try to keep it together.

"I want you to go home for the rest of the day. Ben can handle adding this information into the files."

"And do what, Frank? Wallow in my own misery and despair? Feel sorry for myself instead of catching this bastard?" I stand. "No. I won't run and hide. Let me be an emotional mess, but don't fucking take away my job."

Storming from the room, I return to the sixth floor, wiping tears off of my cheeks while I go about updating the case reports. Stephen doesn't ask questions as I loudly blow my nose and mutter under my breath. Ben comes down a few minutes later, taking a seat at his desk, and handling whatever I missed by walking out. When it's close to four, I pack and go home, making sure to turn on a few lights in the house so I can see. Placing the purse in the study, I shut off my cell to keep Frank from harassing me, which I know he will do, and toss it on the desk.

I head over to the wet bar across from the kitchen and next to the empty living room, snatch six travel-sized glass containers of rum from the micro-fridge, go to the couch in the family room, sit, crack one open, and consume its contents. Frank doesn't know I have these in the house, otherwise he would've dumped them down the sink by now. Tossing the empty bottle into the recycling bin in the kitchen, I head into the bedroom to change into cotton shorts and a matching top, then return to my spot on the couch and continue mourning my friend properly.

Turning on the television, I prop my feet up on the coffee table and drink while searching for something decent to watch, finally selecting an action movie with lots of explosions and sex. Besides starting to feel lightheaded from the alcohol, I'm now horny and ready to fuck, only Sam's not here, so matters will have to be taken into my own hands. Standing, I start heading toward the bedroom where my toys are, only to be interrupted by the doorbell ringing.

Peering through the glass for the front door, I spot Lloyd on the other side. Frank must have sent him when he couldn't reach me.

"What?" I ask, pulling open the door.

"No one can get in touch with you, so I came over to make sure everything is all right."

"I'm fine." I go to close the door, but he shoves his foot between it and the frame, then places a firm hand on the edge.

"Have you been drinking?"

"Ugh, why does it matter?" I gripe, stepping backwards, tripping over my own feet, and nearly falling.

Lloyd grabs my arm to keep me steady while closing the door behind him. Today he's dressed in jeans, a crimson-colored sweatshirt, sneakers, and is wearing his wire-rimmed glasses. Escorting me to the family room, he spots the empty bottles.

"I thought you had this under control," he scolds, scooping them up while I sit. He takes them into the kitchen. "Where are you hiding them?" Placing his hands on his hips, he glares at me like an angry parent.

"Leave me alone." Ignoring the scowl on his face, I go back to watching the movie.

He starts searching cabinets, raiding the fridge in the kitchen, but when he approaches the wet bar, I jump out of my seat.

"No. Don't you fucking dare take those."

"Liv, I have to."

Climbing onto his back, I push him to the floor. "Those are mine. I need them."

Flipping over, he pins me against the carpet. "Why?"

"None of your goddamn business. Now, get off of me." I struggle to move under his grip, his legs pinning mine while his hands hold onto my wrists above my head.

"Frank told me about the video. Nikki's death is not your fault."

"And neither is Parker's, right? Or Matt's? They're dead because someone is trying to kill me. Me, Lloyd! I did this to them!" The tears return, as does the desire to drink.

"No, Liv, you didn't." Relaxing his hold, he brushes my damp cheeks with his soft hand. "None of this is your fault." The lust in his eyes drives deep into my core, but I want nothing to do with him.

"Let me go." Again, I try to free myself, except he doesn't move.

"Calm down first and maybe I will." The hand that had been on my face caresses my arm, then the exposed section of my stomach since my shirt is hiked up slightly. "Are you going to drink anymore tonight?"

"Stop doing that," I demand, noises from the television escalating as the two main characters fuck vigorously.

Lloyd acts as if he doesn't hear me, his fingers tugging on the waistband of my shorts. "I miss you, Liv. I miss us."

"Well I don't."

"Yes, you do." Lowering his head, he kisses me, forcing my mouth open with his.

I manage to free one of my legs and knee him in the groin. He rolls onto his side, curling into a ball while I scramble to my feet.

"Get the fuck out of my house!" I shout, gesturing to the door.

"Goddamn it, Olivia. That fucking hurts," he groans.

"Good. It was supposed to. Now leave."

"I need ice."

"You have that at your house. Clarissa can tend to your injury … or did you forget that you have a girlfriend?"

Carefully, he gets to his feet, hunching forward slightly. "You're a bitch. I don't know why I bothered to come over."

"Because you were hoping to get laid. Don't break my door this time when you leave."

"Cunt." He hobbles to the door and slams it shut, but not hard like before, so the window doesn't shatter.

After locking it behind him, I return to the family room with new bottles from the mini-fridge and continue my pity party. I stop when things start to blur. It takes several minutes to make sure the entire house is locked and the alarm is set. Gone is my need for self-gratification, so I brush my teeth and go to bed, furious with Lloyd.

The rest of the victims have finally been identified, so Ben and I spend all of Wednesday doing notifications. I put together a press release listing the victims and the cause of the fire, with the caveat that it's still under investigation, then email it to the chief for approval. He has a few minor changes, which I make before sending it off to the public relations department. Frank had an early flight, but I did call him the second I woke to let him know that I'm okay, leaving out my encounter with Lloyd. Joe is being released this afternoon, and I have to be at his house by four to keep an eye on him for a few hours while Tanner does a bit of grocery shopping to go along with his husband's new diet.

"I hate rabbit food," Joe complains while we sit in his cozy, warm living room, his feet propped up on the couch.

It's obvious Tanner did the decorating considering how every piece of furniture, rug, painting, and knickknack are coordinated with each other. The various rooms their own canvases, neither one the same.

"The doctors know what's best for you," I counter from my perch in the recliner.

"How much do I owe the funeral home?" he asks, changing the subject.

"They'll be sending you the bill sometime next week. I didn't pick anything extravagant. Just simple. Things Nikki would've approved of."

"What kind of flowers did you select?"

"Roses, which were her favorite. There will be an assortment of color in each arrangement."

He smiles, pleased with my choice.

Tanner invites me to stay for dinner, which is vegetarian lasagna. Joe grimaces at the thought, but cleans his plate. At home, I take a nice relaxing soak in the tub, get under the covers, and fall asleep to an old musical.

Friday morning, I barely sit down at my workstation when my desk phone rings, Chief Daven on the other end.

"Olivia, come to my office. It's important. And bring Ben with you."

After shoving my purse in its drawer, I snag the new detective, then we take one of the two elevators with access to the thirtieth floor. When we step out, the chief's secretary directs us into the office. Ben closes the door, then we each take a seat opposite the big man in charge. Chief William Daven is somewhere in his sixties, dark skinned, with a bulky frame, plump face, and deep, booming voice. He always wears a suit, this one tan colored.

Resting his beefy arms on the desktop, he leans forward. The expression on his face is troubling as he shakes his head. "This isn't going to be easy," he begins, and I automatically fear something has happened to Frank, but if that were the case, Stephen would be here as well. "Detective Candace King was found dead this morning in her car, which was parked outside of a bar called The Vault. She'd been shot in the chest by a striker."

"What?" I utter in disbelief.

"When she didn't show up for work, Director Cruz had one of the guards check her apartment and the bar thinking she might have fallen asleep after a heavy night of drinking. They found the car unlocked; Ms. King slumped in her seat."

"Have you told Frank?"

"He was the first person I spoke to after receiving the call."

"Wasn't she the other detective working the Red Rover Case with Olivia?" Ben inquires.

The chief nods. "Which is why I had her bring you." He turns his attention to me. "I know you're not going to want to hear this—"

"Forget it," I blurt out, interrupting him. "No one is chasing me underground."

"Detective Darrow, I can order you to go into hiding, or place you on suspension so you can leave the country temporarily."

I start to protest, but he holds up his thick hand.

"However, I'm not going to do that. With Frank out of town, I'm down an officer and the Requiem fire is too important to hand off to a rookie detective. No offense, Ben. Stephen has his hands full, so I need you here. But I do want you limiting your exposure outside of work and your home."

"I have a funeral to attend Sunday, Chief, but Ben will be with me. I've asked him to record the attendants. I'm hoping Nikki's killer will show."

"Fine, but if you have to go anyplace else, let me know, and I'll make sure you have an escort."

"Yes, sir."

We're dismissed, and head back to our workstations. Opening the bottom desk drawer, I dig around inside my purse for Sam's phone, then take it into the conference room, closing the door to keep my conversation private.

"Morning, beautiful. What can I do for you?"

"Where's Jake?" I ask, pacing the room, keeping my head down.

"He's doing some recon for me. Why?"

"Shit," I mutter.

"Olivia, what's wrong?"

I tell him about Candace and how I'm on temporary lockdown between home and office. "The chief wants me to have a bodyguard if I travel somewhere other than those two destinations."

"Are you going to listen to him?" Sam asks, sounding greatly concerned.

"Yes. The only thing I have going on outside of work is Nikki's service Sunday, but the new detective will be with me. Along with dozens of other people."

"Bring your gun, and I don't mean leave it in your purse. Have it physically on you. Do you have a backup weapon?"

"There's one I can strap to my ankle."

"Do that, please. I'll see if Jake can quicken his pace and get back here. Where's Frank?"

I'm a little taken aback by the question because it doesn't sound like he's trying to pump me for information, but is asking out of worry. "He's in Prescott tracking down a couple of leads. I don't know when he'll be back. The chief told him about Candace."

"Okay."

"Have you thought anymore about why Joe received that letter?"

He inhales deeply before responding. "Nothing is coming to mind. Does he still have it?"

"Frank does, but it's more than likely locked in his desk drawer, and there's no way for me to get into his office without being noticed."

"Be careful, Olivia. Call me no matter what so I know you're safe."

After hanging up, I open the door and return to my desk, then place the insurance policies into my purse so I don't forget them, along with the keys for Nikki's house to give to her sister if she wants them. Ben and I spend the rest of the day going over our plans for Sunday, borrowing equipment from Hayden, and doing a practice run at the cemetery before the sun sets, checking on the best positions and whether to have him stand in front or off to the side and away from the crowds I expect to be in attendance. I tell him to get there no later than 10:15 a.m. and start filming the second people arrive. At home, I go through my wardrobe, selecting black dress pants, a dark gray, chenille blouse, and a matching blazer, so I can conceal my service weapon. Next, I go into the attached garage, unlock my gun safe, and prepare my other 9mm, finding its holster in a bin at the bottom. After locking the safe, I take the weapon into the house and set it beside my purse on the desk.

Saturday, I spend the day trying to not think about Candace, since that'll only lead me to drink when I need to keep my wits about me. I want to sneak over to the house in Range and jot down what we discovered on the recordings from Requiem, as well as Candace's murder. Maybe tomorrow between the cemetery and club I'll quickly swing by to add the information into the notebook. I busy myself with cleaning, making a grocery list, putting away laundry that I've been neglecting, and blaring music throughout the entire house, drowning out the voices in my head. The ones that beg me to pick up a bottle, even if it's just for a sip. The pounding of the bass drives them back into the recesses of my mind, giving me much needed peace.

Standing under the hot shower Sunday doesn't ease my nerves or anxiety. I barely finished breakfast, my sour stomach giving me issues. After drying, I don the clothes that were selected Friday, attach the holster with my backup gun to the outside of my right ankle, and my service weapon to the waistband of my pants. Running a comb through my hair, I use a flat iron to straighten out a bit of the unruliness, then put on more makeup than I normally do, slip on my chunky boots, grab my purse, and head out in the Halo. I've decided not to stop at the house in Range out of an abundance of caution.

Once I'm over the bridge for Waterside, I head north, then west on the highway until I reach the exit for the outlying regions. The cemeteries are several miles outside of the state proper in federally owned territory since there isn't any room in the states themselves. The closest of the three on this side of Asmor is Parkholm, which is an hour away from Berrin Sector. Passing through its yawning metal gates, I'm greeted by winding roads, manicured lawns, an abundance of flowers, and tall trees. The mausoleum crypt sits right in the center of the massive grounds, nestled quaintly beside a small, manmade lake. My parents' graves are a little farther back. I haven't been to them since my father's funeral, and I'm torn between whether to pay a brief visit or not.

Parking the car in the lot for the granite structure, I check the time: 10:25 a.m. There are chairs set up just outside of the entrance and dozens of large bouquets lovingly placed around a makeshift altar displaying Nikki's urn. After locking my purse in the trunk, I tuck my keys into the pocket of my blazer and approach, sweating instantly from nervousness. Tears run down my cheeks with each thought of never seeing Nikki's smiling face ever again. From one of the arrangements I selected, I remove a red rose and place it in front of her.

"I'm sorry," I whisper, guilt consuming me.

"Excuse me, are you Olivia?" a quivering voice inquires.

Turning, I spot a young woman, possibly in her thirties, with long, light brown hair, green eyes, a round face, prominent chin, and sharp nose. She's wearing a simple black dress, gripping a matching clutch.

"I'm Tabitha," she says, holding out her hand, which I dutifully shake.

"It's nice to meet you. Please, have a seat."

We each take a spot in the front row. I have to watch how I sit considering the weapon I have attached to my leg. Tabitha crosses hers at the ankle, keeping her posture stiff.

"Thank you, again, for doing this. I haven't always been the best sister to Nikki and should've taken better care of her since our parents struggled to." Reaching into her bag, she removes a pack of tissues, using one to dab at her eyes. "Sorry, I don't mean to …" Her voice trails off.

"Tell me about her life. She never mentioned her family."

Tabitha smiles weakly. "That's not a surprise. We weren't her favorite people. Looking back on it all now, I don't blame her for leaving at sixteen. It wasn't a good place for her." She clears her throat. "There's a ten year difference between the two of us. Though our parents refused to admit it, I think Nikki was an accident. One they didn't really want, but being very religious my mother felt obligated to keep the child. I don't have the same views she did. We had a brother. He was two years younger than me, eight years older than Nikki. He died of cancer when he was nine. She was barely a year old when it happened. Our parents were devastated by the loss, leaving me to care for my infant sister. I always thought they'd come around to love her, but they never did. She knew how they felt. That they would rather have Brian alive than her."

"That had to have been difficult."

"It was. Nikki rebelled just so they would notice her, but nothing changed. To them, I was their only child. She hated being left out of everything from family photos to vacations. Our parents would make excuses as to why she couldn't go or participate. I should've tried harder to defend her, but I was enjoying the attention." Tears well in her eyes some more, so she wipes them away before they can fall. "After she left, she would occasionally send a letter or call telling us what she was doing, how she was degrading herself for money. It pissed me off that she was causing our mother and father so much pain and heartache. I blamed her when they died. Heart attacks took both of them one year apart. She refused to come to the wakes, didn't even send flowers."

Taking a deep breath, her body shakes while she exhales. "My boyfriend at the time, who's now my husband, tried to see things from her perspective. He wanted me to realize the pain they had caused her, but I was too stubborn to listen. I didn't invite her to the wedding. For me she was dead like our brother, and I'd made peace with that until the boys were born. My husband insisted they should know their aunt, regardless of what she did for a living. Again, I refused, so he sent the announcements without my permission. I wasn't even sure she received them until your call the other day."

"The policies are in my purse, which is in the trunk of my car."

"I'll collect them after the service."

"You're not going to stay for the get together afterward?"

Tabitha shakes her head. "I'd prefer to remember her my way, not how everyone else knew her. She's still the little girl clinging to my hand on the playground." The poor woman bursts into tears.

I wrap my arm around her shoulder, and we cry together. Tanner rushes over with wads of Kleenex, handing them to us, then goes back for Joe, who's still in the car. When they return, I introduce them to Tabitha. The pair sit beside her and talk while I stand to have a look around, spotting Ben at the far corner by one of the trees lining the road. Cars turn up the lane, pulling into the empty slots, which fill up quickly. Those without a spot, park along the shoulder, some on the grass.

Hayden escorts Alice, both nicely dressed, and wrinkle free. Asher and Tress arrive together in an unmarked CSB car since they're on duty. Dr. Clayton Goff hugs me before making his way to the chairs. Nikki was a patient of his, and he was my alibi from when I was accused of murder. Lloyd has his arm wrapped tightly around Clarissa's waist as they approach, deciding to sit in the back row. Chloe, along with most of the girls and bouncers from the club, join just as Jane arrives.

"Frank told me to come since he couldn't be here for you," she says, pulling me into an embrace. Wearing black pants and a loose-fitting sweater, she holds onto me as if she were my mother. Her wine-colored hair frames her face perfectly.

We wind up standing since all the seats are filled. As the priest begins the sermon, I can't help but glance at everyone, studying their faces, wondering if the person who shot Nikki is here. One by one, everyone approaches the urn, saying brief prayers, setting down flowers, and uttering one last farewell to a dear friend. People remain to mill around, some of the girls talking to Tabitha. Tanner leaves to go prepare the club, so I tell him Joe can ride with me. Ben casually wanders between the groups, recording their interactions without much notice.

"I'll meet you at the club," Jane says, then kisses Joe on the cheek while he remains in his seat.

"Stay here. I'll be right back." I retreat to the car, extract my purse, and then return to the front of the seating arrangements where Tabitha is now talking with Joe. "Here are those policies." After opening the purse, I hand them to her. "I also have the keys to Nikki's home."

"Keep those. We discussed it," she gestures to her and Joe, "and given the situations of some of her friends, the house will be used for them to live in rent free. It's what she would've wanted." She gives me a hug, thanks Joe, and quietly leaves.

"What do we do with all these damn flowers?" he grouses.

"We can take some," Alice comments. "Hayden has a pretty big van."

"We've got room," Chloe states. "They're all going to the club, right?"

"Most of them, but leave a few behind," I suggest.

We segregate those going to the club from the ones remaining while the funeral director and the cemetery's caretaker, remove the urn to be placed inside its crypt. I collect a couple of the roses that have fallen to the ground.

"There's a stop I want to make before we go to Verdigris."

Joe squeezes my arm. "I thought you might."

Once in the car, I drive down the road, winding around a couple of ornate statues until we come to my parents' burial plot. Joe waits while I deposit the flowers onto my mother's grave and stand there for a few minutes, forgiving her for the lies, understanding the choices she made, and acknowledge how much I miss her. Before sitting back down, I remove the holster from my waist, slipping it into the purse.

"Have you had that on this entire time?" Joe asks once we get underway.

"There's another one strapped to my ankle."

He stares at me. "Liv, are you going to tell me, or do I have to guess?"

"I didn't want to worry you."

He snorts. "What else is new?"

"Chief Daven simply wants me to carry a little added protection when I'm away from home. It's nothing, really."

"Uh huh. Well, don't forget to send Tabitha copies of the death certificate when it arrives. She's going to need them for the insurance company."

When we reach Verdigris, Joe has me park in his spot next to his private entrance since the alley is full. I help him out of the car and inside, sitting him down at one of the tables. Nearly everyone who was at the service is here, including Ben, and Joe's best friend, Henry. The flowers are placed all over the dismal surroundings, rolled up blueprints shoved off to the side of one of the booths. Alice and Chloe man the bar while Tanner goes around making sure people eat. Jane keeps me company. I have one drink, then Joe cuts me off. We spend hours talking, laughing, remembering, celebrating the life that was our sweet Nikki.

Six

Monday, Ben, Hayden, and I spend the day in the audio/visual lab reviewing the tape that was made. Each face is examined and run through the motor vehicle servers, matching images to photos on licenses. Everyone is accounted for, no strangers in attendance. Back to square one.

"What about having the Hub run microchips for that night? See who was at the club?" Hayden suggests.

"Our guy is too smart for that. His chip was more than likely removed long ago," I state. "Can you find a picture of Carlos Montoya? Maybe see if the computer can run a comparison."

Ben leans back in his chair, arms folded across his chest. "Who's he?"

"A hitman for the Vilks Cartel. We think he's responsible for what happened to Detective Walker, and possibly the other striker victims. Matt was on his way to meet the man when he went missing."

"Here's a decent photo." Hayden pulls up the video from Requiem, captures a still, and has the software look for identical features, such as face curvature, ear alignment, anything that might tell us who the shooter is. "No match," he mumbles, red letters flashing the same message over both images.

"What about Siem Wolter?"

"Liv, no one has a picture of Siem. We don't even know if the person is male or female. There's nothing. I've checked dozens of times."

"Any other ideas?" I glance between Ben and Hayden, but both remain quiet. "Hopefully Frank had better luck. He's due back late tomorrow night."

Ben and I return to the sixth floor. Sitting beside me at my desk, we go over every piece of information we've been able to gather— photos, witness statements, and reports—to come up with a lead. When it nears five, we stop and leave for the day, then pick up right where we left off the following morning. My head pounds, so I take a couple of pain pills and go up to the breakroom for a Coke. Sitting at one of the tables, I rub my temples and close my eyes, but all I see are flames.

"Darrow," someone calls out, which causes me to open my eyes. "Chief wants you in his office. Now."

Taking the nearly full bottle, I get on the elevator and find Ben waiting for me when I arrive. The secretary ushers us hastily inside, then closes the door. We take our seats and wait since the big man isn't even in his office.

"I don't give a fuck. This is a top priority. All that other bullshit can wait," he bellows from the now open door, then slams it shut. "Hell is breaking loose." Plopping down in his chair, his eyes bore into me while he folds his hands together on the top of his desk. "Olivia, as of right now, you're on vacation."

My eyes widen. "What the hell for?"

Before the chief can respond, his phone rings. "I know. … Give me a fucking minute, I'm in a meeting. … Yes, she's with me. … I'm doing just that! … I'll call you later." He drops down the receiver. "Frank is frantic that I get you out of town."

"Mind telling me what's going on?"

"Director Cruz's car exploded this morning while he was leaving for work."

"What?" My voice cracks as I grow chilled.

"His body hasn't been recovered yet and his microchip is no longer functioning, so for the moment Internal Affairs is going under the presumption he's either missing or burned to ashes. They want to place you into protective custody, and I'm willing to go along with the idea. The only problem is they're short staffed and can't get anyone down here for a couple of days, so I'm pulling a few of our own officers. Therefore, you will be confined to your home until they arrive."

"This is bullshit," I rave.

"Olivia, this is your life we're talking about. You're now the only living witness to the original Red Rover Case."

"What about Frank? He's been working on it ever since I got back."

"He's on his way home right now under my orders and will also be placed into protective custody once the manpower is made available. There will be an unmarked squad outside of your home on Waterside. There will be six-hour rotations. Don't leave for any reason, and don't let anyone inside. Ben will work on the Requiem fire, using that angle as another way to continue investigating the striker murders. The officers are waiting for you downstairs. I'm sorry, Olivia."

Nodding and feeling numb, I stand and go back down to my desk while Ben and the chief discuss the case. After packing up my things and shutting off the computer, I meet the pair of plain-clothes detectives in the lobby. They instruct me to wait in my car until they pull an unmarked from the collection kept on the top level of the garage. Sitting in the Halo, I try to think of why this is happening. We hadn't made any headway on the case, so I don't understand the sudden escalation. Perhaps Frank discovered something useful. I'll call him the minute I get home.

A horn honks and lights flash from a car off to my right. I turn on the vehicle, put it into gear, and start the parade home. Since the detectives have to show their badges to gain access to the island, I decide to enter through the non-residential side of the bridge. Once home, I park the Halo inside of the detached garage, hook it up to its charging station, then go into the house while the officers make themselves comfortable one door down. I drop everything in the study, change into sweats and a T-shirt, then call Frank.

"Where are you?" I ask the second he answers.

"About to take off. It's a four-hour flight, so I'll let you know when I touch down."

After grabbing Sam's phone off of the desk, I call him, but he doesn't answer, prompting me to leave a message. It's close to four, so I make myself a snack, then raid the gun safe—which consists of four handguns, two shotguns, three rifles, and a sniper rifle—carrying everything into the house, placing weapons in each room, along with plenty of ammunition. I draw all the curtains, turn on only a minimum of lights, and hunker down on the couch, both phones in my lap.

Hours pass, so I try Sam again. Still no answer. This time I send him an urgent text message, telling him what happened. Maybe that'll get him to respond. It's not until ten when Frank finally calls back.

"You have officers outside of your home, too?" he asks.

"Yes, with a six-hour rotation."

"Same."

Stretching along the couch, I prop my feet up on the arm rest. "Did you find anything in Prescott?"

"I was able to track down a couple of the partygoers, but none of them remember Nikki. The room she stayed in at the hotel was registered under the record label. The concierge recalls seeing a person matching her description traveling with Dallas. They wouldn't let me review their surveillance recordings without a search warrant. That's what I was in the middle of getting when the chief called to tell me about Cruz."

"Frank, there's more evidence than what I gave you two." I bite my lip and wait.

His breathing quickens as he huffs angrily into the phone. "Olivia Ann Darrow …"

Shit, all three names?

"What did you do?"

Slowly, I tell him about the notebook I've been keeping, the photos I found in Melia's bedroom, the series of numbers I discovered on the back of one of the pictures, the connections we had made, the bracelet from Ronan's ranch, my suspicions, and why I hid everything.

"We need to get that."

"It's at the house in the room where the security computer is kept."

"How do we get there? We're being watched like infants," Frank complains. "Is there anyone you trust to go and retrieve it?"

"Yes, but I haven't written anything down in a week. It'll be incomplete without the updated information."

"You can just tell the person and they can notate it."

"The handwriting will be different, which could get the notebook tossed out of court when it comes time to charge someone."

"Fuck, Liv, you're stubborn as hell."

"I get it from you."

He chuckles. "Yeah, you do. All right, how about this … tomorrow morning, I'll make some excuse about why I need to leave the house. It won't take me long to lose these idiots in Berrin, since the roads are so damn confusing if you don't know where you're going, and I drive fast, making it damn near impossible for them to keep up. Try and sneak out of the house, then I'll pick you up in front of Luke's old home. The chief can reprimand us later for disobeying orders."

"What time?"

"Leave around nine. Take your phone so I can let you know if my plan doesn't work."

"All right. See you tomorrow."

After turning off the lights and television, I set the alarm and bring Sam's phone into the bedroom in case he calls. Lying in the darkness, I do my best to remain positive, hoping we're not making a mistake going after my notes. I should've told him about Sam's spyware, and honestly, I don't know why I didn't. Knots form in my stomach as I close my eyes and work on falling asleep.

I wake at seven and eat breakfast, forcing the dry cereal down my throat, then take a brief shower. I dress in jeans, a light green sweatshirt, and sneakers, then pull my hair into a small ponytail and check Sam's phone. No messages. Setting it down, I go into the den to disarm the alarm and have a peek at my visitors using the camera adhered to the front eave along the right corner of the house. The screen fills with static and I instantly break into a cold sweat. Adjusting to different locations around the exterior, all I get is fuzz. I pick up my cell phone to call Frank, but the device isn't working. Scrambling into the bedroom, I check Sam's and find the same issue.

"Shit, shit, shit," I mutter, hurrying back into the study.

Unholstering my service weapon, I part the blinds for the window above my filing cabinets and glance down the road. No cars. Stuffing my phone into the back pocket of my jeans, I head to the garage and on impulse reach for the keys belonging to the Nimbus, then change my mind and take the ones for the Halo, along with those for the home in Range. Gun in hand, I stay shielded in the house, reaching carefully out of the cracked open door to raise the garage. Once it's lifted, I pause, listening for the littlest noise. There's a button beside the initial one for the detached, so I press it, then wait.

Silence.

I bolt across the motor court, quickly unhook the car from its charger, place the gun onto the passenger seat, and get in. Peeling out of the driveway, the tires squeal, and I barrel down the street. As I start over the bridge, I try calling Frank again.

"The guards are gone!" I shout, my entire body shaking from adrenaline. "My security system was knocked out and my phone just started working."

"Where are you?"

"On the bridge heading toward the mainland."

"Go to the house. I'll meet you there. Hopefully my babysitters are still here and will follow me."

Hanging up, I next call Chief Daven, but he isn't in yet, so I leave a message, then toss the phone onto the passenger seat. On the highway, I exit at Tremont, taking that to Clover. Since I don't have the passcode programmed into the Halo's dashboard, I'll have to get out of the car and manually enter it into the keypad attached to the frame for the hangar-like door. Frank's car is already in the garage when I arrive, the door yawning wide open, so I leave the Halo in the driveway.

"They were gone," he says as I join him, fumbling to get the keys into the lock. "I tried calling the chief, but he didn't answer."

"I did the same thing." After throwing open the door, we rush inside, slamming it closed behind us. "We need to hurry."

Practically running through the living room, we're in the process of entering the bedroom when a breaking noise echoes from the kitchen. There's a back door that leads to the inground pool in that part of the house. Frank draws his weapon from the waistband of his jeans, shoves me behind him, and we retreat the way we came. We're about to turn the corner for the dinette when something outside of the front window catches my attention.

"Fuck, move!" I holler, pulling him back toward the bedroom.

An explosion rips through the garage, sending flaming insulation, sheetrock, beams, and car parts into the house, narrowly landing on us, though we do get knocked down. My jeans and sweatshirt have slash marks with corresponding wounds underneath. We scramble to escape the wreckage, getting singed along the way as our clothes catch fire. Desperately patting out the flames, bullets fly over our heads while we continue to run. It almost seems like we're being purposefully directed into the back part of the house. Pushing the closet door open, Frank bumps into me, and a searing pain tears through my right side, sending me down to the floor. My boss lands on top of me. He moans while trying to move, but we can't go far since we're continuously bombarded. Projectiles miss our heads by mere inches. Frank manages to move just enough for me to slide out from under him.

"Close … the … door," he gasps.

Flipping over, I plaster my back against the floor, then carefully stretch my arm, praying it's not struck by a bullet while smoke and flames pour into the bedroom. Tapping the panic screen, it turns on, so I hit the sensor that'll close the protective door. The steel seamlessly glides out from the wall as the rapid firing continues, projectiles piercing right through the metal like it's paper, embedding into the wall behind us. When the door closes, I look over at Frank.

His skin is paling while copious amounts of blood pool around his still body. Cuts cover his face, and his pants are badly torn, deep lacerations underneath the openings. He has burns on both hands, clothes, and face. Crawling over to him, I take his hand, which is clammy and cooling.

"Frank?" I utter, my lower lip trembling, tears pouring down my face. "Wake up."

His eyes are wide open, emptiness behind them.

"No, Frank. Please, wake up."

Smoke pours through the holes in the door, and I choke, coughing the last of the good air from my lungs. Moving back against the wall now that the shooting has stopped, I hit the link for the CSB station.

"911, what's your emergency?"

"Officer … Officer down," I mutter, pain seizing me from the wound in my side and the burns on my hands and face. A coughing fit ensues for a good couple of seconds, then I try to speak louder. "This is Detective Olivia Darrow, I have an officer down at 308 Clover Street, Range Sector. The structure is on fire, and we're trapped in a panic room off of the bedroom. Door's integrity compromised. Smoke is billowing into the small space."

"Detective Darrow, please stay on the line. Emergency personnel have been dispatched."

The smoke stings my eyes, and it becomes difficult to breathe. I scream as blood runs down my side while readjusting my position so I can open the compartment in the floor. Shoving the cover aside, I lie on my stomach and stick my head into the cool, clean air, drawing it into my lungs slowly. Staring at the notebook and manila envelope tucked safely away, I feel like letting go. I want to fall into an abyss there's no way out of. Fire crackles in the distance, mixed with the sound of wailing sirens. I start slipping from reality, but a wee voice in the back of my head screams for me to hang on, to not give in to the one begging me to die. Things go in and out of focus, my sweatshirt sticking to me while I continue to bleed.

Time no longer exists.

"Olivia!" I hear in the far-off distance. "Olivia!"

The steel door grinds, being forced open by what looks like a large, metallic claw. Eventually, I'm gingerly moved to sit against the wall, an oxygen mask placed over my face, and I'm told to breathe deeply, which only exacerbates the scorching pain in my lungs. The person in front of me continues to speak, but I can't understand anything she's saying due to my heartbeat thumping hard in my ears. She tries to get me to stand, but I shake my head and push away the mask.

"I'm not leaving," I mutter, my voice sounding like gravel.

"Detective Darrow, you have to," she insists, water splashing behind her.

"Let me speak to Hayden." Cough. "I need Hayden."

Scrunching up her face, she appears confused by my request. "Detective—"

"Now."

Standing, she turns and speaks with someone behind her, then continues administering oxygen while her companion in full firefighter gear disappears. He returns with Stephen, who kneels in front of me after the woman has stepped aside.

"Liv, you need to go to the hospital."

I grab his arm, smearing blood on his cotton sleeve. "Listen very carefully." Slow, deep breaths. "I didn't make it. You're not talking to me. I'm dead."

He looks at me thoughtfully, stands, then ushers the firefighters out of the room. The next face I see is Tress'. Her soft, caring smile is comforting.

"Honey, you should go. I'll help Frank."

I shake my head. "Call Chief Daven. Tell him what's happened."

"He's already on his way."

More coughing. "Then allow me to wait until he arrives."

She presses her lips tightly together. "At least let me have a look at your wounds." Carefully lifting up the garment with her gloved hands, she examines the one in my side since it's the worst. "It's not too deep, but you'll need stitches." Next, she checks my burns, which are first degree, and cuts.

"Tress," the chief calls from the doorway, his large frame looming like a giant in the narrow space. "How is she?"

"Hurt. She's refusing to leave."

Lifting my head, I gaze at his sorrowful face. "Take me out in a body bag."

"What?" the coroner exclaims, startled and clearly shocked by my request.

He nods, then pulls Tress outside. I change my focus to Frank, who's now completely ashen, blood no longer seeps from his multiple wounds. The pools drip into the compartment, threatening to short-out the computer and stain the notebook. Grunting, I reach inside and remove it, along with the manila envelope, setting them off to the side away from the red stains.

Chief Daven returns, squatting beside me. "This is what's going to happen. Collins will take photos of the scene, just how it is right now. You can keep your eyes open or closed, it doesn't matter. Tress will return to collect Frank first. He'll be taken out to the van, then Asher will return with the stretcher and another body bag for you. They'll drive you to the morgue, where I will meet up with you in a bit. There are a few things I need to discuss with Collins, Stephen, and the fire chief."

I nod, reach out, and squeeze his hand as a way to say thank you since I'm too tired to speak.

He steps out so Collins can enter the cramped space. She's the supervisor for the forensics department, and Hayden's boss. From my position on the floor, her six-foot stature seems gigantic. Her long, raven hair is in a braid and her dress shoes are covered in protective plastic, gloves adorn her hands, and her rigid face is expressionless, which is typical for her.

"Let me know when you're ready, Olivia."

Taking a couple of deep breaths, I let them out slowly, then close my eyes. Silence fills my world, dead quiet that's greatly unsettling. The next thing I know Tress is rousing me while cleaning my wounds, placing a pressure bandage on the one along my side for the time being. Frank has already been removed, leaving just me. Asher unfolds the black, stiff bag, unzipping it so I can get inside. Taking the notebook and envelope, I hold them firmly against my chest as the bag is closed with just a small gap by my head for air to circulate. I'm lifted off of the ground, placed onto something hard, then taken from the house.

The trek is rough, bumpy with all the debris I'm sure that must be traversed. I want to take a peek and see what remains of the house I love, but I can't ... and I'm not sure I really should. The sirens are no longer wailing, but the lights for the fire engines flash every few seconds overhead. I catch murmurs of conversation, probably from neighbors who've come out to see what's happening. Another bump, then a clicking noise under me, the stretcher jerking and locking into place.

After the doors slam shut, the engine starts, and we move. Several long minutes pass, I think, but I could have fallen asleep again. Tress turns down the zipper just enough for me to see when we're far away from the scene. Asher is behind the wheel.

"Stephen said you were asking for Hayden. He's off today, but Asher called him a few minutes ago just after we got underway. He'll meet us at the morgue."

"Where's Frank?"

"He's on the floor next to you, honey." Her phone rings. "Hello? ... Slow down, Lloyd. ... No, I've got this handled. ... You don't need to come in. ... That's not necessary. ... Then speak with Chief Daven." She abruptly hangs up. "Asshole," she mutters, tossing the phone onto the dashboard. "When we arrive, I'll clean your wounds better since I only did triage. We'll need to remove your microchip, then I'll help you take a shower. We have scrubs you can use since your clothes will need to be collected as evidence. Do you have your phone?"

"It was in the car along with my gun. Can I have something for the pain?"

"When we get to the morgue, which should be in a few minutes."

"Anything left of the house?"

She reaches her hand into the bag to grab mine. "No, sweetheart. It's gone."

The van hits a bump, causing me to wince. Asher turns the vehicle around and puts it into reverse, a loud beeping sound permeates the still air. We wait until he's placed us into park, shuts off the engine, and closes the garage door before getting out. The back of the van opens, Asher unlocks the stretcher, then hauls me out. When the wheels are locked into place, he unzips the bag the rest of the way so I can swing my legs out and over the side. Tress assists me getting down, places an arm around my shoulders, and helps me through the doors that take us right into the refrigerated section where at least a dozen compartments line the walls. Behind them, trays containing deceased bodies, or empty ones waiting for new victims like Frank, reside. After hobbling out another set of doors and into the corridor, she places me in exam room four, which is the first one we come to.

I set the notebook and envelope on the desk next to the computer station for the room. Tress has me sit on the examination table, closes the door, then removes my sweatshirt and starts doing a much more thorough cleaning. This is the first opportunity I've had to check the damage. One of the bullets that struck Frank nicked me just above my tattoo, gouging a narrow groove into my skin. Tress gives me a local anesthetic to numb the area, as well as one in my right wrist.

"The stitches I'm going to use will dissolve over time, that way you won't need to have them removed. Just don't get them wet for a couple of days."

"How do I shower?"

"I'll tape plastic over the bandages. You won't be able to lift your arm for a while because the motion might pull out the stitches."

Once the medication kicks in, she excises the wound, removing the jagged edges, creating a smooth area. She has me lie down to sew me up, then adds an antibiotic ointment, healing gel, and several bandages. Next, she takes a sterile scalpel and makes a small incision—which is no bigger than half an inch, and is slightly deeper than a papercut—into my wrist, forcing the microchip out. I hadn't realized Asher joined us until he places a glass test tube against my skin to collect the chip, then steps into the hallway. After applying a band aid to the tiny wound, she then cleans my burns, but will wait until after I shower to add ointment. I carefully sit up, my body sore all over as a headache forms behind my tired eyes.

"Where is she?" Lloyd's voice bellows from the hallway. "Asher, tell me! I need to see Olivia!"

He bursts into the room before anyone can stop him. The look on his face is one of relief when he notices I'm alive. Hurrying over, he's about to throw his arms around me until he spots the dressings covering my injury and the burns on both my hands and face.

"It's not bad," I say, before he can ask. "Just a graze. I need a shower."

He helps me off the table. "Let's cover that with plastic first."

"I'll handle Olivia, Lloyd." Tress takes the sweatshirt from my hands and gives it to Asher, who's rejoined us holding an evidence bag. "Go call in a prescription for an antibiotic and pain killer, but use Asher's name. He can go pick it up and bring it back here."

"Why does it have to be under his name?" Lloyd protests.

"The chief can explain it to you when he arrives."

She half carries me into the breakroom a little way down the hall, then into the showers at the far end. Selecting a stall—the walls of which rise to the ceiling—I sit on the wooden bench and wait for her to return with a protective covering, cloth tape, a towel, and light blue scrubs.

"Do you need me to wait?" she asks once the plastic is secured to my filthy skin.

"No, I'll be fine. Go tend to Frank."

After she leaves, I pull the off-white curtain closed, undress—which is a struggle—then lean against the dark blue tiled wall, turn on the spout, and wait for the water to warm up. A bottle of cherry blossom-fragranced soap sits on a ledge in the corner, so I pour what I can into my left hand and take my time to carefully bathe, delicately covering the cuts along my arms and legs, cringing when I touch the burns. I'll need to show the other injuries to Tress so she can bandage them as well. There isn't any shampoo, so I use the body wash on my hair, hoping to at least dampen the smoky stench. It takes a lot longer than I'd like to finish showering and drying. Thankfully, the scrubs are easy to get into, but I don't like the idea of being barefoot. When I'm back in the breakroom, I rummage through the staff lockers, which aren't locked, and borrow Taylor's sneakers.

Everyone has gathered in the hallway, including Hayden. I let Asher know the rest of my clothes are still in the shower stall, so he takes a new paper bag and goes to collect them. I return to exam room four, sit at the desk, and use the lone pen by the keyboard to update the notebook with everything that's transpired in the past week. Except today.

A dead person can't document their own demise.

I call out to Hayden as best I can, my voice still raspy from the smoke I inhaled. He hurries into the room. "Don't lose these," I say, handing him the notebook and envelope. "They're the only notes and evidence left in the Red Rover Case. Keep them to yourself. Let the chief know what you find *only* when you deem it's necessary, and if you trust him. Have Asher help if warranted. Tell no one about the spyware, but keep monitoring it and jot down your findings into a different notebook. I don't want this one compromised."

Nodding, he replies, "All right, Liv." Then leans forward and hugs me delicately. "I'm sorry about Frank."

"Remember, don't tell anyone that I'm alive. Not even Alice. No one can know."

"I won't. Stay safe."

The second he leaves, I stand and go over to the wall by the table, lean against it, and slide to the floor, pulling my knees close to my chest.

Lloyd enters and kneels in front of me. "Do you want to talk about it?"

"No," I whisper, the tears returning. "Can I have something to drink?"

"Sure." He stands and exits into the hallway, returning a few minutes later with a cup of water, though I wish it was something stronger. He brushes the hair out of my eyes, the tips of his fingers grazing my wet, tender cheeks.

"Where's the chief?"

"He'll be here in a few minutes," Tress replies, standing in the open doorway. "We can get you a chair."

I shake my head. "The floor feels comfortable. Do you have more bandages? There are additional scraps and cuts that should probably be covered."

Stepping into the room, she goes over to a wall cabinet, removes several sealed packages and more healing ointment, then forces Lloyd to move so she can take his spot. After rolling up my pant legs, she tends to the injuries, which are no longer bleeding.

Staring into the now empty cup, I find myself wavering between numbness and desolation. "It was supposed to be me. I was the target. Not Frank."

"Liv, you don't know that," Lloyd says, positioning himself beside me.

"Matt … Parker … Nikki … Candace … Cruz … and now Frank. All dead."

Moving to the cuts on my arms, Tress comments, "But you're alive. Doesn't that count for something?"

Hard soles click on the linoleum floor. Chief Daven loiters in the open doorway, his beefy arms crossed in front of his barrel chest. "Dr. Rhemick, Dr. Conner, I need to speak with Olivia alone."

"I'll be right outside." Lloyd stands, then Tress finishes and closes the door behind them once the chief has stepped inside.

He pulls over the chair for the desk and sits in front of me, then goes to open his mouth, but I speak first.

"Where were they?" I stare at him, wanting to be furious, only I'm too broken inside.

He lets out a deep sigh, hands falling into his lap. "I don't know. Both units claim they were told to stand down on the protection detail. That Internal Affairs was sending people to replace them. I called up to their offices in Whitebridge and they have no record of such orders, or even the phone calls."

"Did the person give a name?"

He nods. "Brett Ellis. However, when I spoke to the man, he had no knowledge of what I was talking about."

"Brett is the same person who was handling the investigation into the explosion at the home office. He's the one who confiscated my laptop."

A coughing fit strikes, and I plaster my arm against my side to keep the stitches from tearing. Lloyd rushes in with more water. I sip it slowly, then request pain medication.

"Asher just left to pick it up."

"Have him come in the moment he arrives," the chief directs.

Lloyd doesn't move from his spot on the floor beside me.

"Dr. Rhemick, you need to wait in the hallway."

"No," he says defiantly. "Olivia needs me."

The chief's face reddens and a vein bulges in his neck. "She's fine. If her condition changes, I'll let you know."

Lloyd is about to argue when I place a hand on his chest. "Do me a favor and call Joe. I don't want him learning that I've died."

"Olivia, no one can know you're alive," the chief protests.

"I trust Joe and his husband, Tanner. They won't say anything. Besides, the club they own is temporarily closed and Joe's been ordered on bed rest because of his heart attack, so he won't be encountering anyone. He needs to be told the truth. Otherwise, it might kill him, and I can't live with myself if that happens."

The older man glares at me, grumbling under his breath. "Fine, but just those two. No one else."

I nod.

Lloyd leaves to contact Joe before the story breaks, if it hasn't already.

The chief leans forward, resting his arms on his thighs, a perplexed expression spanning his hefty face.

"It was a trap," I mutter, clutching the empty cup. "The security system for my house was knocked out, along with my cell phone. I couldn't call anyone until I was on the bridge." Lifting my head, I glower at him. "They knew where I would go. Who I'd phone for help. This person knows me, personally."

"Does anyone specifically come to mind?"

"No, because they're all dead."

"Who?"

I breathe deeply, my chest rattling as the air leaves my lungs. "Dean, Kane, and Luke."

"What about Lane Murray?"

I didn't mention him on purpose. The chief doesn't know he's dead, nor that I'm the one who pulled the trigger, ending that bastard's life. He used to be the District Attorney for the state, but rigged my murder case to garner a conviction and it backfired, costing him his job. That's on top of a sex scandal that I inadvertently helped uncover. It was how he flirted with Collins during my trial that caused me to question his faithfulness as a husband. She was thrown off the case because of it. Speculation ensued, then weeks later the full story broke. Lane had been forcing women to sleep with him to either get a job in his office or a promotion. His wife filed for divorce and was seeking sole custody of their kids when he supposedly vanished at the end of December.

Shrugging, I respond, "I don't know. Maybe."

"Why were you and Frank at the house in Range Sector?"

Rubbing my temples, I attempt to prevent a migraine from erupting out of the headache that already exists. "While I was at the home office, I kept a notebook detailing everything we were working on, the connections we had made, our theories, lists of evidence that had been collected, my own notes that I didn't share with the others. I wanted something to review as a whole when I was away from the conference room." Feeling guilty, I go on to tell him about the envelope and what it contains, explaining how I came across each item, including the bracelet from Ronan's ranch and what it does. Again, I leave out Sam, his spyware, and the drive I used to load it into our systems.

"Where are these things now?" he asks, his voice controlled and flat.

"Hayden has them. He's the only one I trust at the moment."

The chief frowns, then sighs. "As much as I want to reprimand you for keeping such valuable information from me, given what's been happening I understand your motive behind it. Collins is currently handling the evidence Frank uncovered, but I won't have her interfere with whatever you instructed Hayden to do. For the moment, it's best if the right hand doesn't know what the left hand is doing." Sitting back, his chair squeaks. "Honestly, I don't know who to believe at the home office, or IA. Something doesn't feel right about any of this and it's driving me crazy. I do appreciate the extra initiative you took at creating a separate file for your own investigation. Perhaps with what Hayden finds, we can finally end this nightmare and flush out the shit from our own backyard if there is any."

"Now what?"

He exhales loudly. "Someone is on their way to take you into custody and get you out of the state. Maybe even the country. Your home on Waterside will be locked up and tagged as a working crime scene. There will even be a car stationed outside of it at all times. Is there anything from the Red Rover Case inside?"

"Another one of Ronan's bracelets. It should be sitting on the dresser."

Checking his watch, he asks, "Have you eaten today?"

"Just a bit of cereal this morning. What time is it?" I can't see a clock in the room—which is probably behind me on the wall above my head—so I have no idea if it's still morning or now afternoon.

"Almost two."

I furrow my brow. "Really? How long was I in the house?"

"Quite a while. The fire had to be put out before anyone was permitted inside. The steel door gave the firefighters trouble because the heat had caused it to expand. Some of the hoses were focused on the roof for the panic room to keep the flames from spreading since we knew that's where you were. If you hadn't placed your face into that hole in the floor, and without the access to fresh air like you had, we wouldn't be having this conversation." He stands. "Why don't we go into the breakroom, and I'll have lunch brought to you?"

I nod, he helps me to my feet, and we exit the room together. Lloyd is the only one in the hallway, so I assume Tress has started taking care of Frank, though I wish she'd wait until I leave. Mentioning something to that effect, the chief steps into exam room three to speak with her while I go into the breakroom, taking a seat at the first table by the door. Lloyd joins me, carrying a tube of ointment.

After opening the cap, he squeezes a bit of the velvety substance in his palm, then applies it to my burns. "Joe was relieved to hear you're all right. The news outlets aren't releasing much information, but they did have a helicopter over the house, which he recognized. What they are saying is that two decorated CSB detectives were gunned down this morning and the home they were trapped in was set ablaze. I'm sure everyone else who knows you is panicking. Praying that you're safe."

"They can't know. None of them." My voice is flat, dull, and lifeless.

"I told Joe the urgency about keeping his lips sealed. He assured me no one would hear the truth from either him or Tanner, even knowing what this will do to the girls at the club. He's aware of the importance of maintaining the ruse. Do you have someplace to go?" Lloyd asks, slowly working in the cream.

"The chief has someone coming to get me."

He smiles. "You can always stay at my house."

"Lloyd, we've been over this. Besides, you're dating Clarissa. I have to get as far from Asmor as possible."

Still smiling, he takes on a faraway look. "We can go on a cruise down in the tropics. Spend our time on the beaches, go snorkeling. Enjoy some peace and quiet together."

I grab his wrist, gently pushing his hand away. "No. Stop trying to make a relationship happen when it didn't work the first time."

He places his clean hand on the back of my head, pulling me forward until our foreheads touch. "I nearly lost you today, Olivia. It destroyed me. I don't know what I'd do if you died."

Moving out of his reach, I change seats. "You lost me months ago, Lloyd."

Sorrow fills his eyes. "There's no way for me to get you back?"

"No," I reply adamantly.

His sadness is quickly replaced by rage. His face turning crimson, he slams the tube onto the table, shoves his chair over as he stands, and storms from the room.

Tress stares behind her after she enters. "What the hell is the matter with him?"

"He can't take no for an answer."

Righting the chair, she sits in the one beside me and finishes with the burn ointment. "I swear that man is crazy. It's almost like he believes the world owes him or something. I hate arrogant fucks like that. The chief is having Asher pick you up food, since he's out getting those prescriptions. He told me your concern in regard to Frank. I was just getting him cleaned up so he'll look handsome as always."

I smile, tears falling again. "He has a girlfriend. She was standing with me at Nikki's service."

"Really? That's sweet. It's nice that he found someone."

Referring to Frank in the present tense helps block out the reality I'm not willing to face. A life without him is something I never planned for. He was always going to be around … always. Frank is resilient, stubborn, a mentor, and a friend. He's the father I wish I had. Leaning my head against Tress' shoulder, I bawl. She rubs my back and whispers that it's going to be just fine. My new guardian angel will make sure of that.

My thoughts wander to Jane and how I won't be there to help her grieve. I wish I could talk with my psychiatrist, Dr. Beverly Randall, tell her I'm alive, but not okay. That the rock in my life is now nothing but dust. She's known me almost as long as Frank. He insisted I see her when I started acting out around the age of ten, the start of my horrendous, rebellious years that quickly grew out of control, culminating in a heart-rending event I'm forever haunted by. Frank was the one who took me to the appointments, since my father was either not home or too drunk to care. I've only survived this long because of that man, and now he's gone.

Tress stands to fetch a box of tissues just as Asher walks in with my medication and a greasy paper sack containing a hamburger, fries, and large Coke from Slingers. I eat first, blowing my nose between bites, then take the Vicodin and antibiotic. My lower abdomen starts to cramp, and I know it's not from the food. I ask Tress to run an errand for me, which she's more than happy to do, given she has daughters. She's gone maybe a half hour, giving me time to finish the food without being rushed. I take the purchases into the bathroom, open the package of underwear and box of tampons. It's not that time yet, but trauma has a way of fucking up your cycle. Putting the scrubs back on, I shove everything into the bag to take with me. Including the medication so I don't forget it, along with the tube of ointment and some extra bandages Tress hands me. The three of us remain in the breakroom, but barely say anything since the oppression of the day is hitting all of us.

"Asher, can you move one of the van's out of the garage?" the chief asks, entering. "Olivia's ride is here, and I want him to park inside of the building."

The young man scampers out the door while I take deep breaths, terrified about being passed along to a stranger for protection. Fear of the unknown grips me, seizing me in a tight hold, threatening to suffocate me. Finishing the rest of the Coke, I stand and toss out the Styrofoam cup into the garbage, turn around, and freeze, stunned by who's behind me.

"Hi, Liv," Matt says, running his hands through his light brown hair that has grown a bit since the last time I saw him. He's in his mid-thirties, stands around six feet, is muscular with delicately carved features, and green eyes.

Running up to him, I throw my left arm around his neck since I don't dare stretch the right one. "I thought you were dead," I utter, crying, burying my face in his shoulder.

He wraps me in a warm embrace. "You can't get rid of me that easily." Nudging his head against mine, I lean back, and he kisses me hard.

"Where ... Where have you been?"

"Hiding," Chief Daven responds. "Matt called me a few days after he was attacked. Like you, he didn't know who to trust at the home office. He's been staying with a friend of mine, who patched him up and kept him safe. He'd still be there if it wasn't for what happened today."

Kissing Matt, I whisper, "Don't ever scare me like that again."

"I'll try not to," he teases. "We should get going."

The chief shoves his hands into the back pocket of his black slacks. "Are you driving the car I suggested?"

"Yes, sir. Your friend knows his stuff."

He smiles. "Try to stay off the interstates where you can. It'll add to your travel time since you can't go as fast, but the routes will be safer. Stop only when you have to. You'll need to get Olivia other clothes to wear." He removes a device from his pocket. "This is a satellite phone. Call me in a few days on the number programmed into it, no one else. I'll let you know what we find from the security footage taken at Olivia's house once Collins has it ready."

Grabbing the bag off of the table, I step into the hallway, but stop and enter exam room three. Frank is nicely scrubbed; no trace of blood or smoke remains. A white sheet is spread across his body, draped to his shoulders. Standing beside the examination table, I can't help but feel as if I'm abandoning him. It hurts like hell to see him this way and I wish this morning never happened. He'd still be alive, and I wouldn't have to mourn the last of my family.

Now I'm truly alone.

Leaning down, I kiss him on his cold forehead, tears raining down my face. "I'm sorry. I'm so sorry. I love you, Frank."

Matt has to coax me away, otherwise I'll stay there forever. In the garage sits an old truck with an extended cab covered in rust and white paint. It's horribly dented, the tailgate is missing, but the windows have a thick, tinted film, preventing anyone from seeing inside.

"It runs better than it looks," Matt comments, opening the passenger door.

"Do you have money?" the chief asks once I close the door, dropping the bag onto the floor and reaching for the seatbelt.

Matt nods. "Your friend gave me plenty, along with an arsenal. We'll be fine."

Chief Daven pats Matt on the back. I roll down the window, and he reaches through the opening to hug me. "Stay safe. I need you back here alive, Darrow. Don't disappoint me."

"I won't. I promise."

Matt gets behind the wheel and starts the truck while I secure the window back in place.

Glancing at me, he smiles and reaches out, clasping the necklace in his open palm. "You still have on the pendant."

"I told you I'm never taking it off."

He kisses me.

Asher opens the garage door, and we back out into the night. Making a left onto Cassidy, we travel one block, then turn right onto

McCarthy. Cutting through Berrin Sector, we reach the highway and head west, then onto Route 80 going north. At Interstate 41, we continue west for several hours until we're past the state of Hatley. Taking the exchange ramp for Interstate 43, we again go north, exiting an hour later to stop for the night at a rundown motel where only half of the lights in their sign actually work, and the parking lot is nothing but gravel.

I wait in the truck while Matt goes inside to secure a room. Back behind the wheel, he drives around to the other side of the two-story structure with its sagging roof and parks in front of a door that looks thinner than paper. Reaching behind his seat, he extracts two large duffle bags, hefting them over his shoulders. He then comes around to my side and helps me out since I'm still unsteady on my feet. Clutching the plastic bag, I gingerly walk toward the dark blue painted door, Matt inserts an old-fashioned key, and flips on the lights before stepping inside.

The room smells of mothballs, old sex, and sweat. We set our things down on the table and chairs by the bathroom, not daring to have it touch the floor that's heavily stained with a few mouse droppings.

"I know, but we have to stay low," he says as if reading my mind. "Let me have a look at your wound."

After lifting up the shirt, he removes the plastic I'd left on after showering. The bandage is holding and nothing is seeping, which can only be a good sign. Removing a tampon from the bag, I step into the bathroom to use the facilities, which I do quickly for fear a cockroach will scurry up my ass. Sitting on the edge of the bed, Matt removes his shirt and that's when I notice the healing scar along his left bicep.

"The bullet that struck you was pulled from a tree," I comment, tracing the wound with the tips of my fingers while he kneels in front of me.

"Bastard had me pinned down." He wraps his arms around my waist, pulling me close, and resting his forehead against my stomach. "The only way out was through the forest, but that was after I shot the gas tank. The smoke and fire covered my escape and interfered with his aim."

"What, exactly, did the chief tell you about today?" I ask, running my fingers through his hair.

"That you're being targeted, Frank's death, Candace's murder, that Director Cruz is missing, and how Nikki was used to lure you to Requiem before it was set on fire." He lifts his gaze to meet mine. "I'm so sorry, Liv. I know how much he meant to you. I wish I could've been there to get you through all of that, but I couldn't leave. Not until it was absolutely necessary."

Bending down, I kiss him passionately. "I know, but you're here now."

We kiss some more, and I want it to go further, but I'm too sore and tired. Matt eventually goes into the bathroom while I get under the covers, making sure they're nowhere near my nose. A sole spring pokes me in the back, so I don't anticipate getting a lot of sleep. Before joining me, Matt ensures the door is bolted, the curtains are fully drawn, and the lights are extinguished. It's hard to get close when I'm afraid of ripping my stitches, and it hurts to move. Lying there, my mind takes over, and I torture myself with replaying everything that happened today. As I burst into tears, Matt holds me tightly, reassuring me things will be fine.

Seven

Matt lifts up my shirt, removes the old bandage, adds more ointment, then covers it up with a clean dressing. The water coming out of the faucet is questionable, so he goes down toward the office and buys a Coke from the vending machine in order for me to take my medications. After packing the truck, he drops off the key and we hit the road, pulling over an hour later to fill the tank and grab something to eat. We take Route 92 west and stop at an indoor outlet mall around noon. Nobody pays much attention to us, even though I'm still wearing the scrubs, and no socks with Taylor's shoes.

"You're going to want warm clothes," Matt suggests. "It'll be cold and possibly still snowing where we're going."

With that in mind, I select a couple pairs of jeans, sweatshirts, tank tops to wear underneath and sleep in, cotton shorts, socks, underwear, bras, and a parka, this one in a dark red since the one I currently own is back at the house on Waterside. He has me get boots with a thick, heavy sole, almost like those worn by construction workers, but in black. Matt picks up a few things as well, paying cash for everything. We eat a late lunch at the food court, then top off the tank at a gas station across the way and get back on the road.

In the early evening, we take Interstate 42 heading north. I sit slumped in my seat, staring at the scenery sailing past, occasionally glancing in the side mirror to make sure we're not being followed. The emotional numbness I was experiencing yesterday returns, turning my mood melancholy.

"Liv, talk to me," Matt coaxes, briefly glancing in my direction.

"I don't know what about," I reply, continuing to watch the massive forests fly past as the terrain steepens, jagged boulders lining the road, having fallen from cliffs encroaching around us. The days are starting to get longer, so the sun is just now dipping below the horizon, turning the sky orange.

"Have you spoken to Sam?"

"Not in a while," I lie, then move my attention off the road and onto him. "He knew you were a detective for CSB."

Matt grimaces. "I hadn't realized he was going to admit that to you. It's the reason he recommended me to Wallace, though that was kept strictly confidential. Sam had suspicions about the man, and rightfully so. Calhoun Steel is manufacturing the strikers and selling them globally, not just in Leyon. Wallace is making a mint and is even having a few of his designers creating new types of weapons. Ones that won't be found by metal detectors."

"Did you let Chief Daven know?"

He sighs. "After I went into hiding, but I wasn't able to communicate it to Sam."

"But he has access to these bullets, so he would've already known who was producing them. It's what was in the gun he gave me to kill Lane."

"Yes, but he wasn't sure where the shipments were going, or who the largest buyer is. That's what I was hired to find out."

"Did you?"

"The Friday I returned from San Cadin is when I figured out who the main purchaser was."

"The Vilks Cartel."

He nods.

"Did you tell anyone?"

"Sam, Director Cruz, then Chief Daven after I went into hiding."

I wait a few moments before speaking again. "Do you know Sam is Chairman of the Board for Calhoun Steel?"

I pause for Matt to react, but he doesn't, which means he probably knew way before I did.

"Were you ever going to say anything to me about that?" I ask angrily.

"Eventually, but then things went to hell."

I scowl.

"Liv, don't be mad." After picking up the uncapped water bottle sitting between his legs, he drinks from it, then sets it back down.

"It's kind of hard not to be when you practically begged me to avoid working for the man. Yet, here you are doing it without a second thought."

"I didn't have a choice in the matter. He threatened to have you killed," Matt replies, sounding tense.

"When did he say this?"

"While you and Luke were out touring the Keys. I wasn't going to accept Wallace's offer, but Sam said he'd put a striker in your head if I didn't." He glances at me. "Why did you start working for him?"

"Because he was going to have Frank murdered if I refused." Turning toward the window, I cross my arms over my chest. "Little good that did."

"Do you think Sam is behind the murders?" he asks, his tone less hostile.

"Not at first, but now …" my voice trails off. "I don't know. He sends mixed signals. At times he acts protective, then in other instances I know he's hiding something." Pause. "Did you know he had me launch a spyware program into the home office systems?"

"Are you serious?" Matt's voice rises an octave. "Does anyone else know about that?"

"Just two people not connected with the case who I trust implicitly. One is our forensic lead with extensive computer knowledge, and the other is a coroner's assistant with a penchant for gaming. Both created a program that's attached to the spyware, documenting everything it's doing, what information it's grabbing, and without Sam discovering it exists. The whole thing is being monitored through a reconfigured gaming console."

He smirks. "Not bad."

The cliffs give way to a mighty steel bridge over the Brimher River since it cuts diagonally across the country, ending in Asmor. The tires and axels aren't thrilled with the grating, but endure enough for us to make it across.

"Why did you agree to meet with Carlos Montoya?"

Matt finishes the bottle, tossing it into the back of the cab. "Who told you about that?"

"I'll give you one guess."

He chortles. "Sam. Should've known. I was the only one willing to go and make the delivery."

I furrow my brow. "Is that what Wallace told you, or did you actually hear the other guys in the company refuse?"

He doesn't answer right away. "You think it was a setup."

"Calhoun Steel is making illegal weapons. Carlos Montoya is the hitman for the Vilks Cartel, and you're sent to hand over rifles and standard ammunition? Wouldn't they request the more powerful armaments like they have been? Why purchase run-of-the-mill shit that you can easily get wholesale from one of the other manufacturers? Also, the shooter who targeted you already had the armor piercing rounds. There's no reason to ask for lesser quality projectiles."

He scowls. "I hadn't thought of that. It means Wallace knew who I was."

"But at what point in your employment did he learn that? Obviously not right away. Otherwise, you would've been killed much earlier."

"So, who told him?"

Sitting up, I reach into one of the plastic bags at my feet, remove a Coke bottle and my pain medication, open both, and swallow a pill.

"How are you feeling today?"

Putting the medicine back, I reply, "Like I was hit by a bus. The burns don't really bother me anymore, and neither do the minor cuts.

There are heavy bruises along my calves where part of the house knocked me down when it collapsed. More on my arms and chest from falling debris and when I landed on the hardwood floor of the closet. I'm a fucking mess."

"I'll say," he teases.

I slap him lightly on the arm, which causes him to laugh.

"The Vilks Cartel," he mutters a few minutes later. "Is Carlos the only connection we have to them?"

After drinking some soda, I go into detail about what Candace, Parker, and I found, as well as the financial documents I discovered in my half-sister's bedroom, along with the photographs. He knew Parker had been killed, but not how or why.

"Who could possibly want to murder you?" Matt comments.

"What about the others? Everyone involved with the Red Rover Case is either dead or pretending to be."

"Cartels don't normally target police unless it's a turf war, which this isn't. I hate to say it, Olivia, but maybe the case isn't the connection. Perhaps it's you."

Lowering my head, I reply, "That's crossed my mind as well. Especially since Melia's name is on an off-shoot account for TITAN Industries. The one where all the money is being moved before transferred into thin air. But I didn't really know my sister. We'd only encountered each other a few times before she was killed. The people who knew we were related are all dead." Then it hits me. "Except for Sanford Mecum. Kane's old attorney. Parker went to see him the same time I visited Kane."

"When we reach our destination, we'll phone the chief, and he can have someone look into that."

We stop a few hours later, grab a quick dinner, and check into another motel. This one a little bit nicer than last night's room, but still awful. In the horribly stained bathroom, I finally take off the scrubs, remove the bandage, carefully wash the area, and add more ointment to not only the bullet wound, but to my burns and other cuts as well. The mattress for this bed is lumpy and uneven. The room has a thick pine scent … however, there isn't anything inside to create that fragrance.

Matt exits the bathroom wearing only boxers, turns off the lights, and gets into bed. I curl up beside him, and he drapes an arm around my shoulder.

After a few minutes, he asks, "Sam was protecting you? How?"

"He had someone keeping a close eye on me when I was traveling back to Asmor after the bombing at the home office. The guy stuck around, tracking me when I was working the club, ensuring I made it home. He was guarding me until a few weeks ago. I also saw him one night at The Vault. He passed me a note, which stated that more than one person was watching me. I never did ask him how he knew that or who it was."

"And you actually believe that's what this person was doing?" Matt asks, astounded. "I thought you were smarter than that."

I pull away. "Don't talk down to me. You weren't there when all this shit was going on."

"No, but I know my girlfriend has better sense than that." He pauses. "Or, is there something you're not telling me?"

"I don't believe this shit." He's right, although I'm not about to confess my sins. "No, Matt, I'm not hiding anything from you." I want to flip onto my right side, placing my back to him, but because of the injury I can't. My solution is to scoot as close to the edge of the bed as possible without falling off. "I'm sorry I mentioned anything."

Fuming, he rolls over and grouses under his breath. I ignore him and try to get some much needed sleep.

We've barely said two words to each other all morning. Heading west on Interstate 47, I ride with my eyes closed, wanting to catch up on the rest I've been sorely lacking. Stopping at an oasis for lunch, I use the restroom, take more pain medication, and eat while staring at my food, avoiding Matt's glare. What I really want is a drink, but I don't have any money to buy liquor and I can't take it while on the Vicodin. When we're done, we toss out our trash, fill up the tank, and return to the road. The heater in the truck doesn't work very well, so I bundle up in my parka while Matt puts on an additional sweatshirt. Our next exit is onto Route 87, which runs south of Enris, then up along its western shores.

A few hours later we turn off for a ferry dock, the lights for the marina glowing in the distance like spotlights in the wanning sun. Dozens of cars are in line to board the large boat, while smaller vessels sit moored in the harbor. When we reach the ramp, Matt pays for the trip across the open waters, then follows instructions from one of the crewmen on what lane to park the truck.

"We can either stay in here or go up into the cruise cabin," he says, shutting off the engine. "At least in there we'll have heat."

"How long of a journey is it?"

"An hour if the waves aren't too choppy."

"Maybe they'll have coffee," I comment, unbuckling my seatbelt.

After he opens the door, he folds his seat forward and removes one of the duffle bags, slinging it over his shoulder.

"Why are you bringing that?"

He pulls me closer before responding. "I'm not about to leave our weapons in the truck."

Moving toward the center of the starboard side, we climb the stairs to the third deck, which is enclosed. Grabbing seats in the back row, I watch the bag while Matt goes in search of coffee, returning with two paper cups capped in plastic. He hands me one, then sits. The vessel isn't too crowded and we're shortly underway.

"Where are we going?" I ask, sipping at the hot, caustic substance.

"Kodiak Island. My grandfather built a cabin there decades ago. He used to take me and my brothers fishing during the summer when we were younger. No one uses it anymore since my parents hate making the trip and my siblings are too busy to take care of it."

"When was the last time it was used?"

"I was there in the middle of October for a couple of weeks. Needed a break from sifting through evidence from the ranch. Tomorrow, I'll shop for groceries. There should be enough logs for the fireplace. If not, I can chop up more."

"And no one knows about this place?"

He nods since his mouth is full of coffee. "Except my family, of course, but they all think I'm dead."

I'm troubled by how nonchalantly he mentions it. "That doesn't bother you?"

"It does a little. They knew my job was dangerous, so it shouldn't have been a surprise when they received the call from Director Cruz." He says it so casually, it almost sounds heartless. "Besides, keeping them in the dark makes everyone safer."

"You'll never be able to see them again."

He shrugs. "True, but I'm also not tied down with family obligations."

My face flushes with anger. "So, having a girlfriend isn't an obligation?"

"That's not what I meant, and you know it," he says testily. "I love you, Olivia."

"But?"

Staring at me, he furrows his brow. "But what?"

"There isn't more you want out of life, like a family of your own?"

Standing, he tosses out his empty cup, then retakes his seat. "What could I possibly offer a wife? I'm gone all the time, there's no guaranteeing I'll return from an assignment, and I'd be a shitty father if we were to have kids."

Sam told me once that Matt wasn't someone he could see settling down, that he was merely an in-between fuck for me until the right man came along. With everything Dean put me through during our marriage, the idea of tying myself to someone else for the rest of my life seemed like a horrible idea. Hearing Matt makes me realize that's exactly what I want. A husband … someone to share my life with … a family. I needed it to be him, but now I see that it was simply a fantasy, a wish I sought to come true because I don't want to end up alone.

Placing a hand on my knee, he asks, "What's the matter? You look upset."

I fake a smile. "No, just tired." Leaning close, I kiss him, then rest my head on his shoulder.

As he strokes my back, and with the motion of the ship, I start to doze, nearly spilling the coffee. Matt takes it from me, tossing it into the trash, then goes to use the restroom. A few minutes before we're set to dock, we return to the truck, shoving the duffle bag behind the driver's seat. Everyone slowly gets into their vehicles, the ferry is secured, and the gates lowered. Moving forward in a procession, we drive away from the harbor, turning right at the top of the ridge it sits below. Winding our way around the desolate roads, Matt turns on the high beams to see better because it's pitch black outside. Since there isn't any light pollution, the stars shine brilliantly overhead, exposing constellations I've not seen in a long time.

Eventually, he turns down a dirt road, slowing to traverse large ruts. A lone light shines in the distance, tall pine trees nearly scraping the paint off the vehicle. The rustic house comes into view, a few of the lights on inside.

"I thought you said no one would be here," I state, panicking.

"Those are on automatic timers like the porch light."

He parks the car close to the front stoop, a lone beam casting directly down onto the warped wood of the steps from a single bulb shrouded in metal. Grabbing our things, he searches for the keys in the duffle bag with the weapons, then unlocks the door, turning on a lamp by the entryway. I stay by it while he checks the house, making sure we're the only ones here, in addition to turning on some additional lights. I'm instantly struck by the musty smell, but it's not overpowering. There are a few cobwebs clinging to the ceiling fans in both the living and dining rooms that are currently off, and a bit of dust covers the blades.

To the immediate left is a small dining table ready to seat four. On the right is an alcove with what appears to be three bedrooms and one bath. Straight ahead is the living room with a back door that exits onto an enclosed porch. Halfway through the house on the left is a doorway leading into the kitchen. Much of the interior is done up in clapboard paneling and badly scratched oak wood flooring. Braided wool rugs cover sections of the floor. A bouquet of dried flowers sits in an etched glass vase on a dusty, dark orange charger in the center of the dining table. The living room furniture is done up in red and white gingham with matching throw pillows and blankets tossed haphazardly onto the couch and two side chairs. A pale stone fireplace the focal point for the seating arrangement.

After setting the plastic bags down onto the table, I step into the kitchen, flipping on the light switch that's hidden behind an old-fashioned, olive-colored refrigerator. The room is quaint, the cabinets forming a U-shape with the sink under the lone window to the right, a grimy stove beside it. There's a two-person table right by the doorway, the wood and style matching that of the dining area. A slim door rests behind the table, an empty pantry on the other side. Exiting, I grab the bags, move across the way, and into the alcove where the bedrooms are located, each done in a different shade of blue, all containing a queen-sized bed covered in a handmade quilt, a six-drawer dresser with an attached mirror, and end tables topped with wicker lamps capped in white shades that still have the plastic on them.

I find Matt in the room with a direct entrance into the bathroom. All the others have to go through the door off the hallway. He's busy unpacking our clothes, shoving them into the drawers or hanging things in the closet beside the dresser. Stepping into the bathroom, I notice the motif is pine green, white, and porcelain. A cloth curtain with a forest scene dangles from a rod for the shower and tub. The vanity is a single sink, and the toilet sits behind a half wall that divides it from the rest of the space. Going back into the bedroom, I take off my coat and hang it in the closet. I place the tampons, ointment, and bandages in the bathroom, the unused underwear in the dresser, and the abundance of snack food in the kitchen.

"There's an area at the back of the property where we can get in some target practice," Matt says, joining me. "We'll keep the weapons in the rooms we're going to use the most, making them readily available if something should happen."

"Is it too late to call the chief?"

"He's two hours ahead of us, and it's nearly ten our time. We can phone him tomorrow."

I return to the bedroom while Matt makes sure all the doors are locked, curtains drawn, and turns off the lights. When I'm done in the bathroom, he's standing on the other side of the door, pulls me close, and kisses me ardently.

"I've missed you," he whispers.

"In a few days."

His mouth moves to my neck. "I'm game for right now. We can fuck in the shower."

Closing my eyes, I relish his touch and wish it could lead to more. "As much as I want to take you up on that offer, everything still hurts."

"All right, but be prepared to come like never before." He swats me on the ass, then steps into the bathroom.

I change into my new shorts and a long-sleeved shirt since there's a slight chill in the air, then get under the soft covers. The mattress conforms to my body, and I'm nearly asleep by the time Matt joins me.

When I wake, he's gone and panic ensues, but I find a note on the nightstand stating that he's gone shopping and will be back in an hour or so. Without my phone, and no clocks anywhere in the cabin, I have no idea what time it is. After using the facilities, I go into the living room where the sun is shining brightly through the windows for the enclosed porch. Along the back wall is a lengthy, wooden cabinet with framed family photos resting on top. Four boys ranging in age are covered head to toe in dirt, each proudly holding a fish in their hands. There are more pictures on the fireplace mantel, a few containing a couple I can only assume are Matt's parents.

After looking them over, I retreat to the bedroom and, using my left arm, haul out the duffle bag containing our weapons. I sit on the couch, set the bag onto the floor, and unzip it, revealing a cache of rifles and handguns, along with empty clips, boxes of ammunition, cleaner solvent, a nylon brush, and a few rags. Lining everything on the coffee table, I go about the daunting task of disassembling the handguns, then check the state of the weapons and how much cleaning needs to be done. I methodically scour each component, using the rags to remove excess solvent, as well as wiping my hands. One by one, I put the guns back together, setting them aside to load with ammunition later.

Next, I tackle the rifles, then start slipping the 9mm rounds into the clips. I'm nearly done when Matt returns. Quickly washing my hands, I put on sneakers and help carry in the paper bags as best I can. He bought enough food to last a few weeks. Hopefully we don't have to stay in hiding for that long. Once everything is put away, Matt suggests I take a shower while he cooks a late breakfast. Sitting on the edge of the bathtub, I use a washcloth to clean my skin, still hesitant about getting the stitches wet. When I'm dry, I slather on some ointment, put on a pair of jeans and a black sweatshirt, then return to the kitchen where Matt is dishing out eggs over easy, toast, and crisp bacon.

"After we eat, we'll call Chief Daven. I'm sure he's anxious to hear from you."

Swallowing a bit of food, I have to drink some juice since the toast crumbs insist on sticking to the back of my throat. "I hope Hayden has made headway with my notes."

"Were they in that notebook you had in San Cadin?"

I nod. "But I didn't explicitly mention Sam in any of it. Instead, I drew a profile of a wolf's head in place of his name."

Matt narrows his gaze, clearly annoyed by the remark. "Why did you do that?"

"I wasn't sure where exactly he fit into all of this, and I'm still not."

He stares at me, scowling. "Don't do the guy any favors, Liv. The fucker is just using you to spy on CSB. Once he gets what he wants, your career, and possibly your life, will be over. Why do you think he has a professional hitman on his payroll? To silence those who would otherwise betray him or his businesses. I won't be surprised if Wallace meets his end with a striker to the heart or the head." Clearing his plate, he stands and sets the dishes into the sink. "Men like Sam don't follow the rules, and none are ever properly written for them. You don't get to be on top without devouring those who had once been above you." Matt exits, heading toward the bedroom.

There's truth to his words, but also a hint of jealousy … or is it suspicion? I've been defending a man possibly responsible for Frank's death, which is unlike me. The person I saw for a split second outside of the house right before the garage exploded could've been Jake. He was roughly the same height and build, dressed all in black, including the mask over his face, the baseball cap on his head, and the gloves covering his hands. It was the same person in the videos from both Kane's and Nikki's shootings. I've simply been assuming it's the second shooter Sam had suggested when I told him about the additional shot that was taken at me after Luke was killed. Of course, I'm going off of his word that Jake didn't fire that round. He easily might have, and Sam's been playing me for a fool.

When will I stop being so goddamn naïve?

Finishing my food, I go over to the sink and wash the dishes, then dry them off and put them away. By the time I'm done, Matt returns freshly showered wearing jeans, a navy blue sweatshirt, and carrying the satellite phone. We sit at the dining table since the kitchen feels a bit cramped with the animosity consuming the air. Mainly coming from him. Turning on the device, the phone number we need to dial is already pre-programmed, so Matt just has to hold the '1' button for three seconds, then the other end starts ringing.

"Are you all right?" the chief asks, his voice booming like always, but louder since our device is on the speaker setting.

"We're fine," I answer.

"Good, because the story is officially breaking tomorrow. I tried to stall those damn vultures for as long as possible, but IA gave the go ahead for it to be released. They're spouting bullshit that it makes CSB look bad if we're not transparent with what happens to our officers in a timely manner. The public might think we have something to hide." He growls. "I fucking hate reporters. Anyway, Collins reviewed your security recordings. The attacker appears to be the same one who hit Requiem and killed Kane Cassidy. He first fired his weapon into the back of the house, then raced around to the front and shot at Frank's car. To me, that seems like an odd targeting move. If the initial round was to pull the both of you out into the open, then why hit the vehicle at all?"

Matt looks at me. "Where was the car parked?"

"Inside of the garage. We were in such a hurry that the outer door was left open. The bullet must have struck the gas tank, which is why it erupted."

"Then it was a way to block your escape," the chief states.

"Possibly, but there might be another reason." I bite my lip, knowing my theory that the shooter has a personal connection to me is correct. "With the exception of Hayden, Frank, and the construction company who retrofitted the closet into a panic room, anyone who's been to that house assumes the power box for the security system is in the garage. Taking out that section would disable the cameras, or so they would've believed."

"And no one else outside of those three knew where the true power source and computer were kept?"

Even though the chief can't see me, I nod, then reply, "Yes. Not even Dean."

"Did the guy stick around?" Matt inquires.

"He left once the bedroom went up. We didn't see a car, but a few minutes after the shooter stepped out of the last frame a dark gray van with tinted windows drove past before the cameras were consumed by the flames. Stephen interviewed a few of the neighbors who were home at the time of the attack and none of them recognized the vehicle." The chief lets out a long, deep sigh. "Olivia, I'm going to have Stephen review all of your past cases to see if any of them somehow link up to TITAN Industries or the Vilks Cartel. For the moment, you're the key to all of this."

"I don't know how or why." Clasping my hands, I rest them on the table. "It just doesn't make any—"

"Listen, honey, someone just stepped into my office, so I have to go," the chief says, cutting me off, his voice suddenly strained. "The service technician will call you when the computer is ready to be picked up. It shouldn't be too much longer. No need to phone me back. Love you. Bye." He abruptly hangs up.

"What was that all about?" Matt asks, hand poised to shut off the device, but I stop him by snatching it away.

"Hayden wants to speak with me, and the chief didn't want the other person to know since it might give away the fact that I'm still alive."

He stares at me, bewildered. "How the hell did you get that from Daven's ramblings?"

"Service technician? Call when ready? Pick up? It's code. I'm sure of it."

Scrunching up his face, he says, "All right. We'll leave the phone on for ten minutes, then I'm turning it off."

We only have to wait five.

"Our mutual friend played a new game last night," Hayden says after I answer, placing the phone on speaker so Matt can hear.

"How did he do?"

"Wiped out the enemy on three battlefields. The TITAN never knew what hit him. Complete annihilation. I've got everything recorded to play for you later."

I smile while Matt looks at me, confused. "Are you still going to spectate for any upcoming matches?"

"Of course. Gotta find out who's behind the curtain." With that, Hayden hangs up.

"Does everyone at your headquarters speak in confusing tongues?" Matt asks, taking back the phone, powering it down.

"Remember how I told you that Sam's spyware is being monitored through a gaming console by the coroner's assistant? Hayden is the lead forensic technician helping him. It was his way of telling me that their spectating program has found something."

"Which is what, exactly?"

"Early last week, Asher, the assistant, noticed the spyware had been set into motion after someone searched the word TITAN as an acronym. It hit the Hub systems, financial databases, and business directories."

"Three battlefields," Matt utters.

I nod. "Whomever looked up the company has now erased it from existence, but the spectator program recorded everything. Including the data that was destroyed. All that's missing is the person responsible."

"The man behind the curtain." He leans forward and kisses me hard. "Damn that's good work. Will Hayden inform the chief?"

"Probably not directly, but he'll find a way to coax him into that direction."

He sits back in his chair. "I wonder who interrupted our conversation."

"My bet is Internal Affairs since they're investigating the home office bombing. I'm sure they want to handle the attack on Frank and me."

Matt places a hand on my thigh as we sit sideways in our seats. "Do you know which agent?"

"Brett Ellis."

The puzzled expression on his face is unsettling. "He's not IA. At least, he wasn't the last time we met. He runs the Drug Enforcement Taskforce, but they share the same building as Internal Affairs. Their offices are in the neighboring sector."

"The badge around his neck read IA when he interviewed Candace and me."

Rubbing his chin, Matt asks, "Are you sure?"

"I thought it did." Scrunching up my face, concentrating on the memory, I continue, "Thinking back on the encounter, I could've simply assumed he was from that division since everyone who entered the gym wearing suits were from IA. His ID kept twisting on the chain around his neck, so perhaps when I noticed the 'A', I presumed it stood for affairs not agent. Cruz never actually mentioned who Brett was. Just that he wanted to speak with us."

"But who would've told him to come? There'd be no reason for a drug enforcement agent to be at the scene of a bombing."

"Maybe Cruz called him. The director might have seen our notes on the whiteboard since he had access to the room, which was locked for everyone else. We always kept the blinds drawn for the windows overlooking the hallway so no one could peek inside."

"I hate not knowing," Matt grumbles.

His gaze bores into me, and I sense there's more on his mind, but he isn't ready to talk about it. We stand and go into the living room to finish with the weapons and decide which to use for practice, then stash the others around the house, mostly in the bedroom, living room, and kitchen. Then, we put on our coats and head outside. Matt goes down into the storm cellar, which has an entrance next to the screened in porch along the exterior of the house, and comes back up with a crate of empty glass bottles. Moving to the far end of the property, which spans at least an acre, we're far enough away from any neighbors not to be noticed. Sparse trees and foliage cover the ground, the crisp, dead leaves crunching under our feet as small patches of snow litter the shady areas. After setting down the crate, Matt places the bottles on old tree stumps and a few fence posts, then we spend the rest of the chilly day firing at imaginary stalkers.

Eight

CSB Detectives Killed in Ambush

Is how the main headline reads in the next day's paper, which Matt went out to get while I made breakfast. We wait until we're done eating before spreading the *Leyon Tribune* on the dining room table. Three photos line the top of the article: those from Frank's and my credentials, as well as the remains of the house in Range. The only things left standing are an outer wall for the bedroom and bathroom, in addition to the entire closet Frank and I were in. Both cars are nothing but shells, and debris fills the spaces where the living room and kitchen once stood. This is the first time I'm seeing the amount of destruction and I can't help but cry.

"It's a miracle you survived at all," Matt says, holding me while my tears soak his sweatshirt.

"I almost didn't. The fire department kept a few of their hoses trained on the roof for the walk-in closet since they knew Frank and I were trapped inside. I had it converted into a panic room shortly after Dean almost killed me, but the striker rounds penetrated the steel door with ease, which allowed the dense smoke to filter into the small space. If I didn't have the hidden compartment in the floor of the closet with its own cooling system consisting of fresh air, I wouldn't have made it."

He hugs me tighter, then once I'm calm, we start reading the article written by a reporter familiar to me: Sara Vincent. She not only snared an unprecedented interview with Kane Cassidy after I was charged with murdering Dean and his girlfriend, but she also broke the story on Lane Murray's sex for hire scandal. She's young and quickly rising, which isn't always a good thing in her line of work.

*O*n the morning of Wednesday, March 4th, a 911 plea went out from 308 Clover Street, Range Sector, in the state of Asmor reporting that a CSB officer had been wounded and another was trapped by fire. That desperate call for help came from Detective Olivia Darrow while she and her boss, Supervisory Detective Frank Corro, lay severely injured in a closet of the lone bedroom at the back of the home. They had been shot and the residence set ablaze, preventing authorities from reaching the officers in time. Both were pronounced dead at the scene and an immediate investigation was opened to determine why these brave detectives were at the house, as well as the person, or persons, responsible for the crime.

The home was owned by Detective Darrow, but hasn't been lived in since July. It's known that the pair were working the high-profile Red Rover Case, in which several key members of the Vilks Cartel were slain using the same bullets that murdered the officers: illegal, armor piercing rounds known as strikers.

I stop reading. "What does she mean members of the cartel? We barely linked TITAN to them, let alone the victims."

"Maybe we should call the chief when we're done, and he can tell us where she obtained the information."

Nodding, I return to the article.

What hasn't been identified is the reason these two were at the empty residence. Both had been placed into protective custody, which was unexpectedly revoked by a person claiming to work for the police. Chief William Daven feels the pair were drawn to the home on Clover under false pretenses, then subsequently attacked and killed.

They aren't the only CSB officers associated with this case to have died recently in the line of duty. Detectives Candace King, Parker Haynes, and Matt Walker were murdered in separate incidents last month. Walker's car was found burning on the side of Interstate 47 after an apparent gunfight with an unknown assailant. Though blood was found at the scene matching the detective's, his body has yet to be recovered. Haynes was killed when a bomb detonated at the home office in Whitebridge Sector in the state of Longdale. Internal Affairs is still determining how someone was able to bypass the heavy security for the complex without notice and plant the device in a well-protected building. King was shot point blank in the chest. Her body was discovered in the parking lot of a local bar in Whitebridge when she neglected to show up for work.

We flip to the next page where another photo appears, showing a wrecked car sitting at the end of a long driveway in front of an elegant house with manicured lawns and professional landscaping.

Director Aiden Cruz, who runs the major crimes division, was leading the investigation for the

124

Red Rover Case up until his disappearance on March 3rd. His wife stated that he left for work at his normal time, then several minutes later their house was rocked by an explosion. According to forensics, a bomb had been planted under the director's vehicle and rigged to ignite when the engine started. The home received minimal damage, but it's unclear whether or not Cruz's remains have been found in the wreckage.

Several in the Civic Security Bureau are speculating that Carlos Montoya, hitman for the Vilks Cartel, is responsible for these assassinations. The elusive man has been hiding ever since his escape from custody last year, though sightings of him recently have surfaced. However, neither Chief Daven, IA, nor the Drug Enforcement Taskforce headed by Special Agent Brett Ellis are willing to corroborate the rumors. Neither are they disclosing the exact scope behind the Red Rover investigation, what initiated it, or the killings associated to the case. The victims with known cartel affiliations are businessman Luke Cobb and accountant Larrel Kindreth. The other fatalities tied to this investigation are sex-trafficker Ronan North and convicted killer Kane Cassidy.

Funeral arrangements for Detectives Corro and Darrow are pending.

"I'm surprised she didn't mention Dr. Salvador Tulley," I comment. "He was connected to not only Kane, but Ronan as well."

"But not to TITAN. Who called off the security detail?"

"Someone claiming to be Brett. The person told the officers IA was sending units to take over, so they left. The security system for my home on Waterside was down, as were both my personal cell phone and the one Sam gave me. I couldn't get ahold of anyone until I was on the bridge."

"It also seems the person made the same mistake you did in identifying the office Brett works for, which is odd." He tilts his head to the side. "I wonder if this individual was using a scrambler to disarm your system."

Staring at Matt, I ask, "What's that?"

"A device no bigger than a cell phone. You attach it to the cables for the security feeds if you know where the box is kept and it disrupts the signal, including anything wireless. On the right setting, it can also knock out power for a few seconds, allowing someone to break into a building unnoticed."

"Such as the attached garage where my security system is housed, and CSB's main office."

He nods. "Ronan had a few of them she would occasionally use when retrieving more valuable prey for the ranch. They were in the evidence locker assigned to her case."

"Locker? Cruz only provided me boxes."

"Those would've been in there as well. He didn't give the scramblers to you?"

I shake my head. "Nor the bracelets, if there were any left from the batch you stole."

"Five were recovered and I only took three. Meaning two are unaccounted for if you didn't have them."

"Brett mentioned that his colleagues thought the bombing was an inside job. Do you think Cruz could be responsible?"

"Then why would someone attack him?" Picking up the satellite phone, which was left on the table, Matt turns on the device to call the chief, but the man doesn't answer, so he hangs up.

After donning our coats, I carry the two rifles and handguns that were used yesterday, then head to the back of the property while Matt collects more bottles from the storm cellar. As he sets up the targets on the fence posts, I double check the ammunition in the refilled clips for the 9mms. When everything is ready, I pick up a rifle, load it, nestle the butt against my shoulder, then sight my shot. Inhaling deeply, I wait a few seconds before squeezing the trigger while exhaling, shattering the green glass into shards. We take turns going down the line, then Matt clears the broken bottles, replacing them with new ones. I can't help but recall the image of Cruz's car since it's bothering me.

"Hey, are you all right?" Matt asks, shaking me. "I've been talking to you for like five minutes."

"Huh? Oh, sorry. My mind was elsewhere." Raising the rifle, I stare down the scope on top of the gun, squinting my other eye to get a perfect aim, but hesitate in firing. Lowering the weapon, I ask, "Why was the director's car so far from the house?"

"It was probably moved there after the flames were extinguished."

"That doesn't explain why it was out in the open. Especially when he knew everyone on his team was being targeted. They have a two-car garage, so it should've been inside."

"Unless it's full of storage."

"Then where's the wife's car?" I counter.

"Look, Liv, I have no idea how that man's brain works. There could be any number of reasons why he didn't put the car in the garage."

Tucking the rifle under my arm, I turn and head back to the house.

"Where are you going?"

"I need another look at that photo."

After collecting the remaining weapons, Matt joins me. He opens the back door for the screened-in porch while I lean the rifle against the interior wall. I enter the house, sit at the dining table, turn to the page with the picture of the director's house, and study it very carefully. The section of driveway with the car is heavily scorched to the point where the cement has cracked and buckled. The area closest to the garage has minimal charring with only a bit of smoke staining the exterior doors.

Pointing to the image, I say, "He purposefully parked it away from the house to prevent the fire from spreading. He either knew about the bomb or placed it there himself."

"Then who is Cruz working for: the cartel or Sam? Or maybe Sam is the cartel and his hitman is the allusive Carlos Montoya simply using another name."

"I've met Jake and he doesn't match the description or mugshot."

"Then, perhaps, he took Carlos' place and is using the name to lure out those the cartel is after. Giving everyone a false sense of security … like you."

I roll my eyes. "You're being ridiculous."

"No I'm not," Matt says, fuming. "A man like Sam West can easily do anything with his kind of wealth. He fronted Ronan the money for the ranch—got her into contact with the company that made the bracelets, the small satellite dish that blocked visitors' microchips, and the scramblers. He went to college with Larrel Kindreth, even got him a job with the family mining business until he established himself and opened his own accounting practice. He's known Luke for years, helped him create Lamar Records and launch Dallas' career. His parents ran in the same circles as Richard Cassidy, and they even invested in BluTrend Technologies—which brought him close to Kane. And Dr. Salvador Tulley was his therapist growing up. Sam had big shoes to fill with regard to his father and struggled to keep up with what was expected from him. Hell, even his initials match with Siem Wolter." Snatching the phone off the table, he presses the '1' since he'd left the device on. "Everything leads to Sam being behind the killings." Like before, the chief doesn't answer, so Matt slams down the phone in frustration.

"It doesn't explain the fires in Nok Sector, murdering Nikki, or attacking Frank and me."

"You heard what Hayden said about the spyware and how everything related to TITAN has now been erased. Records of the company no longer exist. Sam got what he wanted, so you became a liability. Frank was involved in the Red Rover Case after you were removed, placing him in the same position as Candace and Parker. Sam probably paid off Cruz to keep an eye on things, then helped mask his disappearance. Nikki might have found out something she wasn't supposed to considering how long she spent on Everlast, then venturing to Prescott for a few days, and the fires were more than likely set to better sell the property without the dilapidated structures."

"If you knew all this, why didn't you say something?" I rave, my anger matching his.

"Because I didn't know who I could trust," he rants, glowering at me. "Not even you, since you lie to me all of the time."

I'm shocked by his remark. "What the hell are you talking about?"

He stands and begins pacing the room. "Sam, Olivia. You seem awfully eager to defend the guy, and I wonder why that is."

"I don't believe this shit," I grouse, tossing up my hands in frustration. "Nothing happened between the two of us."

"How about the time you spent at his casino? The kiss you two shared before going to see Cirque Aérien."

My face flushes as the room turns sweltering. "Luke told you," I utter, my voice barely above a whisper.

"Of course he did. He also said you were fucking Sam, which is why he gave you a suite in his hotel. Is that also the reason he bought you that car?" Matt sits on the couch. "How could you do that to me?"

Still on the chair at the dining table, I lower my head and fidget with my fingers, unsure of what to say or how to even handle this situation. Apologizing isn't going to fix things. What I really want is a drink. Instead, I reach behind my back, unclasp the necklace, and set it on the table beside the phone. Next, I remove my coat, hanging it on the back of the chair, stand, and go into the bedroom where I start transferring my belongings into another room.

Matt lingers in the archway for the alcove, watching me. "Aren't you going to say anything?"

"What's left to discuss?" I step into the room we were sharing, making sure to take the gun that was on the nightstand for my side of the bed. "I slept with Sam." In the new bedroom, I set down the weapon and put away the rest of my clothes. "When this nightmare is over, we'll go our separate ways. After all, you don't want a permanent relationship, whereas I do."

He goes to open his mouth, then closes it, the words he said to me on the ferry more than likely hitting him like a ton of bricks. Walking away, I hear the back door slam. When I return to the living room, the rifle he was carrying is gone, along with the satellite phone, but the necklace is still on the table. I rummage in the cabinet with the photos, finding a couple of books, which I take back into the bedroom, remove my shoes, and get comfortable on the covers to read, fury raging beneath the surface.

When he's not back by the time the sun has set, I get dinner started and a fire going in the fireplace. He enters the kitchen just as the food is ready, takes his bowl, and pulls out a chair at the small table. I carry mine into the living room and recline on the couch.

After a few minutes, he joins me, sitting in the dining room. "I got a hold of the chief and told him your suspicions about Cruz. Apparently, the same thought crossed his mind when he saw the photo."

"Did he say anything about the article?" I keep my gaze focused on the bowl of soup in my hands while I feel Matt's enraged stare.

"It was written with Brett's and Daven's approval. The paper wasn't going to publish it without their consent because of how sensitive the information is."

"What are they hoping it'll do?"

He smirks. "Nothing gets past you. Brett expects someone to rat out Carlos, since hitting police targets goes against some twisted moral code these guys have. The chief wants me to call him in a few days so he can update us on their findings."

"Did you mention Sam?"

"Yes, of course. Why wouldn't I?" he snaps.

"Then you told him about Lane Murray and how Sam gave me the gun to kill him."

Matt lets out an exacerbated sigh. "No, Liv, because then you'll wind up in prison. I kept that part out, along with the spyware. Just that we met the man and how he's linked to all the players involved."

I finish eating, take my bowl into the kitchen, then wash everything in the sink before returning to my room where I grab the book I had been reading and make myself comfortable on the couch in front of the fire. When Matt is done, he places the weapons he used on the dining table and cleans them, adding more bullets into the clips if needed.

This is how we spend the next several days. I'm either in the bedroom or on the couch reading, while Matt tinkers around the cabin or heads out for some weapons practice. The only time we're actually in the same room together is for meals. I try to avoid him more than he does me, since I'll leave a room if he's in it for too long. It'll be nice when I can finally go home and put this all behind me. Wednesday afternoon, he phones the chief, placing the call on speaker so I can listen from my seat on the couch across the room while he remains at the dining table.

"One of the director's neighbors reported seeing a van driving away moments before the car exploded," he says. "Brett interviewed the wife again, asking about Cruz's vehicle. Apparently, it has a remote starter, so with a simple push of the button on the key fob, the engine turns over without anyone having to physically be in the car."

"That would be why no remains were found."

Matt's gaze flickers between me and the phone. "I had Hayden search your house on Waterside. He found a scrambling device wedged behind several cables for your security system. No fingerprints on it though. I'm surprised the guy didn't go back for it."

"He was probably afraid CSB would beat him there," I state, having to raise my voice to be heard. "Any idea how he got onto the island?"

"We're thinking he either rented or owns a boat at the mainland marina, then took it across the water. There isn't a security checkpoint for the wharf on the island, and he more than likely did the same thing when he raided Luke's house. I have officers interviewing the staff at both locations and reviewing their camera footage."

"Is Cruz being listed as a suspect?"

"At the moment, just a person of interest. Oh, and you can rule out Sanford Mecum. He hasn't spoken to anyone in months. Not even his attorney."

I'm taken aback by the statement. "Parker met with him in January."

"There isn't any record of the visit. Who made the arrangements for him to see Mecum?"

"The attorney, supposedly."

The chief lets out an audible grunt. "I'll have the phone records checked. If it turns out he lied about the meeting, then we have another avenue to pursue for the killings and the bombing. Perhaps another cartel connection."

Clearing my throat, I ask, "Can you have someone look into Luke's properties? There was a list we were working off of among the evidence collected, but it disappeared. We surmised the director must have taken it since he's the only other person who had access to the room we were in."

"Are you sure it wasn't Candace or Parker?"

"Positive," Matt answers for me. "They wouldn't have stolen evidence."

"But fabricate a meeting?" I counter, keeping the rest of my comment quiet since both him and Candace stole evidence. She confessed it to me after the bombing. I told her to turn everything over to Brett, so I can only assume she did.

"I'm sure he had a valid reason. I knew Parker. He was one of the good guys." Glaring at me, Matt asks, "What about Sam West?"

"Brett is interviewing him. We have the statement Frank took when he questioned Mr. West about Calhoun Steel and Wallace Shaw. From what we've gathered so far, he's clean, as are his financials. There's nothing tying him directly to the Vilks Cartel or TITAN Industries, but we'll keep looking. Call me again in a few days."

Matt shuts off the phone, and I go back to my book. After a few minutes, he comes over and sits on the couch, looking pensive. "I hate this."

"Which part?" I ask, retaining my focus on the words, though I'm not actually reading them.

"Us fighting. The fact that you won't stay in the same room with me for any length of time. I don't even know how your injury is doing."

"It's fine. I can now shower normally, and finished both the antibiotic and Vicodin yesterday. There isn't any pain or discomfort. Tress did a great job sewing me up."

Adjusting his position, he turns to face me since I'm sitting lengthwise on the couch. "Frank's funeral is scheduled for tomorrow. I read it in the paper this morning during breakfast. The article didn't mention where he's being buried."

Looking up, I set down the book, using my finger as a placeholder. "And mine?"

"Friday, but unlike his, yours will be private."

"Can't have everyone there when the corpse isn't." I go back to reading.

"I shouldn't have said what I did on the ferry."

"You were just being honest."

He reaches over and takes away the book. "Don't block me out when I'm trying to have a serious conversation with you."

Pulling my knees up to my chest, I wrap my arms around my legs, encasing myself in a protective cocoon.

"I was married once, right after graduating from the academy. She hated the hours I was putting in to get moved into the major crimes division. I spent more time at the home office than I did with her. It lasted less than a year. Knowing how grueling the job is, I decided never to get involved with anyone seriously. One-night stands with cadets became my thing, though that was against regulations. But it's easy to sneak around and not get caught."

"Lots of people put career ahead of family and relationships."

"You don't."

I shrug. "That's just who I am. We're not all the same."

"Being married to Dean didn't deter you from the idea?"

"Sure it did, but it wasn't until you said you never wanted to have a family of your own that I realized I'd been lying to myself. The thought of winding up alone is terrifying. Fucking whomever you want only satisfies you so much, then it becomes monotonous, and you're left feeling lonely in the end." My ire starts to rise. "If all you were looking for was a quick screw whenever you were in town, then why give me the damn necklace and tell me that you loved me?"

"Because I meant it. You can still be in love with someone and not want a commitment."

"That doesn't work for me." I stand, snatch the book from his grasp, and go into my bedroom, shutting the door.

Instead of reading, I bury my head in a pillow and cry, but not over another failed relationship. For the loss of a reality I've been desperately clinging to. Life is always going to do whatever the hell it wants, and I should stop trying to reroute the torrent river I'm floating down. I need to ride the current until it ends. Take the beatings and lashes from the waves and rocks as they pass, then keep going. No longer clasp for tree branches as if they were lifelines to pull my ass free from drowning.

Standing and heading into the bathroom to wipe my face, I discover Matt has left the house. He doesn't return until after the sun has set, a rifle in his hands, which he leans against the living room wall while I go into the kitchen to get dinner started. We eat quietly in our designated spots, avoiding each other whenever possible. I decide to go to bed early, so after brushing my teeth and using the facilities, I put on cotton shorts and a matching tank top, turn off the lamp, and get under the covers. Lights from the alcove turn on, shining underneath the door, then go out since Matt has probably turned in for the night as well.

I'm starting to doze when the door for my room creaks open. Reaching for the gun on the nightstand, I carefully pick it up.

"It's me," Matt says, closing the door, so I put down the weapon.

"What do you want?" I ask, lying back on my side, tucking my arm under the pillow.

The bed shakes, the covers lift, and I feel him slip in beside me. "I can't stand being in bed alone." He moves closer, his hot breath hitting my neck. "I love you, Olivia." Wrapping an arm over my waist, he nestles his head against my shoulder blade. "Please desire me as much as I need you."

Pushing my hair aside, he nuzzles my neck, his one hand grazing my searing flesh while the other works on rolling me onto my back. Our mouths, meet and the world disappears. His fingers glide down my stomach, then under the waistband for the shorts, and work their way inside of me, thrusting in and out with a gentle force. I instinctively moan, arch my back, and work on disrobing. His lips tease my nipples, sucking on them, lighting me up inside. Moving on top of me, Matt takes off his pants, pushes my legs apart, and enters. I bend my knees and drag my fingernails down his back.

"Stay with me," he whispers, sweat soaking our bodies. "I don't want to know what life will be like without you in it."

Finding his mouth, I shove my tongue inside as a way of submitting myself to his request. He entwines our hands together, pushes them above my head, and fucks me harder. The headboard bangs loudly against the wall, our voices rising to match pitch as we both beg for more. I turn him onto his back, pin him to the mattress, straighten up, and ride him. He places his hands on my hips and closes his eyes.

"Goddamn it, Liv," he moans loudly. "Fuck!"

He grips me hard while he comes, holding me tightly to ensure not a single drop is spilled. Bending down, I kiss him passionately while he tries to catch his breath, then slide onto the bed, lying on my side. I'm barely given any rest before he pulls me onto my knees and fucks me from behind. The orgasm that follows comes in waves, each one more intense than the previous. He pulls out, and I soak the sheets, then he slips back inside.

"We'll have to designate this room for fucking," he groans in my ear. "The other one strictly for sleeping."

"And the third?" I ask, another round of orgasms seizing me.

"Bondage?"

The laugh escaping my lips comes out like a sigh. "Fuck, yes."

Nine

During breakfast, Matt puts the pendant back around my neck, then kisses me before retaking his seat. This is what I'll accept from life. Not necessarily a full-on marriage, but someone to spend my days with and fuck until I can't breathe anymore, which fits with what he wants. Hopefully, this works out for the both of us since I'm tired of jumping from one relationship to another.

"Who do you think Parker went to visit if it wasn't Sanford?" I ask between bites.

"I'm not sure. As far as I knew, he didn't know anyone in Asmor."

"Cruz placed him at the same hotel you stayed, and he mentioned seeing Verdigris, so he definitely was there." I wait a few seconds before continuing, "He and Candace took evidence. I told her to turn it over to Brett after Parker died."

"Something must have been bothering the both of them to have broken protocol."

I chuckle. "Or they thought like you do and simply stole whatever was handy to use for themselves."

He shakes his head adamantly. "No, neither of them would've done that."

"Then why did Parker lie?"

Matt shrugs. "I don't know."

After cleaning the dishes, we take a shower together, prolonging our time under the hot water, which eventually runs cold, and we haven't even lathered our bodies. We dry, dress for the inclement weather, and go out the back door to get in some more practice before we're buried in the several inches of snow yesterday's paper predicted. An hour later, I'm struggling to hold the weapon since the cold, damp air has seeped into my bones.

"Why don't you return to the house and get a fire started? I'll cleanup," Matt suggests.

I kiss him before retreating to the enclosed porch, resting the rifle against the wall, then entering the living room. After removing the parka, I toss it onto one of the chairs, set a few logs into the fireplace, add a bit of kindling, and strike one of the long, wooden matches kept in a tin on the mantle. As the flames come to life, I go into the kitchen to get something to drink. Opening the cabinet, I grab one of the juice glasses, close the door, and am reaching for the refrigerator handle when something on the counter catches my eye.

Sitting next to the fridge is a plain silver band alongside another ring containing a three-karat diamond flanked by two rubies.

My engagement and wedding rings from Dean.

The glass in my hand slips, shattering into fragments onto the floor while my throat clenches shut, making it nearly impossible to breathe. Stumbling sideways, I hit the table, remembering that the satellite phone was moved here this morning along with a handgun. But when I turn to grab the weapon, it's gone. I take the phone, turn it on, and hold the '1' button while stepping into the living room to search for another gun, blindly walking into a dense mass. Gazing upward, my mouth hangs open and I forget how to speak since my brain has ceased to function.

"Hi, babe," Dean says, grinning. His once short, dark hair is now pulled back into a ponytail nearly as long as mine. I feel insignificant compared to his six foot four height, and the muscles covering his body have doubled in size—made even larger by the bulky sweater he's wearing—and his skin has a bronze glow that it didn't before.

I go to scream when his massive hand covers my mouth. He spins me around, causing me to drop the phone onto the floor, then wraps his other arm around my waist and holds me tight against his firm body.

"Thought I had you back at the house in Range. Boy was I surprised to learn you survived. Shall we wait for the boyfriend to join us?" He pushes me toward the living room, and turns until we're facing the back door.

In the hand securing me to him is a CS .40, the same weapon used to murder Nikki. I squirm for freedom, kicking him in the shins, then slamming my head back, making contact with his chin.

Grunting, he slips the one arm from my mouth to my throat, then places the barrel of the gun against my temple. "You know I'll do it," he utters through clenched teeth.

I freeze in place, blood pumping loudly through my veins. Every muscle quakes, and I sweat in terror. It feels like hours pass before Matt finally returns.

"Hey, Olivia—" he begins, entering the still room carrying his rifle, then stops when he notices Dean.

"Put it down," my husband demands.

He hesitates, angering Dean.

"You know what's in the chamber, so unless you want to see her brains everywhere, do what I say."

Slowly, Matt lowers the gun to the floor.

"Kick it out of reach."

He does, sending it under the side table containing his family pictures. "What do you want?"

"The two of you dead."

"Why? We won't tell anyone you're alive, Dean. Let Olivia go and we can talk this out."

My captor cackles. "How did you ever make detective spewing nonsense like that?" He shakes his head, then tightens his hold on the weapon. "Aren't you the one who placed a gun to the back of my wife's head at Liutas Ranch? How close were you to pulling the trigger when I fired first?"

I swallow the lump that's formed in my throat. "You killed Ronan?"

"The bitch needed to go. She became a liability … and she was fucking you." His body shakes in rage. "I knew where you were going, even without the tracker on your car. I followed the next day and waited in the forest across the street. Parked a half mile away so the vehicle wouldn't be spotted. Not only did I play the video you two made shortly after it was received, but I also caught the live show. Ronan left the curtains open in her bedroom, and with the scope on the rifle, I saw everything." He presses his lips to my ear. "The recording I sent of Crystal and me was made the night you took off from the hair salon." He squeezes my throat. "I should've killed you both then."

"Do you know how close those rounds came to hitting me?" My voice pitches up unintentionally.

Dean lowers his arm to my waist, then starts nuzzling my neck. "This asshole was about to pull the trigger and you're mad at me?" He playfully bites me. "I saved your life, babe. Just like I'm about to do now."

Aiming the weapon, my husband fires. The bullet strikes Matt's chest, splaying it open, and continues through the door. He falls to the floor, blood spilling from the wound like a flood.

"No!" I scream, breaking away from Dean and rushing to my boyfriend's side.

Dean comes over, grabs my hair, and pulls me away. "He's dead, Liv. Nothing you can about it now."

"Let me go!" I shriek.

He throws me to the floor, then kicks me in the side. "No one is going to hear you. The neighbors are too far away."

Groaning, I pray the stitches haven't ruptured, and, at the moment, don't notice any blood soaking my top. Gripping my side, I do my best to stand, but Dean knocks me down.

"It's been you this whole time," I whimper, cowering into a ball to protect myself.

He kneels beside me, resting the gun against his lap so I can see it. "Except for Luke. Someone else tapped him, but the shot to the window you were next to, that was me." Smiling, he leans closer. "Who was it, Liv? I know you have his name rolling around in that brain of yours." He taps my forehead. "Tell me."

"I don't know, I swear." Tears flow down my cheeks as I continue to tremble.

Raising the gun, he presses the hot barrel against my chest, scorching the sweatshirt.

"Dean, please," I beg.

Standing, he grabs me by the collar, hoists me to my feet, then raises the weapon high into the air.

"Dean, don't!" I shout, praying the chief is listening on the other end from wherever the phone landed.

The gun comes down, striking me on top of the head, knocking me out.

Ten

My mouth feels like cotton since there's something wedged between my teeth. It hurts to open my eyes while my body rocks in rhythm with the road underneath us. A black tarp is draped over me, concealing my existence from anyone outside daring to look in. Dean probably did this before we got onto the ferry, which means I've been unconscious for at least an hour or more. My ankles are tied, and so are my hands behind my back. I test the tension in the ropes binding me, but windup grinding them farther into my skin. Using the fingers on my right hand, I touch what feels like metal enclosed around one of the fingers for my left, realizing they're my wedding and engagement rings. Dean always hated it when I took them off. I guess this is his way of letting me know we're still technically married, that I'm his to do with as he pleases. Not being able to move my head, I can't tell if Matt's pendant is still around my neck, but I wouldn't be surprised if it's not.

Aching all over, I somehow manage to kick whatever is behind me, hitting a seat.

"Stop it, Olivia," Dean grouses. "I'll let you out in a minute."

The vehicle makes a hard left, then comes to an abrupt stop. Dean turns off the engine and slams his door shut, which is followed a few seconds later by the sound of another one opening. He flings the tarp over to the side and grabs my feet, dragging me across the carpeted floor before I can kick him. Picking me up, he carries me over his shoulder and away from the van that was seen fleeing my burning home. I try to bend my body to view something other than his tight, firm ass, catching a pair of feet in black sneakers to our left.

"Take care of the stairs and the door, then get us in the air," my husband orders.

He starts climbing, the ground dropping away, metal steps taking its place. Crouching, he arches carefully through a doorway, then straightens up and drops me into a dark leather upholstered seat. Looking around, I notice we're in a private jet. An armed man with a thick beard and bald head boards, then presses a button in the panel next to the door, recalling the stairs. Once everything is secured, he disappears behind me and into the cockpit. Dean saunters to the back of the plane, goes behind a door, and returns a few minutes later, the sound of a toilet flushing in the background.

He jabs a finger in my face. "Behave."

"You're a fucking asshole!" I shout the second the gag is removed. "How the hell are you alive?"

Laughing, he frees my hands and ankles, tossing the ropes onto one of the seats across the aisle before sitting in the chair opposite mine, facing me, a metal table enlaced with mahogany between us. I take that moment to rub my wrists and check the wound in my side, which is still holding. Glowering at him, I start to remove the rings when he reveals the gun hidden under his sweater and tucked into his waistband.

"Don't even think about it, babe. You know the kind of punishments I like to dole out when you disobey me."

Lowering my hands into my lap, I sit back in the chair as the plane taxis, noticing Matt's necklace is gone. A few minutes later we're in the air, heading for God knows where.

"Answer my question," I growl.

"I think the better one to ask is whether or not Crystal is dead." He chuckles. "She is. The bitch was shocked when I pressed the gun against her head and pulled the trigger. This was after I shot the guy fucking her. She really couldn't say anything when he climbed on top, considering her jaw was broken. The violence seemed to stimulate him far more than it does me."

Something clicks. "Carlos Montoya."

"The leader for the Vilks Cartel wanted him dead and for me to take his place, so Luke and I did the man a favor. Two birds, one stone. It's hard to tell burnt bodies apart."

"What about the dental X-rays used to identify your remains?"

"Aaron handled that. See, he was already working for Luke before I 'died'." He uses air quotes around the word. "Guy was a genius when it came to manipulating records, moving them around to cover up the body switch. No one knew the difference. Poor bastard didn't deserve the bullet that went through Luke's head and into his."

"Lane tried to convict me for your murder," I rave. "What if he had succeeded?"

Dean shrugs. "Oh well."

I slam my heel into his shin bone.

He reaches over and slaps me hard across the face, splitting my lip. "Someone's gotten feistier," he says, smirking. "We're going to have so much fun."

"Shoot me. Get it over with already."

"First, the gun is filled with strikers, so I'd wind up taking down the entire plane, which isn't good for me. Second, I don't want you dead. I just like to get you all riled up with the thought that your life might possibly end by my hand. It's entertaining, and a turn-on. Consider it foreplay." He winks.

"That was something you were never good at."

Scowling, he says, "Watch it, or I won't be nice to you." Spinning his chair around, he reaches into what appears to be a wet bar. "Still drink rum? I made sure to bring plenty since it's going to be a long flight."

Turning back, he places an unopened bottle of the liquor onto the table—the brand identical to the one Dallas served during his New Year's Eve party—and two cut-crystal tumblers. After filling both glasses, Dean passes me one, but I don't touch it.

"Dallas knew this whole time that you were alive, didn't he?"

My husband sets down his empty glass and refills it. "Yes. He's the one who drove us on his boat to pick up Carlos from Kinney Airfield in the Jadan Keys."

"And Nikki recognized you at that party Lamar Records held in Prescott, which is why she fled."

He nods. "The dumbass shouldn't have invited her. I don't know why the hell he did. He's the reason she's dead."

"No, you are. Just like you're responsible for Frank." I pick up my glass, throwing the drink in his face. "How the hell could you do that?" Rising from my seat, I beat him about the head, finally venting my wrath.

He shoves me away, knocking me into the chair beside us. His complexion reddens as he sets down his glass and removes the gun, placing it on the table. Using the sleeve of his sweater, he wipes away the liquid, stands, grabs my arm, and drags me onto the floor, where he raises a fist to hit me in the side.

"Not the right!" I scream, holding up my hands to block the blow.

He studies me for a brief second, lowers his arm, and lifts up my sweatshirt, spotting the newly formed scar that's still healing. "How did you get this?" he asks in an even tone.

"One of the bullets you shot at Frank hit me. It wasn't too deep, but Tress still had to stitch it closed."

His fingers caress the wound, his hot skin a far contrast to my cold flesh. "A few more inches to the left and you wouldn't have made it."

"I almost didn't because of the fire." Knowing better than to explain more, I don't continue with the reason about how I survived. It's better to let him believe the cameras around the house were destroyed instead of capturing his every movement.

Dean relaxes his hold, but doesn't let go. "Frank was the target, not you."

"But you used me to draw him away from his home, like you used Nikki to get me to come down to the club."

"I knew you would go to the place in Range since it meant safety once the security system for the house on Waterside stopped working. Frank was always your go-to person in an emergency. He was the first one you'd call or turn to, never me, and I'm your husband." He sounds pained by the admission.

"You beat the shit out of me, Dean, and constantly cheated … even with my own sister."

He scowls. "How did you find out?"

"I saw the pictures. Melia had them hidden in an album."

"Luke should've destroyed those after he used them to blackmail her. Honestly, at that time I didn't know you two were related."

I scoff. "And that's supposed to make it all right? What about the fact that you loathed Kane, but accepted money from him anyway?"

"It was compensation he owed me. As was signing TITAN Industries over to me before he went to prison. It was all arranged through Luke, so nothing ever showed in that asshole's name when CSB came to seize his assets. I wasn't allowed to collect from the Victim's Reclamation Act like you were." He stretches his body on top of mine, stroking my cheek with the back of his rough hand. "Cruz said you were getting close to the truth, which is why the others had to die."

"Is that why he tried to blow me up?"

Dean sits up, appearing shocked by the news.

"Did he neglect to tell you that? The bomb he rigged to detonate when the door for the conference room at the home office opened was for me. I was always the first one in and he knew it. Except that morning I overslept, and Parker wound up being the one who triggered the explosives."

"You're lying."

"Ask him yourself. I'm sure he's already at the place you're taking me to."

Dean seems to ponder it over for a few seconds. "I'll let Siem deal with him for that fuck up."

I startle. "What? He's not Cruz?"

My husband smiles, lying on top of me once again. "No, babe. Siem is a whole other monster. One you'll get to know quite well."

My heart pounds as my pulse races. Could Matt have been right? Is it Sam?

Fuck, what do I do?

Dean brushes his lips against mine. "It's been a while for us, and the flight is at least six hours." He wraps one hand around my wrists, shoving my arms above my head, while the other tugs at the zipper for my jeans. "We could make the best use of our time together, and I've missed fucking you. The women on the island aren't fond of the same things you are. They scream from the pain I cause instead of groaning in pleasure like you do." He kisses me, but I don't return the gesture. "Did the boyfriend fuck you like I used to? Like Luke did? Shall we see if I can still generate the animal inside of you?"

His mouth envelops mine, nearly suffocating me while I struggle under his weight. He has my pants and underwear down around my ankles while he hurries to free his hardened cock, thrusting it firmly between my legs. He then rushes to undress me the rest of the way, tossing our clothes onto the chair beside us, his grunts growing louder in volume.

"You're disappointing me, Liv," he whispers, nibbling on my ear. "Relax and let go."

"No."

He smacks me across the face. "Do it," he demands.

Scared that he might hurt me some more, I give in and come without much effort, pleasing Dean. He pulls out, forces me onto my knees, then plunges his cock into my ass, howling with delight. Tears pour down my face while his fingers thrash against my clitoris, causing me to orgasm and soak the floor beneath us.

"Fuck yes, babe. This is more like it." Clamping his hands on my hips, he holds me firmly against his waist as he comes, shuddering with delight. Resting his head on my sweat-drenched back, he breathes heavily. "We're going to have so much fun together, and this time there won't be anyone getting in our way." He stretches to reach the wet bar, extracting a towel, which he uses to clean up.

I pull myself up onto wobbly legs and grab my sweatshirt to redress, but he stops me.

"I said it's a long flight. You can put your clothes back on when we're done."

"But I'm cold."

He stands, goes over, and opens the door for a closet beside the bathroom, taking out a thick, plush, dark red comforter. Before giving it to me, he retakes his seat, has me sit in his lap, then wraps the blanket over the two of us, cocooning me against his chest. Since his arms are free—mine holding the folds close together—he pours us more rum, then presses the glass to my lips so I can drink.

"Why were you on the rooftop when Luke was shot?" I ask, working through my second glass, hoping to numb the pain and heartache that I feel.

"To kill him, only someone beat me to it."

"You knew we were in Prescott?" I ask, surprised by the statement.

"The arrogant fuck told me about the trip, but never explained what it was for. He wanted me to protect him since he suspected his life was in danger. Idiot never realized he was dead even with me there."

I pause a few minutes before continuing the conversation. "How did you know I was still alive?"

He places a finger against my lips. "No more questions."

Setting down the glass, he moves everything to the other side of the table, removes the comforter, then has me back on the floor in the same spot I was before. He's rougher this time, interpreting my moans of anguish for those of gratification. Between drinking and sex, I'm completely worn out and a bit drunk by the time the plane is ready to land. I struggle to dress, which causes Dean to cackle with pride. We buckle into our seats as we make our final approach, the tires squealing when they contact the runway. Outside of the small windows, the waning sunlight glistens off tall canopies for the dense forest just beyond a row of empty hangars. Slowing, we gradually turn left, then come to a stop. The man from earlier exits the cockpit, goes over to the panel by the exterior door, and presses a series of buttons. The instant the door opens, thick humidity infiltrates the cool space, the sounds of birds and other mysterious animals floating in with it.

Once the staircase is lowered, Dean forces me out of the seat and helps me down onto the tarmac since I'm struggling to find my footing. What I thought was forest is, in fact, jungle. The clothes I'm wearing aren't meant for this climate, so I immediately sweat, causing everything to cling to me. There are at least a dozen hangars, most of them empty, with several watch towers rising out of the dense foliage in the distance. Thick light poles begin to glow, casting the entire field in sheer brightness.

"Phone the main house and tell the boss we're here," Dean says to the pilot. He then nudges me in the back, grabs my hand, and pulls me alongside while making his way toward a sandy path leading away from the plane.

"Where are we?" I mumble, swatting at tiny gnats trying desperately to tag along.

"The island of Ilusor, but the main house is on Nolita, so we'll take a boat."

Wooden lampposts with iron grating line the trail that winds through the vast overgrowth. Besides birds, I catch the sounds of croaking frogs, with the occasional lizard scurrying in front of us. Those animals I don't mind, but I hate snakes and spiders, so I cling closely to Dean, fearing something will drop from a branch and land on my head. Crashing waves break through the noise as the tree line recedes and we come upon several docks, speedboats moored to their pilings. Guards with automatic weapons slung across their shoulders patrol the area, each dressed in shorts and tank tops to accommodate for the heat.

Dean signals for one of them to get into the farthest boat, then we head in that direction. It's similar to Sam's except the color is dark blue—not red—with black accents, and is streamlined much like my Nimbus, where the front narrows to almost a point. Black leather captain's chair and three passenger seats make up the interior, while a heavily tinted windshield bends over the front seats, acting as a partial sunroof for the rear passengers. Unlike Sam's, this boat is lacking ornamentation that identifies its owner.

Dean has me sit in the back with him while the driver and another guard untie us from the pier, then pushes us out into the water just as the engine starts. After backing up a few feet, we turn around and head away from the island. Off in the distance to the right, left, and straight ahead I spot lights twinkling, but because of the encroaching night I can't discern their exact range or location compared to ours. The breeze being kicked up by the speed over the open water helps cool me off, but the mugginess remains, rousing the bile filling my stomach from all the rum sloshing around inside. I do everything I can not to throw up.

The lights up ahead grow larger, exposing several docks and more guards patrolling the beach. We pull alongside one of the wooden piers and stop. Dean helps me out of the boat, then the driver backs up and leaves. My husband escorts me down another sandy path illuminated by waist-high lampposts made from brushed nickel. This trail is much longer than the previous one and branches off into three directions when we're no longer in view of the water. We keep to the center, and through the thick foliage I catch snippets of a wrought iron fence and more lights.

Winding to our right, the path transitions from sand to crushed stone. Emerging on our left is a two-story mansion with stucco walls painted the color of wheat, and burnt umber roof tiles. It's also beautifully landscaped with philodendrons, areca palms, hibiscus flowers, orchids, and tiger lilies. The front entry consists of an immense porch holding Romanesque-style columns supporting balconies for the upper floor. A round, bubbling fountain sits at the center of a pair of steps sweeping up to the entry, railings matching the columns grace the stone walkway. We head up to the double-hung French doors with etched glass inlayed into white oak.

Dean doesn't bother knocking and simply presses the lever for the handle, pushing open the door onto a grand foyer with a set of staircases curving up on both sides, flanking a series of steps leading down into the rest of the house, a large planter the focal point for the enormous space. The interior of the house is painted white, stunning blue tiles cover the floor, and expensive oil paintings adorn the walls. We continue deeper into the house, coming upon three doorways, the one to the left has a closed set of double doors, while archways transition the hallway to our right into a small gallery and a great room in front of us.

The tile changes to plush, navy blue carpeting in the great room where an elegant seating arrangement consisting of two couches and identical loveseats are covered in a light gray woven material with a sharkskin pattern. A white oak coffee table rests in the center, while end tables and a sideboard flank the furnishings. Along the walls on either side are built-in bookcases that house various statues made from ivory and marble, glass and porcelain vases, and old, heavily worn books, as well as what appear to be family heirlooms. At the far end of the room, the entire wall is floor-to-ceiling windows overlooking the back of the house, which is a little hard to see at the moment from my vantage point.

Sitting on one of the couches facing our direction is a breathtaking woman with long, wavy, raven-colored hair, round face, pointy nose, and an olive-complexion. She sits with one leg crossed over the other and a bare arm delicately draped along the back of the couch. Her sleeveless dress is dark crimson like her lips, cut down to the navel exposing some of her large breasts, with a hem that squeezes her thighs tightly together. Gold bracelets cover one wrist, a diamond ring on her right index finger, and a partially filled snifter clutched delicately in her left hand.

She smiles as we enter, lines forming under her fierce brown eyes. "This must be the ever elusive Olivia Darrow." The exotic accent flowing from her mouth isn't what I was expecting. Standing, she sets the glass down onto one of the end tables and saunters over, swinging her hips as if in a rhythmic dance. Even though she's barefoot, she's a good inch taller than I am with an athletic physique. When she holds out her hand, I tentatively shake it. "Pleased to finally meet you. I'm Siem Wolter."

My eyes widen in surprise. "You're a woman."

"Most people expect me to be a man, since many feel a woman can't possibly run a cartel," she says, chuckling, then frowns. "This includes my older, practically worthless, brother."

Instantly I know she's referring to Director Cruz. "The two of you look nothing alike."

"Same father, different mothers. He was raised in Leyon, while I grew up in Navital, then here to learn the ropes from our father when I became of age." Getting closer, she reaches out and touches the cut on my lip, causing me to flinch. "Dean, did you hit her?"

Firming up his grip on my arm, he replies, "My wife has a tendency to mouth off."

"Hopefully she learns her lesson soon." Siem gently pushes my face to one side, then the other before tugging on the sweatshirt and making a disapproving noise when she notices the jeans and heavy boots. "Where was she?" the woman asks, running her fingers through my hair as if checking for fleas.

"Kodiak Island."

"I hear it can get cold there this time of year. Thankfully, we don't have such dreadful weather down here near the equator." She purses her lips. "The two of you look exhausted. Dean, take her upstairs so you both can shower. I'll have one of the maids bring you dinner. Tomorrow, I expect you both at breakfast."

We go back to the foyer, take the stairs on the right, then turn left at the top of the landing where a lone spiral staircase reaches up to a third level. There's a bridge connecting the two halves of the second floor, leaving an opening for the great room below, the elongated windows extending to the second story. We enter a suite with a large bedroom, bath, walk-in closet, and a private balcony. The walls are painted in a light cyan, the ceiling a pristine white, and the soft, deep carpet is cream-colored. A king-sized bed leans against the wall it shares with the stairwell, white linen curtains are pinned around the four poster-columns for the canopy, and the dresser with a matching chest of drawers made from white oak sit against the opposite side.

Closing the door, Dean directs me into the bathroom decorated in pale, sea green tiles and shell-shaped sconces. It has a single vanity, no bathtub, and the shower stall is in the corner of the room, large enough to hold several people. Fluffy, cotton towels dangle from rods on the wall perpendicular to the door, matching the rug strewn on the floor in front of the shower.

"Go ahead and get in," Dean instructs. "I'll wait in the hallway for the maid, then join you."

When he leaves, I hesitantly open the stall door and reach inside to turn on the water, noticing two showerheads dangling from the ceiling, each cascading warm liquid like rain. Leaning against the wall, I work on removing the boots, but wind up slipping to the floor, hurting my sore ass. With quivering hands, I take off the rest of my clothes and carefully use the facilities before getting wet. This is the first opportunity I've had to be alone. Sitting on the tile floor of the stall, I pull my knees up to my chest and bawl. I've lost too many people that I love in such a short time and don't know how much more I can take.

Nikki … Frank … Matt.

Who's next? How long will I be trapped here? Is there no escape?

The stall door opens, Dean stepping inside, naked. I hadn't even heard him enter. He hauls me to my feet, plasters my back against his chest, then takes his time rubbing the soap all over my body. His fingers play with my nipples while his hard cock thumps against me. Pressing his hands on the tops of my shoulders, he pushes me over so I bend at the waist and fucks me from behind. I'm so sore that every motion is painful, but that doesn't seem to faze him. This won't be the last of his torment for today.

Before his supposed death, I was starting to believe my husband was a sex addict, among other things. Now I'm convinced. For once, I want him to abuse someone else instead of me. He mentioned there are women here, so where are they being kept? I won't be surprised if the Vilks Cartel also participates in sex trafficking besides drugs. Both very profitable endeavors in our perverted world.

Tears continue to run down my face, mixing with the water and soap, but I make sure Dean doesn't notice when he spins me around, shoving his tongue down my throat. To appease him, I return the affection.

"I knew you still loved me," he utters in response. "You're forever mine, Liv. Nothing is going to keep us apart this time. I promise."

I fucking hate that word. There's been only one person who's maintained their assurances, and that's Sam. Not that any if it matters now. Since he isn't Siem, what's his connection to TITAN and the cartel? Do I even want to know?

When we're finally done, we dry, and I wrap myself in a towel before returning to the bedroom. Sitting on the bed is a silver tray and two covered plates, each containing a steaming lobster, diced roasted potatoes, and green beans. Dean dresses in lounge pants before heading downstairs to get us drinks, bringing back an entire bottle of rum and two glasses. I'm not in the mood to eat, but it's been hours and my stomach is rumbling. Taking my plate and old-fashioned glass, I sit on the floor, mainly to distance myself from Dean, but he decides to join me. Given the events of the day, I drink more than I probably should and eat very little. Leaving my dishes on the floor, I crawl onto the bed and promptly pass out.

Eleven

The pounding in my head is what wakes me, not Dean biting my shoulder while his arms are wrapped around my waist. Lying on my stomach, my head sideways on the pillow, I spot the sun filtering brightly through the gauze curtains draped in front of the doors for the balcony. My towel is nowhere in sight. I can barely move, mainly due to my husband lounging against my back. And also because everything hurts and, for the moment, I don't know why.

"God, I love you," he whispers, pushing my hair away from my face, kissing my cheek. "Breakfast should be ready. Siem won't like it if we're late."

Sitting up, he swings his legs over the side of the bed, grabs my hand, and pulls me off of the mattress, directing me into the bathroom. I use the facilities before getting into the shower, though I don't see the point in taking one since we did last night. The hot water does help loosen my tight muscles, alleviating some of the building headache. It's now I notice the damage done while I was unconscious. Teeth marks cover both breasts, but the skin isn't broken, and there are love bites—deep red bruises—on the insides of both thighs. The stitches on my right side are still intact while the rest of me aches and throbs.

"Last night was so much fun," my husband whispers, pulling me against him.

"You've gotten considerably worse since being down here."

He nibbles on my ear. "I'd like to think of it as improving. Besides, no one will see them except for me."

Once we're clean, Dean hands me his towel after drying off since mine is still in the bedroom. He then dresses in jeans and a rugged, short-sleeved, red shirt, while I don black shorts and a blue marble tank top that he hands to me from the bottom drawer of the dresser.

"Where did you get these clothes?" I ask, gingerly holding them as if they're poisoned.

"Does it matter?"

I glare at him.

"They were left here by someone who's no longer on the islands." He comes over to me and places a hand under my chin, lifting my stare to meet his. "She won't be returning for them, babe, so don't worry." He kisses me gently on the lips.

Shaking my head, I reluctantly dress, then after running my fingers through my hair, I haphazardly pull it back into a ponytail. While Dean finishes getting ready, I slip on a pair of sandals he has stashed on the floor of the closet, which probably belong to the same mysterious woman. He escorts me down to the foyer where we pass through the archway beyond the stairs and into the gallery. To the right behind a series of columns is the dining room, a table made from cypress prepared to serve a party of four. The oriental rug covering the hardwood floor underneath appears hand stitched, and there's a buffet table in a niche in the wall toward the back corner.

Dean directs me to a wet bar that sits between it and another staircase leading to the other half of the second story, then mixes and pours us each a Bloody Mary using ingredients from the built-in fridge beneath the marble counter. After taking the drink, I wander the ornate room, admiring the oil paintings. The one hanging above the buffet table stands out. It shows a vast ocean with four islands of various shapes and sizes surrounding a fifth, and they're each labeled: Termore, Ilusor, Tenace, Antiris, and Nolita—the latter being in the middle.

TITAN.

Dean stands next to me. "I doubt those idiots at CSB will ever realize that TITAN Industries is an acronym for these islands. Even if they do, there isn't anything that can be done about it. No one has jurisdiction down here. Not even Navital, which is twenty miles to our west."

"If it were only that simple," Siem comments, joining us. Today, her raven hair is neatly plaited at the base of her neck, exposing her bare shoulders, a floral-printed halter top encapsulates her robust chest, while her short, tight, beige skirt accentuates each step she takes toward us. In her grasp is a pair of sunglasses with gold frames and dark lenses. "Still, there are those who wish to shut me down and will do anything to make it a reality. Even if they don't have the authority to do so."

"What's housed on the islands?" I gesture to the painting.

She smiles, drapes an arm over Dean's shoulder, and leans into him. Surprisingly, he looks uncomfortable. "Termore has all my coca plants and marijuana greenhouses, since the temperature has to be carefully regulated. Ilusor contains the airfield, hangars, and docks. Tenace is where the factories and employee housing are kept. Antiris … well, that's something else altogether." She snickers slyly. "Nolita is where the main house and guest bungalows are situated."

Staring at the image of Antiris, and knowing what is more than likely being kept there, I ask, "How many women do you have imprisoned on the island?" I nod, indicating the landmass.

She purses her plump, painted lips, then using a manicured nail polished in dark red, she trails the outline of my husband's ear. "Dean, you've been a naughty boy. Bragging to your wife about my possessions. What else have you told her?"

He swallows roughly. "Nothing, Siem."

Smiling, she pats him on the ass. "Good boy. Have a seat and I'll see what's keeping Aiden." She disappears through a doorway beside the wet bar.

Gripping my waist, Dean propels me into a high-backed cushioned chair, then takes the seat next to me, close to the head of the table where I assume Siem will be sitting. Fine white China with a silver band around the outer edges rest on a hand-woven tablecloth in a herring bone pattern containing various hues of blues and greens. Goblets sit next to small bread plates while neatly polished silver adorns the pressed, dark blue, cloth napkins. A silver candelabra resides in the center of the table—its candles dormant— and is flanked by crystal vases filled with freshly cut flowers.

"I've never seen you afraid of a woman before," I state, sipping the drink.

He places his glass onto the table. "You don't know Siem like I do."

I can't help but laugh.

"What?" he asks, scowling.

"Just picturing the two of you in bed together, and for once someone else giving you orders instead of the other way around."

He mutters inaudibly under his breath.

Our hostess returns, two older women wearing gray maid's uniforms covered with white aprons trailing behind. One pushes a silver trolley containing plates filled with eggs benedict, bacon, and toast. The other woman carries carafes filled with water and orange juice. Taking her seat at the head of the table, Siem orders the pair to start serving.

"Aiden should be along shortly," she says, unfurling her napkin and setting it into her lap. "He's staying in one of the guest bungalows since I refuse to allow him to reside in the house." She turns up her nose as if disgusted by the idea of sharing space with her brother, then changes her attention to Dean. "Later this morning, you'll leave for Asmor to pick up our next guest."

Dean glances at me, a worried expression on his face. "What about Olivia?"

"She'll remain here." The horrid woman smiles, noting his discomfort with the idea. "Don't worry, your wife will be perfectly safe as long as she behaves."

He reclaims his drink. "I don't plan on snatching the woman until either tomorrow or Sunday. So it'll be at least a day or two before I return."

My stomach tightens, making eating difficult. "Who?"

He smiles. "No one you need to concern yourself with, Liv."

"That's fine." Siem picks up her fork to cut into her food. "Olivia and I will become great friends in your absence."

I notice the wheels turning in Dean's head since he's more than likely conjuring images of what happened the last time he left me alone with a woman, and it doesn't sit well with him in the least. This instance will not end like it did with Ronan.

That was a mistake I sort of regret.

The former director of CSB's major crimes unit enters just as the maids finish. I glare at the short, robust man while he sits across from Dean. His black hair and mustache are in desperate need of a trim. The top two buttons for his white linen shirt are open and the garment is already sweat-stained. His khaki shorts are a bit tight around the waist, practically cutting him in half.

Noticing me, an expression of immense satisfaction creases his face. "Nice to see you, Olivia." Furrowing his brow, he adds, "You don't seem surprised to find me here."

"That's because I'm not," I snarl. "Perhaps the next time you fake your death, you should hire a professional so it doesn't look so sloppy."

His face turns crimson, and his lips tighten into a thin line. "What the hell are you talking about?"

"Well, for instance, don't park your car so damn far from the house when it's typically kept in the garage. Or have your getaway vehicle spotted by neighbors. An unfamiliar van in an otherwise peaceful neighborhood garners a lot of attention." Smiling, I continue, "But don't worry, I'm not the only one who figured out it was simply a ruse."

"You're lying," he says, clasping a butter knife tightly in his grip.

"I'm sure you still have a loyal contact or two at the home office who can tell you what Internal Affairs might be doing with regard to locating your whereabouts. After all, you're number one on their priority list now that several detectives are dead, and each one connected directly to you. Obviously, you cut out your microchip before fleeing, otherwise they'd be here by now."

His chuckle is unsettling. "Sweetheart, no one can touch me. They never could. That bomb I planted wasn't just for you."

Dean's manner darkens and a vein bulges in his neck. "You claimed the explosives were set for Parker. Not once did you mention Olivia being your intended target." He reaches for the weapon tucked inside of his waistband, but Siem places a hand on his arm, stopping him.

"Oh, please. You're just as gullible as she is." Aiden nods toward me. "Of course the bomb was meant for Olivia. I knew her routine and that she'd be the first one into the office that morning. She figured things out before I could properly cover my tracks." He glowers at me. "Asking to visit Kane Cassidy, the database searches you conducted, the copious amounts of notes you took that I couldn't locate when you skipped out of town the weekend prior, and your damn theories written on the white boards. It all needed to be destroyed."

"You were spying on us?" My mouth gapes open.

"I had to. There were cameras and microphones hidden all over that conference room, along with the one next to it, so I heard your conversations with Detective Corro, which is what added him to the list of targets for Dean to eliminate. I removed the devices the afternoon I planted the bomb so they wouldn't be found."

"Did you swipe one of Ronan's bracelets to keep your microchip from being detected on the grounds?" I ask, incensed. "Matt said there were two still in the evidence locker you neglected to show me." I cock my head to the side. "I bet you also used a scrambler to disarm the security cameras and locks so the break-in couldn't be tied directly to you."

He scowls. "You're so fucking clever, but you weren't the only one I was after at the home office. There were additional loose ends that needed to be taken care of, which were handled in one fortuitous shot. Two of my detectives, who had been aiding the cartel, were waiting by the conference room for her to arrive that morning. I had asked them to retrieve a couple of files knowing the explosion would kill them as well. They were getting anxious about how the Red Rover Case was progressing and became a liability, so they had to go." He frowns. "I did hate losing Parker though, but it was easy putting the bullet into Candace while she was passed out in her car after a heavy night of drinking."

"You killed her?" I ask, stunned, believing it had been Dean.

"She didn't leave me much of a choice. The bitch was going around ranting to anyone who would listen that I was the one responsible for the blast. I knew her death would be tied to the Red Rover Case, since that's what everyone believed was the reason for Parker's … and mine when the time came."

"So your solution was to murder those involved? I was merely speculating on the connection between the killings. There was never any substantial evidence to back up my theory." At least none that he's aware of. I don't dare mention what I found in my sister's bedroom, which is what really ties everything together for me. "Your paranoia is what led to your demise, not anything I did or found."

His anger swells. "Who were you scheduled to meet that Sunday?" he blurts out, startling me. "You promised to share information about the case if that damn reporter dug up details on the cartel. I couldn't take the chance of someone else figuring things out like you did."

Siem and Dean remain silent while the two of us bicker. The pair listening intently to every word spoken.

"Then you go after the reporter, not me. Besides, I never saw Sara Vincent. She canceled at the last minute, which you would've known since I know you had my cell phone tapped." Reaching for the Bloody Mary, wishing I had something stronger, I finish its contents rather quickly to calm my frayed nerves. "I was never going to say anything to her. I'm not an idiot like you."

His scowl slowly turns into a grin. "Still, Parker's death provided the results I wanted. His girlfriend backed off her requests for details about the slayings that weren't included in the press releases. Otherwise, there'd be another body tied to me, as you put it."

"That's why he was in Asmor? To see her?" I ask, perplexed. "I thought he was dating Candace?"

Cruz chortles. "They were simply fuck buddies. Though I think Candace cared more about him than he did for her. Sara is the one he was really involved with, pumping him for stories before officially going through proper channels. Fucker was blindsided by the cunt." He turns serious again. "It still doesn't explain how you knew about the car."

Now it's my turn to smirk. "The *Leyon Tribune* ran a story concerning your disappearance in conjunction with Frank's and my murder. Matt picked up a copy of the paper to see if anything about the killings was mentioned. An article, written by Sara—so I guess your threat to her had little effect—included a photo taken after the fire had consumed your vehicle. Because of its location on the driveway and the fact that there was very little damage done to the house, the entire incident appeared staged." I take a bite of food, chewing it thoroughly before continuing. "Look up the article yourself. I assume you somehow have access to the internet down here. Otherwise, how else would you be able to keep tabs on the money being stolen from your accounts?"

Siem stares at me bewildered, then glances between Dean and Aiden. "What is she talking about?"

The pair seethe, furious glares shot in my direction while their breathing turns heavier and more forceful with each passing second.

Does she not know? Fuck!

"Isn't that why I'm here?" I ask, dreading how the two will respond. "Because you think I know where it is, and who might be behind the theft?"

"No, Liv," Dean replies, enraged. "You're here to work for the cartel in whatever capacity Siem needs. Especially when it comes to matters with CSB. You still have access to all their information, including the HUB, which we'll need to expand the business."

"You're insane," I utter, astounded by the request. "There's no way in hell I'd help you." I go to reach for the water carafe when he grabs my wrist tightly, nearly cutting off the circulation to my hand.

"You don't have a choice, babe. It's either that or I put a bullet in your head right here." He fingers the grip of the gun tucked in his waistband.

I'm used to Dean's threats, but this one feels different … genuine and foreboding. However, I find myself saying, "It's better than being a part of this nightmare."

Releasing me, pain and sorrow fills his eyes. "Don't say things like that."

"Explain this matter," Siem demands, her gaze boring into me.

"Well, someone in their little group—I'm not sure who—placed my half-sister's name on an offshoot account to store the cartel's money before it was laundered through TITAN Industries' holdings. The problem now, they don't know where the fuck it is, or who's behind the theft." I glower at Aiden. "You murdered the only links you had to those accounts. Melia was already dead when you started assassinating your associates, severing any hope of recovering the money. And all of the evidence that might have led to the person responsible was destroyed in the bombing."

Siem drums her manicured fingernails on the table. "How much is missing?"

Dean clears his throat. "A quarter of a billion dollars." He takes a deep breath. "We thought we could keep the theft hidden, then Sanford had Melia killed because she stole documents from Kane's house and refused to give them back without compensation. After that, Aiden put his people in place as a way to keep tabs on the other players. Including you." He points to me.

Aiden smiles smugly. "Before coming here, I closed those accounts and transferred the money into a new one to stop the hemorrhage. Also, I deleted all record of TITAN Industries from CSB's databases to keep anyone from possibly piecing things together."

"At least you're good for something," his sister utters, her brow furrowed and her manner icy.

"What I can't figure out is why the two of you," I gesture between Aiden and Dean, "have spent the last two months burning down Centurion properties in Nok Sector of Asmor. At first, I assumed it was to get a better price for the land without the decrepit structures, since TITAN took ownership of them after Kane went to prison. In addition to help finance the purchases of Luke's properties, such as Club Deviant and Ataxia Arena. But now I realize it's more than likely to replace the stolen money before Siem realized it was gone, and you have to explain to her why." I pause. "Did you know that the last fire killed fifty-six people? Nothing like drawing unwanted attention to yourselves with mass murder."

Siem slams down her fork, then pushes back her chair. "If you'll excuse me, I need to make a phone call. Dean, come with me." She abruptly stands and they quickly leaves, her heels clacking on the floor as she rushes toward another part of the house, my husband hurrying to catch up.

"You just can't keep your damn mouth shut," the former director gripes. "I should've had Dean kill you at the cabin on Kodiak instead of drag you down here."

"How did you know Matt was alive and took me there?"

The smile puckering his lips causes me to shiver. "His body was never found, and I had officers searching everywhere while they recovered the car. If he'd been killed, his corpse would've turned up quickly. As for the cabin, where else is there better isolation? I knew about it because he'd mentioned the place in the past."

Since I have him alone, I decide to question him some more. "Are you the one who told Wallace that Matt was a CSB officer? You knew he was working undercover at Calhoun Steel. Is that why the pathetic coward setup a meeting with Dean, who was posing as Carlos, so Matt would get killed because Wallace was terrified of having his underground business exposed?"

"I don't know. You'd have to ask him." Aiden focuses on his food, which is getting cold.

"Chief Daven says a new officer is at the plant posing as an informer for CSB. I can only assume it's someone loyal to either you or the cartel. Is that so the new weapons can get made without outside interference?"

He ignores me, shoveling bacon into his arrogant face.

"What were you going to do with the list showing all of Luke's businesses? You could never purchase them *and* payback the money."

"That's exactly what I was going to do," he answers after consuming some juice. "I would've easily made five times the amount missing, and my sister would never have been the wiser."

"Are you the one threatening club owners in Nok Sector?"

He laughs. "Don't be ridiculous. I'd lose money doing that."

It's several long minutes before Siem and Dean return, both reclaiming their seats and finishing their breakfast without uttering a word. When the maids come to clean, Siem stands and picks her sunglasses up, off of the table.

"How about we take a tour?" she suggests, slipping the dark lenses onto the bridge of her nose.

Dean pulls out my chair, places a hand on the small of my back, and escorts me outside as Siem leads the way, with Aiden traipsing behind. We make our way down the path alongside the house toward the docks where two boats are waiting, one filled with heavily armed guards. The four of us get into the vessel containing just a driver, then take our seats. The glare from the sun reflecting off the open water hurts my eyes, so I use my hand to shield them. We swing around Nolita, heading northwest and toward the island of Termore, if I'm recalling the map correctly. It takes roughly ten minutes to reach the mouth of a waterway that divides the extensive piece of land; several wooden bridges span the narrow river to connect the two sides. Our speed slows to avoid creating wakes. Through the foliage I notice men and women laboring hard in the hot weather, tending to not only coca plants, but various vegetable crops and fruit trees as well.

"We grow a lot of our own food," Siem says, sitting beside me. "There's also a farm on the far southern end of the island since items can be difficult to transport. Several of the workers fish around the islands, but they're heavily guarded at all times. Whatever we can't create or catch, we buy from a couple of the shops in one of Navital's lesser secured ports, or import it from Leyon when Dean happens to be in the country on business."

Coming upon a pier, our boat idles to a stop, then we're tied off to the moorings and disembark. My husband keeps me practically plastered to his side while Siem and Aiden saunter ahead. The guards in the other vessel remain in the water. Sweat seeps from my pores, and I'm drenched in a matter of minutes. Marching through the mangroves, we eventually come upon rows of small mounds of disturbed dirt, and I know immediately what it is: a graveyard.

Aiden looks around, puzzled. "Why are we here?"

Dean shoves me toward an open pit, and I nearly fall in.

"This whole thing is very troubling," Siem says, clutching her hands together, rage underlying her words. "I've worked hard to protect my family's lands and keep those with authority from discovering everything that we do. Now, however, it's all been compromised, placing my livelihood at great risk. It's unfortunate, but I can't afford to keep careless people around. No matter who they are."

My husband removes the gun from his waistband and raises it, pointing the weapon at me. "I swear you pull this shit on purpose, babe."

I grin and shake, realizing I'm never going to leave here alive. "Perhaps this time I did."

The seconds pass like hours, his arm never faltering. I close my eyes, not wanting to see the striker leave the barrel. The shot that rings out isn't deafening, and I don't feel any pain. It takes me a brief moment to realize I'm not injured. Opening my eyes, I spot Aiden collapsed on the ground clutching his side, blood pouring from a wound, soaking his clothes.

"Fuck!" he shrieks. "Why did you shoot me?"

"Because you risked everything our father worked hard to create!" his sister rants. "And for what? Your own greed?"

"I saved this cartel! If it wasn't for me, you'd be wasting away in a Navital prison. Everything I've done has always been to protect you and these islands. He's the idiot who set fire to a full nightclub." Aiden points a bloody finger at Dean. "And murdered two CSB detectives, even though one of them isn't technically dead." I know he's referring to me. "If anyone has placed our lives at risk, it's him."

Dean fires again, this time hitting the former director in the chest, killing him.

Siem turns to my husband, holding out her hand. "Give me the gun."

He doesn't hesitate in turning it over, which shocks me.

She aims the barrel at my head, her stance firm. A lump forms in my throat, and my trembling worsens. At the last second, she turns away from me and fires. The striker narrowly misses Dean by inches and the slug lands somewhere in the dirt behind him. Gripping his chest, he falls to his knees, quaking, his skin suddenly pale.

"Next time, it won't be a warning," she says, then walks away still holding the weapon.

Glowering at me, his fury is apparent. "What the fuck were you thinking?" he raves. "Are you trying to get me killed?"

"It would make my life so much easier."

Standing, he steps over and hits me across the face, adding another cut. This one at my brow line. "Goddamn it, Liv. Don't jeopardize this for me … for us," he adds at the last second while pacing in front of me. "You have no idea the deals I had to make so nothing will happen to you when I'm not around. Siem will do anything to get what she wants. Including torturing you to find out who has her money."

"I was being honest. I have no idea who's stealing it, and Cruz destroyed everything we had on the case." Then his words hit me, and I shudder. "What kind of deals?"

"Ones that'll keep you safe for the moment." Snatching my hand, he drags me back toward the boat where Siem is waiting.

"Take Olivia to the house and make sure she doesn't leave," the woman orders her guards, while my husband forces me onto their boat. "I'll be back momentarily." She and Dean board the one we initially rode in and depart.

After turning around, we follow them out of the waterway and back onto the ocean, but they soon disappear from sight. We dock on Nolita, then I'm escorted to the main house, guards positioned at every point of entry inside and out. The cool interior air is welcoming and needed. I head upstairs to tend to the cut, which isn't deep. Since I'm the only one on the second floor, I decide to do some exploring.

Behind our room I discover another balcony and a hidden staircase to a third story. At the top is a lone open archway leading into what appears to be a den with plush, beige carpeting, pale yellow walls, a teak desk, and nearly a dozen plasma screens adhered to the walls, each containing six individual images of footage from around the property. It seems Siem has cameras situated all over the islands, even around her own home.

I spot her and Dean standing in front of one of the hangars, its doors yawning open while the plane is being prepared for departure. He appears apprehensive, nervous almost, especially when she caresses his arm. He turns, climbs the ladder into the plane, and Siem moves out of the field of vision. Not wanting to get caught in a room that I probably shouldn't be in, I head downstairs and pour myself a drink from the wet bar, then take it into the great room to sit and wait for her return. I select a seat on one of the couches facing the wall of windows that overlook a koi pond which butts up right against the rear of the house. There's a small, wooden bridge separating it from an inground pool, and a covered lanai sits off another wing I've yet to see. The water looks inviting, and I miss swimming, but now isn't the time to reclaim my forgotten hobby.

Lost in thought and drawn to the landscaping mere feet away, I don't realize Siem has joined me until I catch her reflection in the glass.

"Dean tells me you enjoy being in a pool. I do as well, but hardly have the time. You should take advantage of the opportunity while you can." Her words sound ominous. "Before he and I returned to the table earlier this morning, I quickly reviewed the article you had mentioned to my brother. The photo depicting the remnants of your home were quite horrific. It's amazing you were able to survive at all."

Clutching the tumbler in my hand, I avoid the discussion.

"Does the topic make you uncomfortable?" she asks, nestling into the seat across from me and crossing her legs at the knee, which hikes up her skirt ever so slightly.

"I just don't like being reminded of the family taken from me on that day."

She purses her plump, pink-painted lips. "Before you came here, I did a bit of research, as I do with anyone who might come work for me. I, too, lost my mother at a young age. She was murdered by a drunk driver. When my father found out, the man was never seen or heard from again." She pauses. "The one who perished in the fire handled your mother's homicide case, correct?"

I nod, hoping not to break into tears. "But it wasn't the blaze that killed him. It was the striker that Dean shot." Lowering my head, I stare into my half-empty glass. "It almost killed me, too."

"Your husband was very distraught when he thought you had died. He was virtually inconsolable."

Lifting my gaze, I stare at her. "I sincerely doubt that considering he was the one responsible."

"Assume what you want, but upon his return he beat one of my girls to death out of anger and severe distress."

"Now that I believe," I say, grimacing. "He was probably fucking her at the time."

She doesn't deny the statement. "Dean is unpredictable when it comes to you, and I see that as an immense problem."

I finish my drink. "What are you going to do?"

"Well, for now, nothing because I need him."

"And when you no longer do?"

She smiles, sending chills down my spine. "We'll see." Standing, she comes over and places a hand on my shoulder. "Why don't you enjoy your stay? Relax and have a bit of fun. I won't tell your husband." She winks, then departs.

I simply refill my glass and drink to forget.

Twelve

I don't remember much of Saturday, considering I spent the majority of the time emptying the wet bar of its contents. Siem wasn't too thrilled with the lack of refreshments I left for her, so she ordered one of the guards to replenish the pilfered stock. He was heading to Navital anyway to procure items for a party she's hosting Monday. Apparently, it's her monthly gathering of buyers looking to purchase women for their sex trade. From what I've been able to overhear—when I'm sober enough—is that there will be roughly a handful of men arriving early that morning. Names haven't been disclosed, but there isn't anyone for me to inform if I did happen to find them out.

By Sunday, my head is pounding, and my stomach is sour. One of the maids brings breakfast to the bedroom since I'm not in any condition to navigate the stairs. I force myself to consume the runny eggs, salty bacon, and bland fruit, knowing I need to stop feeling sorry for myself and work on getting out of here. After the food is gone, I place the thin, metal tray on top of the dresser, then step into the bathroom to take a shower, allowing the hot water to rain down on me for several long minutes. I have to borrow Dean's razor to shave my legs and under my arms, as well as my pubic hair since I've grown to despise having any after Nikki waxed me almost a year ago. Once clean, I wrap up in a towel, then rummage through the drawers, finding khaki-colored shorts and a forest green tank top, donning both. Running a brush through my hair, I decide to leave it down around my shoulders, slip on the sandals I wore the other day, and head downstairs now that I feel human again.

When I reach the foyer, I follow the slight noise of tinkling glass, which leads me into a section of the house I've yet to explore. Passing the dining room, I sidestep around the massive kitchen and enter an elegant family room decorated with hard maple flooring, slate gray painted walls with white trim, and midcentury-modern furniture covered in dark blue cheviot. A set of curio cabinets constructed from dark metal and glass flank a large watercolor painting adorning the wall by another wet bar. Maids are busy dusting, vacuuming, and preparing the room for tomorrow. Turning to glance outside, I spot strings of lights are being hung between the lampposts that are spread across the large, brick patio. Cushions for the lounges around the pool are being hand scrubbed and dried before placed back into position.

"The rest of the decorating will happen tomorrow after my guests arrive," Siem says, sidling up beside me.

Today she's wearing tight-fitting black pants with a silver halter top and matching stilettos. Her makeup is flawless and her perfume—a sweet, lilac fragrance—is stronger today than it has been on previous occasions, and her long, raven-colored hair is straight, allowing the locks to dangle gracefully above her waist.

"I don't want anything to ruin the party, and the weather down here can be unpredictable at times." Focusing her attention on me, she glowers. "We must improve your wardrobe before the occasion. I'll have one of the maids find something decent for you to wear. In the meantime, Dean should be back shortly with my new acquisition. He phoned from the plane advising they're close to landing."

"Is that why you're all dolled up? To make an intimidating first impression?"

She laughs. "Don't be ridiculous. A very close and dear friend of mine will be flying in this evening ahead of the others. The two of us have certain business that must be attended to before the festivities begin." The smile crossing her lips is wide and seductive, and her eyes sparkle with anticipation. "Come, let's meet Dean at the airstrip. He's most anxious to see you."

I follow her out of the front door and down the path to the dock where a boat containing several guards waits. The sun blazes overhead with a bare minimum of clouds in the air, which is unbearably humid. In the distance, toward the south, dark clouds loom, threatening to storm.

Siem takes notice and scowls. "I do hope the rains hold off until much later. My visitor might not be able to land if the weather is too severe, and I'm so looking forward to seeing him." A sparkle returns to her eyes, along with a devilish grin.

When we arrive on Ilusor, the guards accompany us through the jungle, and we wait by one of the empty hangars. After a few minutes, I spot the plane approaching. My nerves tighten since I'm unsure of the reason why Siem had me join her. I know it's not for Dean's sake, so perhaps it's because I might know the person he's bringing to the islands.

But who? The one responsible for alerting the cartel that I was still alive?

Everyone, with the exception of a couple of people, believe I'm dead. And no one I know has any connections to drug running or sex trafficking. The ones who did were all murdered.

I grow queasy as the plane touches down onto the tarmac, then slows once it gets closer to the hangar. After the engines are shut off, the staircase is lowered, and Dean descends carrying a squirming body—wearing torn jeans, a rumpled, long-sleeved, white shirt, and black boots—over his shoulders. Her screams are muffled by more than the black sack covering her head. Plastic zip ties bind her hands behind her back, and her legs are secured together at the ankle. Siem nudges me forward, following a few paces behind as more guards join us.

"Hi, babe," Dean says, then drops his captive onto the blackened surface. Her screams of pain pierce my core. "I brought you a gift."

Lying on her side, the woman struggles to sit up, her entire body shaking as she sobs uncontrollably. Under the tears in her clothing are remnants of dried blood and deep scratches, probably sustained during a fight. Studying my husband, I'm paralyzed with fear, terrified to discover who's shrouded beneath the sackcloth.

"Don't be shy, Liv. She won't bite," Dean teases, nudging the poor thing with his leg.

I cautiously approach, then kneel down onto the hot pavement. The woman's cries are now simple whimpers. When I reach out, she cowers at my touch, shrinking away while I work on loosening the tie for the bag over her head. The first thing I notice is her shoulder-length burgundy hair, which is blocking most of her face.

"Taylor?" I gasp, then quickly remove the sack the remainder of the way and push back her hair to see her better.

She stares at me, bewildered. Tear stains have soaked her cheeks, smearing whatever makeup she had on. A gag has been placed around her mouth, so I untie it, allowing the rough material to fall to the ground.

"Olivia," she bemoans, then rests her head against my shoulder and continues to bawl.

Stroking her back, I glare up at Dean. "Why the hell is she here?"

He grabs her by the back of her shirt collar, wrenching her away from me. "Because she owed us a favor."

"I already did what you wanted!" Taylor shouts. "Now let me go!"

"What …what is she talking about?" I ask, glancing between my husband and Siem.

Dean shakes the frightened, young woman. "She's the one who alerted us that you survived the fire. She's also the reason you're here, Olivia, instead of still in your cozy cabin on Kodiak Island with the bastard you were fucking. What was his name? Matt? How I enjoyed putting a striker through his heart."

"You said no one would get hurt." Taylor looks pleadingly at me. "They promised."

"And you were a fool enough to believe us," Siem says, stepping up to my side, placing her hands on her hips.

Standing, I ask, "How did you know I survived the attack?"

She momentarily stops fighting for her freedom. "Lloyd let it slip when I asked about the shoes missing from my locker." Her eyes grow hard as they bore into me. "You should've seen the panic on his face when he noticed my reaction. He tried to cover up the mistake, made excuses about how he was still grieving the loss of his beloved Olivia, and that he was struggling to come to terms with reality, which was why he misspoke. When I didn't buy his bullshit, he swore me to secrecy, but I had already made the deal with the cartel … with Dean, to monitor you and tell him everything you were doing."

Anger pulses in my veins, and I ball my hands into fists. "You knew he was alive?" I ask, seething. "Why didn't you say anything?"

"Because I couldn't! It would've cost me everything!" She moves her focus back to Siem. "Where is she? Where's my sister?"

The older woman steps toward Taylor, then places her hands on either side of the young woman's face, gently moving it back and forth as if examining her. "I sold her several weeks ago. Received a generous price for such a young thing."

Taylor spits in the woman's face. "Bitch! She was only sixteen! How could you do that?"

After wiping the moisture off of her cheek, Siem slaps the scared, young woman hard, her manicured nails slicing through Taylor's skin, cutting it and drawing blood. "That little whore owed me. Along with several of those other castoffs from Ronan's ranch. I saved her life. Otherwise, she'd have been buried with the rest of her friends." Siem turns to me. "The ones CSB didn't find." She runs her fingers through Taylor's hair, admiring it. "It's unfortunate that your family refused to pay for her release, and that her noble sister failed to come through in saving her before time ran out."

The tears return. "I tried."

Siem smiles. "I know you did, my dear, but everything must come to an end when agreements aren't kept."

Taylor stiffens, her eyes widening with horror. "What are you going to do with me?"

"I'll need to assess you first before making my final determination." Siem signals for the guards. "Take her to the boat and wait for me."

The heavily armed men seize Taylor by the arms and drag her toward the jungle while she screams. Dean saunters over to me, places a hand behind my head, and shoves his tongue into my mouth. He doesn't come up for air until Siem clears her throat.

"Why don't the two of you return to the main house? Dean, ensure Olivia is better dressed since we have company arriving in a bit."

He appears confused. "Who? The auction isn't until tomorrow evening."

She smiles, a twinkle appearing in her irises. "It's someone very important and special to me. He's been down to the islands many times before, and you've met him on several occasions. It's Sam."

My heart stops, my blood runs cold, and everything around me slowly goes out of focus. I quickly and desperately regain my composure before either notice.

Dean pulls me against his chest as if protecting me from an attacker. "Why does Olivia have to be there? None of this pertains to her."

Siem narrows her gaze. "It's imperative that she familiarizes herself with those heavily involved in my business. That is if you still want her to join our endeavors. Otherwise, I can find something else useful for her to do."

"Fine," Dean grouses. "Hopefully he has some good news about the missing money."

That's who she called Friday? Sam? The program he had me install into the databases; it was for Siem, not himself. Fuck! But wait. That would mean she already knew the money was missing before I told her. She seemed genuinely shocked by the news, so then Sam must have implemented it for another reason, which is what?

Betrayal eats away at my soul while the three of us make our way to the docks, Siem boarding the boat with her guards and Taylor, who's now cowering on the floor of the vessel. Another takes Dean and I to Nolita where we head for the house, then our bedroom the second we enter. Sitting on the bed, I remove the sandals and think of what to do and say when Sam arrives while my husband hops into the shower. Nothing comes to mind, leaving me anxious and worried.

A few minutes later, Dean exits the bathroom completely naked, his wet, dark hair falling just below his shoulders. He rummages through the dresser drawers, donning beige, linen pants and a tropical print shirt. I'm surprised when he leaves his gun on the nightstand instead of tucking it into his waistband. Perhaps that's due to the company supposedly arriving. The temptation to grab it and shoot my husband is overwhelming, but then the guards would rush into the room and end my life without hesitation. I have to know the full extent of Sam's involvement with the Vilks Cartel and I can't do that if I'm dead.

After searching the closet, Dean pulls out an asymmetrical, silk skirt in pale green with a matching blouson. "Change into these," he says, handing me the garments. "There aren't any shoes to go with it, so you'll have to wear the brown leather sandals. Luckily, they're decent enough to pass Siem's criteria." He points to the discarded pair on the floor.

"And what about tomorrow?"

"You're not going anywhere near those piranhas. You'll stay in this room until they leave on Tuesday. I'm not thrilled with Siem insisting you meet Sam, but you do need to know her closest associates since you'll be working for the cartel."

"This isn't what I want for my life, Dean. Why couldn't you just leave me well enough alone when you went underground?"

Grabbing my waist, he pulls me close. "Because we took vows, Liv, remember? Until death do us part." He leans down so his moist lips brush against my ear. "And since neither of us is technically dead, those words still stand." He kisses me fervently, his hands wandering under the tank top, groping me. "I love you, babe. Please love me like you used to."

His mouth moves to my neck while he works slowly on undressing me. He takes the skirt and top, tosses them aside, then guides me backwards to the bed, laying me across the soft covers. I do my best to not get caught up in our past, when we genuinely cared about each other, but it proves difficult, and I find myself unbuttoning his shirt, followed by his pants. His hardened cock thumps against my thigh, throbbing with anticipation, but he doesn't force anything to happen. He yelps when I grab him, then guide him inside of me. Our lovemaking is gentle, the passion intense. Sweat coats our bodies as we soak the sheets. Our mouths devour each other, craving everything we have to offer. He takes to my tit, which causes me to moan. My entire body shudders when I achieve orgasm. The wave flows up and down, hitting every nerve, setting them on fire. Dean hollers as he comes, and his eyes roll into the back of his head. It takes several long minutes for us to catch our breaths.

"I think you need to shower again," I say, tugging on his soaked locks.

"Only if you join me."

When we're under the hot water, I let Dean wash every inch of me. His touch electrifies me in ways I'd forgotten. His fingers massage and lather the soap into my flesh, working their way around my most sensitive of areas. Closing my eyes, I gasp when his newly erect cock slips into me. His thrusts are drawn-out, extending our time and arousal. He bites my shoulder while I wrap my arms around his neck as best I can given our awkward position. Using the suds, he strokes my nipples, waking them from their brief slumber.

Leaning my head back, I succumb to his desires. "I'm yours, Dean. Fuck me however you want."

"Just like this," he whispers. "Always and forever."

"Yes, please."

Again, he hollers when he reaches his climax. Mine isn't as intense as before, but I actually don't mind this time. It takes a few extra minutes to wash off, then he steps out of the stall first, handing me a towel from the rack before retrieving his from the tiled floor. I wrap it around myself, securing it at my chest, then return to the bedroom. Dean is just about finished buttoning his shirt when there's a knock on the door. He opens it slightly, mutters a few words to whomever is on the other side, then closes it.

"The food for tomorrow has arrived, so I need to go to Ilusor and make sure we have everything before bringing it over. I shouldn't be gone long." He kisses me, retrieves his weapon from the nightstand, then leaves.

I take my time getting dressed in the skirt and blouson. Stepping into the bathroom, I hang up the towel on the metal rack before combing my hair, working out all of the knots. I try not to dwell on Sam's impending arrival while making my way downstairs and into the family room. One of the maids pours me a glass of rum from the wet bar that's still stocked, which surprises me.

"Here, Miss Olivia," she says in broken English.

I thank her, take the drink, and exit onto the deck. Colorful umbrellas stand wide open, shading cushioned wicker lounge chairs. Taking a seat, I recline and sip the delicious liquor, desperately wanting more.

"Don't you look comfortable," a familiar voice says behind me.

My nerves prickle. "When did you arrive?" I ask angrily, not bothering to turn around, my gaze focused on the clear, inviting water for the pool.

"A few minutes ago." Sam moves around my chair and sits sideways on the lounge beside me, his hands clasped at the knee.

I briefly glance at him, noting the white, linen suit with a pale yellow dress shirt underneath, and brown leather loafers on his feet. His champagne-colored hair is a bit longer since the last time I saw him, there's some stubble on his chin, and his chestnut eyes cut right through me.

"I'm surprised to find you out here alone."

I finish the drink, then roll the warm glass between my palms. "Dean is on his way to Ilusor, and Siem is currently on Antiris."

"And Aiden?"

Glaring at Sam, my anger turns into hate. "Dead." I'm in the process of opening my mouth again when he places a finger to his lips.

"The walls have ears." Instinctively, he reaches for my face, probably noticing the cuts, but I pull away. "Did he do that to you?"

"Like you care." Fuming, I head back into the house and refill my glass.

He follows, helping himself to a tumbler of Scotch.

"Are you all right?" he whispers, his cologne tantalizing my senses.

"Of course I'm not. You used me."

He leans against the wall, sips his drink, and smiles. "How?"

But I don't get a chance to answer.

Siem saunters into the room. "Darling!" she exclaims, then rushes over and throws her arms around his neck before kissing him deeply on the lips. "Why didn't anyone tell me that you were here?"

"I wanted to surprise you," Sam replies, appearing to relish her in his arms.

She glances around the room, mystified. "Where are your things? I didn't see them in the foyer."

After setting his glass down onto the marble top for the wet bar, he guides her over to one of the couches and sits closely beside her. "I had my security place them into a bungalow."

She scowls. "That's ridiculous. I insist that you stay in the main house like you always do."

Leaning back, he drapes his left arm along the back of the couch behind her, then brushes his right arm across his thigh, cinching up the sleeve and exposing a silver bracelet. I immediately recognize it as having come from Ronan's ranch. I thought for sure he had his microchip removed long ago, considering where he travels and some of the business he conducts.

Perhaps I was mistaken.

The object catches the woman's attention. "Where did you get such a lovely thing?" she asks, grabbing him to have a better look.

With Siem's attention occupied, she doesn't notice him staring at me. "My fiancée gave it to me."

She looks up at him, horrified. "You're engaged? When did this happen?"

"Fairly recently, which is why I'll be staying in a bungalow."

Her cheerful demeanor quickly sours. "If I had known you were getting married, I never would've invited you."

He places the arm from the back of the couch around her shoulders, pulling her tight against him. "You and I both know that isn't true."

She rests her hand on his leg, stroking the soft fabric of his pants with her delicate, well-polished fingers. "Who is this woman that's stolen you from me?"

"It's none of your concern, my dear."

Repositioning herself on his lap and brushing her lips against his, she says, "I bet I can get you to change your mind." Then she proceeds to shove her tongue down his throat, and his hands climb up the back of her shirt.

Rage for both of them eats away at me, taunting me to lash out, but as much as I want to explode, I can't. Not while I'm still trapped on these islands with nowhere to run. Finishing my drink, I rapidly exit the room before doing something I'll regret. Feeling lost on where to go, I step outside and trot along the shoreline, putting as much distance between me and the house as possible. Dean will be furious when he returns, but at the moment I don't give a damn. I wander until the coast bends toward the bay that sits at the mouth of the island. When I reach the end, I turn and head back, coming across Dean halfway.

"I was starting to worry," he says, wrapping an arm around my waist. "Siem said you left and no one was able to find you."

"I doubt they looked hard enough," I grumble.

"Let's return to the house."

When we enter, the pair are now in the great room, fresh drinks in their hands. Dean pours me one, then plasters himself against my back, obviously showing Sam whom I belong to.

"Is this your wife?" he asks, coming over to us and extending his hand for me to shake.

"Yes," my husband answers, disdain thick in his voice. "Olivia, this is Sam West."

I shake his hand and pretend to be nice. "It's a pleasure to meet you."

"Dean, you neglected to tell me how beautiful she is." His eyes twinkle while he smiles. "Your husband raves about you constantly. I'm so glad we finally got a chance to meet."

Escorting me to the other side of the room, Dean asks, "What news do you have?"

"Well," Sam begins, then consumes a bit of his drink, "Wallace was arrested the other day on weapons charges. It appears someone let slip to CSB that he was illegally manufacturing striker ammunition with intent to sell."

Siem crosses her legs at the knee and grins. "Does that mean you're finally in charge of the entire company? No more board of directors bullshit?"

"Like you wanted." He raises his glass toward her in a makeshift toast. "Of course, this means I'll need to relocate some of the business down to Navital in order to continue making the armaments that you want. Since they're not as strict on gun laws, it shouldn't be too difficult."

Dean appears rather annoyed. "Have you found the money?"

Sam sits beside Siem, who nestles herself closely to his side. "Unfortunately, no. Whomever was stealing hid their tracks rather well." He finishes his Scotch. "I've decided to shut down TITAN Industries to stop the bleeding."

Siem furrows her brow. "My brother told me he closed all those accounts and moved the finances into another, more secure one."

"He did, but I don't think it's wise to continue using the fake company to front your money laundering. Who knows what kind of deal Wallace may try to broker in exchange for information."

Sitting up straighter, she places a hand on his cheek and beams. "You always have my best interests at heart."

Removing her hand, he kisses the back of it. "Why wouldn't I?"

Dean takes a seat in a high-backed, cushioned chair by the wall of windows, pulling me onto his lap. "He's still a liability we can't afford to have."

"I'll leave that up to you." Sam tips his glass in my husband's direction. "But, enough about business. I want to get to know Olivia better."

Dean stiffens.

"What would you like to know?" I ask, provoking the tension for shear enjoyment.

"How did a gorgeous woman like yourself wind up with a bastard such as Dean?"

Siem laughs while my husband grows furious. He places a hand against my back and digs his shortened nails into me. Thankfully, the blouson is absorbing most of the force, but it still hurts.

I will have marks later.

"We met at a bar shortly after I graduated from the CSB academy, and he's been a pain in my ass ever since."

Dean pretends to chuckle at the comment.

Sam's gaze lingers on me longer than it should, which my husband notices. "Are you still with CSB?"

"No," Dean answers rather hastily.

Thunder cracks outside as the storm we spotted earlier finally rolls in. The winds pick up, causing a torrential downpour. The lights flicker momentarily while lightning flashes brilliantly across the sky.

"Good thing I arrived when I did," Sam says, chortling. "What time tomorrow are the others set to land?"

"Around early afternoon," Siem replies. "The party won't begin until later in the day, then Tuesday is when the real fun starts."

Sam smiles wickedly. "Will Olivia be joining us?"

"Absolutely not," Dean answers, balling his one free hand into a fist, and practically shattering his goblet containing whiskey with the other.

Siem glowers at him. "Yes, she is. How else is she to learn where her position in the cartel will be?"

"What do you plan on having her do?" Standing, Sam relieves Siem of her empty glass to refill it.

"Entertain my buyers while they drink, in addition to preparing them for the auction. She'll be quite busy."

"Sounds exciting." He hands her back the drink, but doesn't reclaim his seat. "Perhaps I'll help introduce her around to your guests while Dean is managing the security and you're welcoming the others as they arrive."

"That won't be necessary." My husband nudges me to move so he can stand, then I sit while he goes to pour me another drink, taking my old-fashioned glass with him, even though it's not empty. "My guards already have their assignments for tomorrow and Tuesday, so Olivia will be on my arm, not yours."

Sam bows partially at the waist. "Just offering some assistance." He turns his attention to Siem. "How many are coming?"

"Eight, not including you. Along with whomever they trust to accompany them." She drinks her red wine. "It's a little larger than normal because I have more to sell. My recruiters have been very fortunate as of late. It should be an extremely profitable event."

A few minutes later one of the maids announces that dinner is ready, so we retreat to the dining room. Siem and Sam banter like old lovers, while Dean fumes under his breath. After we're done eating, Sam calls for several of his guards to come to the house and escort him to the bungalow he's chosen to occupy, much to Siem's disappointment. They carry umbrellas to protect the arrogant man from the pounding rain. I head upstairs while Siem and Dean argue about tomorrow.

He slams the bedroom door after entering. "I don't want you leaving this room until the party starts," he orders, then undresses, tossing his clothes into a pile on the floor in the closet. "If Siem didn't need Sam, I'd put a striker through his head tonight while he slept. He was ogling you too much."

"I barely noticed," I lie while sitting on the edge of the bed, removing my sandals. "He's not my type anyway."

"Sam West is every woman's type, Liv. If not for his looks, then for his money."

I step into the bathroom. "You almost sound jealous."

He joins me, placing his hands on the upper part of my arms. "No, just leery. I don't trust him."

"At least that's something we have in common."

Wrapping an arm around my waist, he turns me until I'm facing him. "Are you sure?"

I don't like the sneer he's displaying. "Yes. Why wouldn't I be?"

"It was his casino you, Luke, and Aaron were staying at while in Prescott. Was Sam going into business with your late boss?"

Trying not to show my sudden unease, I make sure my voice is calm and even toned. "I don't know."

Placing a hand under my chin so his fingers dig into my cheeks, he starts to squeeze. "The car you were driving when I shot Luke, it was the same one in the driveway at the house in Range Sector. Where did you get it?"

"Luke rented it so I could run errands."

"But that's not what you were doing that fateful morning. The three of you were heading to the same location. I know because Luke called me before you left the casino. However, he neglected to specify where. He didn't trust his new supposed partner, which is why I was on the rooftop to make sure nothing happened to him en route. Even though Aiden had already given me the go ahead to murder my former friend." He leans his face close to mine until they're practically touching. "Was it Sam who had him shot?"

"Dean, you're hurting me." I grab his wrist and work on prying him loose.

"If the car was simply a rental, then why did you keep it?" He shoves me into the vanity, pressing himself against me until I cry out from the pain of the granite countertop burrowing into my back. "Did Sam give it to you?"

"No," I mumble, tears welling in my eyes. "Please, Dean, stop."

"Why did you keep the car?"

"It was a gift from Luke," I blurt out, praying the lie works.

Dean releases me, rage still deeply welled in his eyes.

I rub my face. "He surprised me with it that morning. I thought it was a rental until I found the purchase agreement in the glovebox after he'd been killed. It was in my name."

"Why is Sam pretending he doesn't know you?"

I shrug. "You'd have to ask him."

A loud crack of thunder echoes outside, shaking the house, and causing the lights to flicker before finally going out.

"Shit," Dean grumbles, then exits into the bedroom and redresses. "I'll be back in a bit. Get some sleep."

After he's gone, I breathe a sigh of relief even though my anxiety has skyrocketed. Fumbling in the darkness, I use the facilities, brush my teeth, and change into something comfortable to wear to bed.

Thirteen

Dean didn't return to the room until well after three in the morning. The power was knocked out on all five islands, so once the storm had passed, he went to each to make sure the guards were handling things appropriately. A couple of the trees close to the house came down, so the sounds of chainsaws wake me up from a restless sleep. While my husband is out preparing for the guests' arrival, I'm served breakfast in bed per his instructions. After setting the now empty tray on top of the dresser, I take off the T-shirt and shorts I wore to bed and get into the shower. When I'm clean, I dry my hair before wrapping the towel around my body, securing it at my chest. Just as I step into the bedroom, there's a knock on the door.

"Miss Siem would like you to wear this for the evening," one of the maids says, handing me a colorful, silk sundress with spaghetti straps, along with a cosmetic bag. "This also came for you." She digs into the pocket of her uniform and removes a card-sized envelope, handing it to me.

I thank her, close the door, and set the dress and bag onto the bed so I can open the nondescript note.

> I know that he's hurt you and he will be dealt with later for that. I'm so sorry about Frank. Knowing how close the two of you were I can't imagine the pain you've been going through. Right now, Olivia, you need to trust me no matter what I say or do. Everything that will happen tonight is to protect you from further harm. I love you. Please remember that.

It's not signed, but I recognize Sam's handwriting. To keep Dean from finding it, I remove the bottom drawer for the dresser, shove the note with the envelope all the way to the back, then reinsert the drawer.

His words are ominous, foreboding, and chilling. Adding to my already fraying nerves. I'm sure one of his bodyguards delivered the letter, meaning he didn't actually have the desire to do it himself. Or he didn't want the maids to recognize him as the writer. Either way, it doesn't take away from the fact that he's planning to do something at the party.

Noting the time displayed on the small clock on top of the nightstand, I don the clothes I wore to bed, slip out of the room, and quietly go up the stairs to the third floor. The alcove with the monitors is devoid of people, so I take a seat in the lone, rolling chair, and study the images being captured by the various cameras. The first person I spot is Dean with several of his men securing boats to a couple of moorings, Siem is busy greeting several parties who've landed on the airstrip, and Sam disappears into a ramshackle building with a sagging roof, chipped stucco exterior, and hardly any windows—none of his guards are visible in the camera which surprises me.

I stay seated for quite some time, studying the faces of those arriving, counting the number of guests they've brought along. All are relatively older men, with a few younger ones thrown into the mix. The gathering of eight is quickly exploding into at least twenty or more. I'm not sure where Siem intends to house them all. Over an hour passes before Sam finally emerges from the derelict building, then hastens to an awaiting boat where his guards are stationed. The next time he appears is on the shores of what I assume is Nolita. Siem is still by the hangars for the airstrip, and Dean's guards are starting to launch the first boat of guests. Knowing my solitude could be compromised shortly, I leave.

In the bedroom, I sit on the mattress and look through the cosmetic bag, finding a bottle of dark blue nail polish. Assuming I'm to wear it, I spend the next half hour carefully applying the sticky substance several times to both my finger and toenails. After they dry, I step out onto the balcony since I'm unsure about how much time I have to waste until the party begins. I'd prefer a drink in my hand at the moment, but there isn't a way to ring for the maids to bring me one.

Leaning against the railing, I notice the flurry of activity going on below as men in starched white uniforms rush in and out of the front door. Many of them have sun-kissed skin, causing me to wonder if they normally work in the fields on Termore. Curious about what else is happening, I once again leave the bedroom and step out onto the balcony at the rear of the house. High-topped tables are being placed on the concrete patio around the pool. A crystal fountain has been assembled with matching champagne flutes encircling it, while cases of the bubbly drink rest on the ground waiting to be opened.

Something latches onto the back of my shirt and pulls me inside.

"I thought I told you to stay in the bedroom," my husband raves, shoving me.

"I got bored."

"Well, you won't be for long. Siem insists that you be present in the great room when everyone enters the house. Once introductions are done, the party will begin in the family room and move out onto the patio. If I'm not with you, then one of my guards will be. Did the maids bring you something to wear?"

We retreat to the bedroom where I show him the dress stretched out on the comforter. The mosaic pattern covering the delicate material is filled with luscious dark colors matching the polish I was given.

"Put it on," he demands.

I step over to the dresser in the hopes of finding some panties that may have been left behind by the woman whose clothes I'm currently wearing. Locating a black, lace thong, I remove the shorts and T-shirt, then don the garment like directed. The front is open down the center, exposing my entire torso with very little fabric to conceal my breasts, ceasing just above my belly button. In the mirror above the dresser, I notice the back of the garment drops to my tailbone. The hem barely covers my thighs, so if I bend over too far everyone will get a good show.

Dean scowls. "I'm not allowing you to wear that."

"You honestly think there's a choice here? Hasn't it crossed your mind that Siem will use me however she wants, regardless of your feelings?"

He doesn't answer, but continues to fume under his breath.

"What am I supposed to do?" I plead, looking for some guidance.

Clenching his jaw, he replies, "Finish getting ready. I'll be back shortly." He slams the door on his way out.

Picking up the cosmetic bag, I head into the bathroom. After combing my hair, I find a bottle of mousse under the sink, so I apply a small amount to keep the fly-away strands in place. Next, I put on the makeup, doing my best to cover up the cuts on my brow and lip, as well as the dark circles under my eyes from the lack of sleep I've been suffering. Back in the bedroom, I rummage through the closet, looking for a pair of high-heeled shoes to go with the outfit, but all I find are flipflops, a couple of sneakers, and sandals too worn to be of use. As I take one last look in the mirror, there's a knock on the door, causing my stomach to churn.

"Miss Olivia," the maid from earlier says after I've opened the door, "Miss Siem would like to see you in the master suite."

Following her along the hallway, we traverse the stairs, and before entering the great room, we turn left toward a pair of French doors with frosted inlaid glass. The older woman knocks, but doesn't wait for a response and hurries away.

"Come in," Siem calls in a sing-song voice.

Entering, I step into a lavish seating area with pristine hardwood floors that expand the length of the entire room. Furniture matching that of the great room sit angled to each other in conjunction with a set of glass-paneled doors leading onto a private lanai. Off to the left of the seating area is the main bedroom with a king-sized canopy bed blanketed in black lace and satin. Siem is standing at the foot of the bed helping Dean with the bowtie for his tuxedo. I hadn't realized that he keeps clothes in here as well.

"Don't you look ravishing," she praises, her eyes sparkling with excitement.

"Why did you give her that dress?" my husband asks, stepping away from his boss in fury.

"Because Olivia needs to look perfect for tonight." She purses her lips. "But there are a few things missing."

She disappears behind another door, returning with a pair of open-toed shoes in a glimmering gold. Next, she steps over to a freestanding jewelry cabinet and removes a thick, gold bracelet and thin-chained necklace with a compass pendant dangling at the end. The shoes are a little big, but not uncomfortably so, and the pendant hangs right at my breastbone, drawing attention to it.

"That's much better," she says once I have everything on, then tucks a few pieces of hair behind my ear. "I'd give you earrings, but your lobes aren't pierced." Her hot skin lingers a bit too long against my face, which forces Dean to get between us.

Gripping my wrist, he pushes me behind him. "I still don't think Olivia needs to be a part of this."

"Don't be ridiculous, of course she does," Siem says dismissively. "In fact, I already have an offer for her."

"What?" I nearly shout, becoming sickened by the thought.

Dean releases me, lifts up the back of his coat, and wraps a hand around the grip for the gun hidden in his waistband. "We had this discussion already, Siem. Olivia is not yours to sell."

She smiles wickedly. "No, but you've forced my hand, dear boy." Turning for the dresser, she places a silver bracelet on her wrist to match the tone of her form-fitting, red dress. "If it wasn't for your and Aiden's carelessness with my money, she wouldn't be in this predicament. I need to make back those millions somehow, and seeing as you owe me for the loss, what better way to reclaim it than through your wife's virtue?" Noticing his stance, she carefully approaches us. "Or would you rather I take it out of you? There are several guests inclined to solicit for your companionship … if you get what I mean. However, I highly doubt you'd be inclined to partake."

Dean lets go of the weapon, then buttons his coat. "How much is someone willing to pay for her?"

"Are you fucking serious?" My eyes widen in astonishment as I move away from the pair.

"Five million so far," Siem replies, ignoring me. "But that's simply for an hour of pleasure. I'm hoping to procure more when the others get a chance to see her and all she's worth."

Dean glares at me, wrath in his eyes. "Who?"

"Sam West."

"Anyone but him, Siem," my husband says, grabbing my arm so I don't get away.

She gets closer and runs the tip of her polished nail along the ridge of his face. "Then you had better hope someone else comes through." Kissing him on the cheek, she heads for the door and leaves.

"Dean, don't let her do this," I beg, tears welling in my eyes.

Placing his free hand under my chin, he stares intently at me. "I need time to think, Liv. For now, play along." He kisses me hard on the lips. "You won't be awarded to anyone. I promise."

I want to feel a bit relieved, but I don't. Not even when we enter the great room where one of the maids instinctively hands me an old-fashioned glass filled with rum. Dean has me sit in the same seat I occupied last night, while he stands by my side, a gentle hand on my exposed shoulder. A doorman greets the men as they enter, each wearing black tuxedos, and a few are escorted by gorgeous, young women in formal gowns. They seem to be more for show than actual wives or girlfriends. Waiters wander the room and foyer carrying silver platters filled with hors d'oeuvres and champagne. Several of Dean's guards are strategically positioned in a few of the doorways into the dining room. Briefly turning in my chair, I spot more on the patio. I'm a little surprised by the amount of security, considering these guests are here to have fun, not to start a war.

A couple of the older men approach, shaking hands with Dean, but it's clear from how the others are behaving that they fear my husband. The occasional weary glance in our direction confirms my suspicions. Those I do chat with appear nice and cordial. However, there's an undertone of testosterone and sexual tension from each of them.

I feel like a fresh cut of meat on display for purchase.

After a few minutes of scanning the room, I spot Sam by the planter in the foyer talking to a group of what appear to be first-time visitors, according to their nervous and eager behaviors. The tuxedo he's wearing is probably the same one from Dallas' New Year's Eve party, and he looks extremely handsome in it. I find myself growing wet at the thought of possibly having an hour with him tonight, though I sincerely doubt that's going to happen.

"Dean, I want to introduce you to a couple of people," Siem says, wrapping her arm around his.

"I'm not leaving Olivia alone."

"Nonsense, she'll be fine. Besides, it's hard for the men to have a good look at your wife if you're hovering over her shoulder."

He begrudgingly leaves, and the pair turn the corner, heading toward the family room.

I have yet to touch my drink, and as I'm about to, a champagne flute is thrust into my face.

"I thought he'd never leave," Sam says.

Taking the glass, I set down the other onto a small side table next to me. "He won't be gone long." I have to force myself to sip the beverage and not consume it all at once like I desperately want to. "I heard you're already putting in bids on some merchandise."

He pulls a chair over and sits. "I would hardly call you merchandise."

"Then why do it?"

Clasping my hand, he says, "Did you read the note I sent?"

I pull out of his grip. "Yes, but it doesn't change whatever game you're trying to play."

"This isn't a game, Liv." His jovial tone turns serious as he leans closer to keep our conversation more private. "There's so much I want to say to you, but this isn't the ideal place or moment. Just know, I plan on getting you out of here by any means necessary before all hell breaks loose and you get caught in the middle of it."

Studying his demeanor, I notice the intense expression on his face. "Where's Jake?"

Sam places a hand on my arm. "He's not the one you should be worrying about."

My spine prickles, and when I turn my attention toward the foyer, Dean is standing there glowering at us. Sam's gaze follows mine, and he stiffens at the sight of my husband.

"How many guards did you bring?" I whisper while continuing to nervously stare at the man who holds my life in his abusive hands.

"Five, why?"

I finish the champagne, and hand him back the glass. "You should've brought more." Standing, I make my way over to Dean, who places an arm around my waist and escorts me outside to the pool deck.

He and I stand at the table closest to the champagne fountain, which is being filled with the light-colored liquid. It cascades down the various levels like a waterfall. A waiter comes around with small plates of caviar, designer crackers, flavorful cheeses, and thinly sliced meat, setting one down on our table. I eat a bit of the cheese and crackers, but have no desire to touch the caviar. Dean requests one of the young men to bring me a drink and to refill his whiskey.

"Exquisite," someone mutters behind me when they pass.

"Very alluring," another comments, leering directly at me from a few feet away.

Fingers graze the outline of the red angel wings on my back, sending uncomfortable shivers down my spine. "How lovely," Siem says, appearing beside me. "What other tattoos do you have?"

"A lily on the inside of my right ankle, and an exploding star on my right hip."

She smiles. "I'll need to let a few of the interested buyers know. They'll pay extra for that."

"Don't do this, Siem," Dean says, pulling me against him. "Olivia has money … we can pay to replace some of what's been lost. She received a very substantial settlement from Kane Cassidy's estate after the torment and torture he put her through. It's yours if you leave her alone."

"As much as that is a tempting offer, I'm afraid she can't afford the price. You see, the newest bid I have is twenty million dollars. But don't worry, she won't be leaving the island. Just your bed for the night." Chuckling, she saunters away.

"Now what?" I ask as the waiter returns with our drinks.

"I'll think of something."

Over the course of the next several hours, I nurse the rum while Dean banters with the men who've come to solicit me. I do my best not to lash out and make matters worse, but I refuse to accept the situation. I'd like to believe that my husband is thinking of ways to get me out of this. However, the more he discusses the idea with my so-called admirers, the wider his smile becomes.

He'll sell me off to anyone, so long as it isn't Sam.

Normally, I would drink heavily to put this miserable evening out of my mind, inducing a well-deserved blackout. Unfortunately, I can't if I'm to save my own ass.

Hungry eyes rake over me from a distance. Whispers of desire float along the air with the muffled melody of music wafting out of the family room. With night settling in, the temperature starts to drop and a chill washes over me. I do everything possible not to show it, fearing I'll give someone an opportunity to offer me their jacket, thereby allowing them to paw at me.

"Gentlemen, may I have your attention please?" Siem calls while standing on a stool that's been placed on the bridge between the koi pond and the pool, tapping the crystal for her glass to silence everyone.

Dean returns to the table and stands behind me, blocking any chance for escape.

After all eyes have turned to her, she continues, "I'd like to take this moment and thank you all for coming. It's nights like these that I look forward to and long to have them more frequently."

The men all chuckle, while the few women in attendance hardly make a sound. They're either too drunk or heavily medicated on some type of illegal substance to even realize what's taking place.

At the moment, I envy them.

"With tonight being the first of many for my new personal assistant," she nods in my direction, causing heads to turn in unison, "it's sure to be an extremely profitable endeavor having her as part of the family. A most generous offer of fifty million dollars has been made to spend one evening in her lovely company. I just hope the man's fiancée doesn't find out." Siem laughs, and so does everyone else.

A lump forms in my throat, and I start to feel lightheaded. Shaking, I have the urge to sit, but Dean won't let me move an inch. He's plastered himself right against my back, his hands cinched tightly around my biceps, the heat from his body nearly sweat inducing.

Siem lifts up her glass. "I give to you, Sam West."

Applause and cheers erupt from the crowd while Sam heads over to the hostess, shaking hands along the way, being congratulated for his accomplishment.

Relief washes over me until I catch Dean mumble, "Fiancée?"

"What she doesn't know won't hurt me," Sam quips, then chortles with the rest of them. Gradually, he and Siem make their way over to us, grins on both of their faces. He holds out his hand in anticipation of me accepting it. "Shall we go?"

Dean's heavy breathing encapsulates the air, forcing everyone to take notice and grow very still. The only sound to be heard is the music and croaking frogs out in the jungle.

"Don't worry, I'll return your wife back to you in one piece."

He doesn't relinquish me.

"Dean," Siem says furiously, "let her go."

His glare bores into Sam, then over to Siem. Shoving me forward, my husband stomps away and disappears into the house.

The party returns to a lively atmosphere. Drinks are poured and food is consumed.

"Have fun you two." Siem kisses Sam on the cheek before returning to her guests.

Taking my arm, he places it around his, and we make our way into the family room. Passing the dining room, I notice Dean in quiet conversation with a few of the guards toward the back by the alcove where the buffet table is. Dread permeates my core when I catch a few hastily thrown glances in our direction, but I don't think Sam notices. When we exit through the front door, five armed men wait at the bottom of the steps, then encircle and escort us away from the house. I recognize them as Sam's security, but it doesn't ease the fear rising inside of me.

"When can we leave?" I ask once there's some distance between us and the main house.

"Not until tomorrow. There are cameras all over the islands and we don't need Dean or Siem spying us on one of them while we try to escape."

"No one goes into the room on the third floor," I comment.

"That isn't the only location with monitors. Besides, Dean carries a small, portable display that alerts him whenever something sets off one of the many hidden sensors. He's never without it."

"I've never seen it. Staying here longer than necessary is a horrible idea. It gives Dean a chance to come up with a plan to kill either you, me, or the both of us."

"Siem will keep him in line, Liv. After all, *he* works for *her*."

I hold onto Sam tightly. "You don't know him like I do."

He places his hand around my waist. "Relax, Olivia. It's going to be fine."

Along the tree line for the jungle are a row of small, one-story bungalows that sweep up the coast, each with a front porch facing the beach. We turn down the stone-filled path for the first building, climb up the few steps to the porch, then enter. Lights are already ablaze in a small living room decorated in pale yellow and white. It shares the space with a galley-style kitchen and dining room that has a back door. Off to the left is an archway expanding into what I can only presume are bedrooms.

Sam's guards take up positions both inside and out, while he guides me to the master suite to the right after passing under the archway. Light gray walls and hardwood floors make up the medium-sized room with a queen-sized bed topped with a matching quilt. A black suitcase lays open on top of a cushioned chair along the wall for the closet, and toiletries rest on top of the dresser.

Sam closes the door, locking it, then pulls me into a firm embrace. "I was so grief stricken when I thought you'd died."

Moving out of his grasp, I slap him hard across the face. "You knew Dean was alive this whole time!" I rave, incensed.

He rubs his reddened cheek. "Of course I did. Who do you think helped him escape the boat after shooting Carlos?"

"You're a fucking bastard! You're the reason Frank is dead!" When I raise my hand to hit him again, he seizes my wrist. "Let go of me!"

"Stop it, Olivia! I'm sorry about what happened! If I had any notion of what Dean was up to, I would've stopped him!"

I wrench myself free, nearly stumbling back and losing my footing. "That's a bunch of bullshit, Sam. Everything that comes out of your mouth is a fucking lie. I knew you were treacherous. Matt warned me, but I didn't listen." Heading for the door, I struggle with the simple lock, tears coating my face, blurring my vision. "If we somehow manage to survive escaping here, I never want to see you again."

His warm hands gently wrap around my biceps. "You don't mean that."

Turning, I shove him. "You've destroyed my life!"

"Where is Matt?" he asks, crossing his arms over his chest, ignoring my outburst.

"Dead. Dean killed him, then kidnapped me and brought me down here."

Glaring intensely at me, anger pulses in Sam's eyes. "Why were the two of you together?"

"What the fuck do you care?" I move over to the other side of the room, standing in front of a set of windows covered by white, gossamer curtains. "I'm sure you're happy he's out of the picture."

The smile creasing his face is subtle, but enough.

"You're a goddamn asshole."

He chuckles. "Who now has you all to himself."

I'm about to argue the statement when the lights cut out, throwing the entire bungalow into utter darkness.

"It's probably a residual outage from the storms last night," Sam comments, his voice close.

But I know better. "Do you have any weapons in this room?" I ask, searching my way toward the dresser.

Several loud thuds echo from the hallway outside of the door. It's quickly followed by glass shattering and the sound of a metal canister skirting across the flooring, gas hissing into the room.

"Shit," Sam grumbles, groping for me, grabbing my arm, and flinging me to the floor where he lies on top of me.

I start to cough, then choke, while Sam does the same. The smoke stings my eyes, causing them to burn and the tears to return. I begin to claw at my throat, desperate for some breathable air, but there isn't any to be found. Sam's body becomes heavier, crushing me since he's probably already unconscious. I do my best to remain alert, listening for any noise as to when Dean's guards might be approaching. However, I can't keep my eyelids open, and my fighting becomes useless, so I succumb and dread waking up.

Fourteen

My throat burns, my head throbs, and my neck feels stiff. When I go to rub away the pain, my arms won't move. Opening my eyes, to my horror I realize that my arms are pinned behind me, tied together while my ankles are secured to the spindly legs of the wooden side chair I'm sitting on. Lifting my head, I work on getting a better idea of my surroundings.

The walls of the structure are built from wood planks, the floor a concrete slab with partitions that rise waist-high, separating four stalls in a circular formation in the center of the main room, each with a hook suspended from a chain in the ceiling above a drain in the floor. Hoses snake over racks in the far corners, water dribbling from their ends. The roof is tin. Large hay bales sit stacked in several corners, along with buckets and grooming brushes, more than likely for horses. Industrial-grade fixtures dangle from the support beams, casting harsh light around the surprisingly large space, illuminating areas with heavy amounts of a dried, brownish substance. Along the eaves are awning-style windows, their panes opened by a crank that extends practically to the floor, darkness the only thing seeping inside.

Across from me tied to an identical chair is Sam, his hair dangling down in front of his face while his head rests against his chest. His tux is torn at the shoulders, cuffs, and the shirt underneath has blood spatter, from what, I don't know. Moaning, he rolls his head slowly, gradually lifting it, exposing a broken nose, blood caked down the front of his mouth, and bruises forming under both eyes. Staring at me, it takes him several long seconds to realize who I am.

"Liv, are you all right?" He winces, the pain from his injury finally registering.

"I told you not to fuck with Dean," I scold. "I'll be surprised if we get out of this alive."

Moving his arms, Sam tries to loosen the bindings, but the ropes are too tight. "Shit," he grouses, which is soon followed by a heavy sigh, sounding almost like relief. "He didn't take the bracelet."

I glare at him, puzzled. "Why should that matter?"

He doesn't get a chance to answer when a door somewhere in the distance bangs, the noise followed by a series of heavy footsteps. Dean, along with two of his guards, turn a corner at the far end on the right side, which is covered in the same wood paneling as the rest of the room, causing it to blend in. Each of the men have a rifle strapped across their shoulders and a holster containing two handguns around their waists. Dean simply carries a thick-bladed hunting knife, a swagger in his step and an expression of triumph gleaming across his face. He's no longer wearing the tuxedo, but plain, black pants and a matching short-sleeved shirt, exposing the broken arrow tattoo on his left bicep.

Approaching, Dean pulls his arm back and slams his closed fist hard into Sam's face. "You were told to stay away from her," my husband raves, seething.

Spitting out a glob of blood onto the concrete floor, Sam raises his head, and I spot a deep gash in his lower lip. He glowers at Dean. "Where's Siam?"

My husband smiles wickedly, his eyes sparkling with insanity. "She's at the main house." Sauntering over to me, he plays with the knife, twirling it in his beefy hand. He stops beside me, grabs my hair, wraps it into his fist, and violently yanks my head back.

I holler from the sudden pain. He adjusts his position so that Sam can see the tears welling in my eyes. Dean places the tip of the knife against my throat just under the left side of my jaw, his arm relaxed across my chest.

"You disappoint me, Liv," he says, though he continues to stare at Sam. Dean's fingers twirl through my hair, dislodging strands.

I involuntarily yelp with each tug.

"Getting engaged to this piece of shit while you're still married to me. Could you stoop any lower?"

"We're not engaged, Dean. I swear," I reply, my voice trembling, along with the rest of me.

Sam's breathing quickens, his face turning red. "It's true, Dean. Olivia isn't anything to me, but a quick fuck. Some entertainment while I'm down here. You're overreacting."

"Am I?" he shouts. "Luke sent me a video that he took with his phone of the two of you kissing in the lounge of the Prestige Theater the night you all went to see Cirque Aérien."

"It was one kiss, Dean. What's the big deal?" Sam tries to shrug, but can't because of his arms being confined. "How many women have you fucked since I helped fake your death? Plenty."

"We're not talking about me. Just my wife," he says furiously through gritted teeth.

"So, it's fine for you to do whatever the hell you want, but not her?"

"I own her!" For a brief second, Dean moves the knife away from my throat. "Olivia belongs to me and no one else!" He jabs a finger in Sam's direction, then turns and stares at me mournfully. "But, perhaps, she's too tempting for other men." He caresses my cheek with the back of his hand, and I cower. "They'll always be a threat to our happiness."

Tears fall down my hot face. "Dean, don't," I beg.

Setting the tip of the knife underneath my jaw close to my ear, he slowly pierces the skin. I shriek, knowing my life is finally about to come to an end. Blood trickles down my neck, soaking the strap for the dress.

"Stop!" Sam screams. Dean momentarily ceases slitting my throat. The terror on Sam's face is genuine. His eyes wide with shock. "It's not Olivia's fault. It's all mine. If you're going to kill anyone, kill me. Not her."

"Have you slept with her?"

"No," Sam replies adamantly.

Releasing me, Dean takes a few steps toward Sam, then stops. "But you were going to tonight."

"Someone was. You and Siem were making damn sure of that by the way the two of you were conning and bargaining your way through the buyers tonight. I saved her from those vile wretches you call friends." Sam's chest rises and falls rapidly, his rage showing with every word. "If you knew half of the things that I do about those men, you'd have gotten Olivia off of this island, not keep her prisoner on it."

Dean lifts the knife, which had been held down along his side. "It sounds like you care about my wife. You didn't give a damn about the other women we've sold, or even the ones you've bought from Siem over the years. Why her?" He nods in my direction.

There's a lengthy pause since Sam isn't fast enough with a response, and Dean catches the quick glance the terrified man sends in my direction.

My husband's jaw tightens. "String him up."

One of the guards goes over to a winch attached to the back wall and starts lowering the hook for the stall Sam's chair is sitting in. The other removes a hunting knife similar to Dean's from his boot, along with a cord of rope from his back pocket, then ties Sam's ankles together before freeing them from the chair. When the chain is low enough, the hook is placed behind Sam's back and he rises into the air only a few inches, but enough to keep his feet from touching the floor. His arms bend at an awkward angle because of how they're secured, making him arch forward. The guard puts the knife back into his boot, while the other locks the winch into place.

Dean steps over to another stall and comes back with a length of heavy lead pipe. "She can't see your face in this position, and I want her to witness the agony you're about to go through." He raises the new weapon above his head, and it comes crashing down onto Sam's shoulder.

The scream that leaves his mouth nearly shatters my eardrums. He's now hanging vertically, his left shoulder grossly dislocated. Dean swings the pipe again, blowing out Sam's left knee. He shrieks, the sound of anguish reverberating off of every wall.

"Dean, stop!" I yell as loudly as possible. If Jake is on the island, I pray he's somewhere close enough to hear me. "Let him go!"

After tossing aside the pipe, which clatters onto the floor, rolling against the partition, he rushes over and wraps a hand around my throat. "Do you want to take his place? I can easily finish what I started with you." Resting the full blade of the knife against my throat, his fingers shake enough for the weapon to scratch my skin.

"It's all right, Liv," Sam croaks. "Everything will be okay."

Hearing my nickname escape the other man's lips sends Dean into a frenzy. Turning, he lunges at Sam, driving the knife into his side. The scream from Sam's lips is broken because of his raw throat. Blood flows to the floor, pooling at his feet, collecting dust from the concrete I didn't know was there. Dean slashes Sam across the chest, tearing through the tuxedo like paper. I can't watch the horror, so I lower my head and cringe with each sound of flesh opening and Sam hollering in pain, his voice becoming weaker with each passing second.

"Dean," a muffled voice crackles over a portable radio attached to the waistband of my husband's pants. "Dean, we've got a problem."

Breaking away from the torture, Dean's hand, arm, and knife covered in blood, he removes the device and presses the button along the side. "What?" he demands, annoyed at being interrupted.

"We have incoming helicopters. At least a dozen of them." The man on the other end sounds nervous.

Shifting the knife into the hand with the radio, he reaches into his back pocket and takes out a small, portable display, which he turns on and begins scrolling through various images, pausing when he gets to one in particular. "So?"

"They're military helicopters coming in from the west. The flag for Navital painted by the tail rotors."

Curious as to how someone is able to see that much detail in the dark, even if it is through a camera that more than likely has night vision capability, I peek toward the open windows behind me and notice the sun is starting to rise. Orange and red streaking across a cloudless sky.

"Alert the men in the towers on Termore and Tenace to fire on them. Get the others prepared for a ground assault." Dean clips the radio back onto his waistband and shoves the display into his pocket. "You two," he points to the guards who had accompanied him, "head to Antiris and help with getting the girls down into the bomb shelter."

"What about Siem and her guests?" one asks, removing a gun from his holster and handing it to Dean.

"I'll deal with them." When they're gone, Dean turns back to Sam, who isn't moving. I can't even tell if he's breathing. Especially with the amount of blood that's now collected on the floor, his wounds seeping, coating everything in crimson. My husband smiles. "I guess you're no threat to me anymore. To anyone, really." He chuckles, then comes over to me, placing a bloody finger under my chin and lifting my face to meet his. "I wish we had more time, babe. But all good things are bound to come to an end." Raising the gun, he aims it at my forehead. "Tell Frank hi for me."

An explosion rips the right side of the building apart, knocking Dean to the floor and me over in the chair. My ears ring from the blast and everything blurs. A scraping noise catches my attention, but it dissipates when the beams supporting the tin roof comes crashing down, blocking the only exit out of the structure. The bales of hay burst into flames and smoke fills the air. I desperately work on freeing myself, the ropes digging farther into my skin with each motion. Gunfire and flashes of red echo into the disintegrating building, along with shouts of commands in a language I don't understand.

The wood-paneled walls ignite as the fire spreads, the crackling of flames the only sound I'm able to focus on. Terror seizes me in its paralyzing hold. The growing smoke stings my eyes and fills my lungs, choking me into a coughing fit.

"Olivia!" someone yells as the wall behind Sam shifts, sliding open on invisible rails, revealing a misty, chaotic morning.

The two figures rushing toward me are barely recognizable, their voices dulled by the throbbing in my head.

"I'll get her. You help Sam," the second man says, kneeling beside me. The bindings around my wrists and ankles give way. "Head that way." The man points in the direction he and the other entered in from.

Keeping my head low as possible, I do my best to remain focused on the fresh air outside, letting it guide me out of the burning building. When I'm several feet away, I grip the closest tree for support, coughing until the smoke clears my lungs, then turn my attention back to the structure. The two men emerge with Sam draped between them.

The first one I recognize is Jake, Sam's hitman. He's dressed from head to toe in dark green camouflage, his short, brunet hair covered in soot, along with his face. His square-shaped jaw is clenched, the muscles under his short-sleeved shirt rippling while lugging Sam toward me. Over his shoulder is an automatic rifle and a holster carrying two high caliber guns.

To my surprise, the other man is Special Agent Brett Ellis. His clothes are all black, his face filthy from the smoke, sweat drips down his furrowed brow, and the nostrils of his broad nose flare with each step. He's armed with the same weapons as Jake, in addition to several serrated blades secured around his waist.

They lower Sam to the ground in front of me. Jake starts working on him while Brett comes over to me, gripping my arm, and shaking me free from the shock desperately trying to take over.

"Olivia, are you all right?" His light southern drawl is music to my ears.

I stare at him, fury rising inside of me to a volatile point. "Where's Dean?"

"The Navital army will deal with him. We need to get you and Sam on a chopper and off of this island."

Shoving his hand away, I lift my legs one at a time and remove the stupid high-heeled shoes Siem gave to me, tossing them aside. "Which way did he go?"

"Toward the docks," Jake responds, pointing behind him and the building now fully engulfed. "I need help with Sam. If we don't move him now, he won't make the trip."

Grumbling, Brett presses a button on a collar tucked under his shirt and calls for assistance. At least I think that's what he's doing, considering I can't understand anything he says. It's now I realize they're both wearing voice collars and earpieces, which is why I don't hear the response.

Stepping over to Jake, I hold out my hand. "Give me one of your guns."

He doesn't hesitate and unholsters a weapon, slapping it into my palm just as a dozen men in army fatigues join us. "Make sure to put the bullet through his fucking head."

I glance at Brett. "Are you coming?"

We race for the docks, and I try not to think about what I might be stepping on in my bare feet. My sole focus is finding Dean before he manages to escape. When we come upon a river, it's now I realize that we're not on Nolita, but Termore. Bodies float in the water—a mixture of cartel guards, Navital soldiers, and field workers. Brett jumps into the lone boat moored to the rickety dock, while I toss off the ropes holding us in place. Once I'm onboard, he revs the engine, turns the wheel, and steers us out into open water.

"Dean is probably heading to Ilusor where the airplane hangars are," I shout to be heard over the roar of the waves and wind, both hitting us at high speed, while I stand beside Brett, clinging to the rail along the edge by the captain's chair.

He adjusts our course, using the onboard navigation system as his guide. "Does he know how to fly?"

"No." There are so many questions I want to ask, but now isn't the time. Hopefully we both live through this so they can be answered later. "But several of his guards do."

"Where are the women being held?"

"Antiris. There's a bomb shelter Dean is having the men move them into."

Briefly removing one of his hands from the wheel, Brett informs whoever is commanding the soldiers. The only word I recognize is the island's name. After some time, Nolita passes on our left, the sounds of perpetual gunfire and explosions reverberating from the tranquil land. Knowing it's another ten minutes before we reach Ilusor, I decide now is a good time to at least find out a few things.

"How did you know where we were?" I ask, gripping both the railing and gun tighter.

Brett keeps his focus on the water around us, watching for any cartel boats that might try to stop us. "Did you notice the bracelet around Sam's wrist?"

"Yeah. Ronan used them on her ranch to block the signals from the microchips in everyone's wrist."

"It's the same one you gave Hayden in the manila envelope with your notes and photos from the Red Rover case. He found a way to reverse its programming, turning it into a beacon. You wouldn't believe the number of hits that lit up across the world when that happened."

A pit forms in my stomach, and acid rises in my throat. "Were they dead or alive?"

He momentarily stares at me. "What do you think?"

I try not to.

"Anyway, Hayden changed the frequency of the one Sam wore so the others wouldn't interfere when he came down here."

"And the army?" I gesture to a helicopter heading for Ilusor.

"We've been working with them for several years to bring down the Vilks Cartel. That all changed when you exposed Cruz, and Matt was killed." Brett looks at me, sorrow creasing the corners of his eyes. "I'm sorry. I know how much he meant to you."

"Where is he?" I ask, my voice cracking with emotion.

"Back with his family. They held a private memorial for him yesterday. He was laid to rest beside his grandfather, which is what he wanted."

"How did you know I was brought down here?"

The island comes into view, and the boat slows. "We'll discuss that later."

There's just one other vessel moored and I'm hoping it's the one Dean used. Otherwise, who knows where the hell he might be. We barely come to a stop when I jump onto the dock, then sprint for the runway. Brett has a hard time keeping up, shooting at guards hidden in the foliage while I dodge a couple of strikers. They slam into the trunks of nearby trees, splitting them open. I want to fire back, but I'm saving the bullets for Dean.

Who knows how many I'll need to use on him.

The winds kick up the closer I get to the hangars, since the helicopter I spotted moments before has now touched down, its propellers spinning even though no one is inside. A handful of men lay dying or wounded across the tarmac, but none of them are Dean. I plaster myself against the outer wall of the farthest hangar, Brett joining me practically out of breath and drenched with sweat. The temperature has risen with the sun and his clothes aren't conducive to a jungle environment.

"What now?" he asks, checking the ammunition in his rifle.

"We search each building one at a time."

"Here." He hands me a gun from his holster. "You're going to need both of them. I'll cover your back."

Taking a deep breath, I lift both weapons in front of me and round the corner, exposing myself to the open hangar. Empty. The next two are as well, but the fourth has a few guards hurrying to store crates onboard an airplane. Brett decides to aim high while I shoot low, killing three of the five and severely injuring the other two. Gunfire erupts from a hangar across the way, forcing the two of us to take cover inside. While Brett fires back, I search the guards. All of their weapons contain strikers, so I swap out my guns, and hand a couple to Brett. He gets on the radio, hopefully advising the others to our location and how we're pinned down. Briefly glancing around one of the corners for the hangar door, the light from the sun glints off of something shiny and metallic.

"Shit! Brett, run!" I shout before the man across the way can pull the trigger on a grenade launcher resting on top of his shoulder.

The two of us scramble out of the building, making it a good distance in separate directions when the grenade hits the airplane, blowing it and the hangar to splinters. I'm knocked to the ground, adding to my injuries as I badly scrape my arms and legs across the concrete and asphalt. I can't see Brett through the thick clouds of black smoke, so I quickly continue making my way around the tarmac, dashing between the various buildings, trying to avoid being spotted, ignoring the shooting pain traveling up and down my body. Crouching behind a stack of tires, I survey the area. Next to the hangar where the grenade was launched are barrels of gasoline. Using the top of the tire stack to steady my aim, I fire at them.

The detonation shakes the ground, nearly collapsing the building. Three men run out, two of them on fire from the fuel that splashed over everything. The third appears singed, but otherwise all right. He limps toward the helicopter, a gun in his hand. I aim at his right shoulder and fire. He cries out and drops the weapon, but keeps heading for the chopper. I stand, move away from the tires, and shoot again, this time at his legs. The striker tears through his calves, causing him to collapse face-first onto the tarmac. With both weapons in front of me, I cautiously approach Dean, who's hollering from the wounds, making me grin with wicked amusement.

When I'm beside him, I slip my barefoot under his torso, and shove him over onto his back. He smiles, a stream of blood sliding out of the corner of his mouth.

"I thought I had you back there," he says, laughing, his face contorting into a grimace. "How many lives do you have?"

I smirk. "More than you, babe."

He smiles. "Are you sure about that?" Trembling, he lifts his hand and points to something behind me, but I don't dare turn, knowing it could be the last thing that I do.

I jump when a shot rings out, my composure faltering a bit, until Brett steps beside me, his rifle aimed at my husband. "At least someone has your wife's back even if you don't," he says, pressing the tip of the barrel into Dean's forehead, burning the flesh with the hot muzzle.

Pushing Brett's weapon away, I move closer to my husband. "You shouldn't have come after me, but you just couldn't leave well enough alone."

"I'll always be after you, babe. Until death do us part."

"You got that right." Pulling the trigger, the striker leaves the gun and pierces him between the eyes.

His skull splits open, exposing his newly mangled brains, blood flowing everywhere. Stumbling backwards a few feet, I collapse onto the ground, drop the guns, and bawl. Brett kneels in front of me, lowers his weapons, and pulls me into an embrace. The adrenaline that had been pumping through my entire body suddenly ceases, shock finally setting in, and I blackout.

Fifteen

The smell of disinfectant is overpowering, but welcoming. Opening my eyes, I have to blink a few times until they focus on the sterile room around me with its painted white walls, windows covered in thick drapery, and a dormant television attached in the corner by the ceiling. A white curtain with dark gray dots is spread between the uncomfortable hospital bed I'm on and probably another one on the other side. White sheets and a gray blanket cover me from head to toe, an IV line sticks out of my left arm attaching me to a bag filled with a clear fluid, which drips quietly every second. I slowly lift up the covers and find I'm clad in a lovely thin, light blue gown that more than likely ties in the back. My arms and legs are bandaged, as is my forehead and the small incision Dean created along the right side of my throat.

Clipped to the handrail is a call button, which I push, summoning a nurse into my room. She chatters away while checking my vitals and plumping the pillows under my head, but I don't understand a word she's saying.

"Where's Special Agent Ellis?" I ask, my voice barely above a whisper.

She stares at me, puzzled, then grins as if understanding and leaves. A few minutes later Brett enters, a bandage covering his left hand and one just above his right eye. Today he's dressed in a suit, his official credentials clipped to the belt holding up his tan pants.

"You've been out a full day. How are you feeling?" he asks, pulling over a chair that was under the window.

"Sore. Where are we?"

"The military hospital in Navital. You were airlifted from Ilusor and brought straight here. Colonel Bolivar is out in the hallway. He wants to ask you a few questions."

I pull the blanket up to my chin as a way to hide. "Who is he?"

"He's in charge of the drug task force for Navital, and the person I've been working with since Siem began growing her father's empire."

Rolling my head to the side, I look away from Brett. "I don't want to talk to anyone."

"Olivia, you don't have a choice here. You're the only witness we have to everything the cartel has been doing as of late."

I turn and stare at him. "Where's Siem?" The real question I want to ask is where's Sam, but I can't bring myself to utter his name.

Brett lowers his gaze. "We found her face down in bed. She'd been shot with a striker through the back of the head. We suspect Dean is responsible given the time she was murdered. At least according to the maids, who heard a violent altercation between the two of them."

"What about the others on the island? The ones she invited."

"They're in custody on sex-trafficking charges. A few of them are talking simply to get a lighter sentence, but they don't have the knowledge that Colonel Bolivar feels you do."

"Why?" I toss up my hands in frustration. "Because my husband was the man in control? That he murdered everyone who ever got close to me, so I must have known what went on inside of his mind? I don't know shit about the cartel and its workings. I was his prisoner, not his confidant," I snap.

"But you figured out the connection between TITAN Industries and the assassinations … Director Cruz's involvement … who the wolf was—a person we've been after for years."

I can't help but laugh, which causes my head to hurt. "You think Dean was the wolf? God, you're stupid."

He bristles at the remark. "What the hell does that mean?"

"Did you ever think to ask yourself how Sam West knew who the leader of the Vilks Cartel was when everyone else in the world didn't? That he just so happened to volunteer to come down here and supposedly aid in a rescue attempt?" Lowering my head, I start picking at the blanket, hoping to dispel my growing anxiety. "He played you all for fools." A lump forms in my throat. "Me more than anyone."

"If it'll make you feel any better, Sam has always been on our radar." The chair squeaks, and I look up to find Brett sitting closer to the bed. He leans forward and keeps his voice low. "Sam doesn't go anywhere or do anything without us knowing about it."

I narrow my gaze. "Are you sure? Jake can't be at his side all of the time."

Brett startles at the comment. "H-How did you know?"

"Why else would the two of you have come to the islands together? The both of you wearing the same communication devices as the army. Where is Sam, by the way?"

He clenches his jaw. "Two floors up recovering from surgery."

I glower at the special agent. "You like Sam, don't you? Is that why you haven't arrested him yet for purchasing women, like you've done with the others?"

Standing, Brett straightens his suit coat, since it's now bunched around his waist. "For your information, Olivia, Sam rescues those women using his own money. Returning them to their families so they don't wind up as slaves like so many others. He's managed to save over twenty young girls from Siem's clutches. That's why he remains free." After shoving the chair back into place, Brett makes his way to the door. "Get some rest. We'll be leaving for Asmor on Friday. I'll make sure you have something to wear for the trip." He doesn't quite slam the door on his way out, but it's enough to project his anger toward me.

A few minutes later, the nurse returns to unhook my IV, then brings me a tray of food. I eat what I can since I don't really have much of an appetite. After she takes it away, I go into the bathroom to use the facilities and get back under the covers. Colonel Bolivar doesn't come in, which gives me a bit of relief. Over the next day and a half, my dressings are changed, my wounds cleaned some more, and I'm permitted to take a much-needed shower. Friday morning while I'm eating breakfast, Jake enters carrying a brown paper bag.

"These are for you," he says, setting it down on the foot of the bed.

"Where's Brett?" I ask, grabbing the flimsy handle, dragging the bag over to me. Inside are black leggings, white ankle socks, a pair of sneakers, underwear, and a beige sweater with long sleeves.

"He's waiting for you in the lobby." Jake remains standing by the end of the bed, hesitant to leave. "Sam wants to see you."

Pushing the tray table away, I toss back the covers. "I have nothing to say to him." Taking the bag, I head for the bathroom, closing the door to change in private.

"He cares about you, Olivia," Jake says from the other side of the door.

I throw the horrible hospital gown onto the cool tile floor and start dressing. "If that were true, then he would've told me about Dean, and Frank would still be alive." The sweater exposes my midriff, which leads me to believe Sam is the one responsible for the clothes I now wear, not Brett. He probably told Jake what to shop for. I'd tear them off if there was something else available.

"He had no way of knowing what was going to happen. Don't blame him for something Dean did."

I yank open the door. "Bullshit, Jake. I could've told you. I would've warned you about that asshole, but Sam's ego got in the way, and it cost me everything." Grabbing the shoes, I push my way past him and return to the bed where I sit on the edge to put them on.

"Sam loves you, Olivia. He was serious when he proposed."

"He told you about that?" I ask, livid.

"Of course he did. Why wouldn't he?"

After the shoes are on, I stand and approach Jake, my hands balled into fists down along my sides. "Do you think he'd be this open if he knew the truth about you? Somehow, I doubt that." As I start to move past him, he forcefully clutches my arm.

"When they found Lane Murray's body, who do you think directed them toward Luke as the trigger man? Sam could've easily tossed you to the wolves, but he didn't."

I jerk free. "You're making it sound like I owe him."

"Then call it even. He couldn't save Frank, so he chose you instead." Jake steps in front of me, blocking my escape. "Daven suspected you had murdered Lane given your past history together, and because no one could account for your whereabouts when the former district attorney went missing. Especially when your microchip reported you being at the same airstrip as Lane when he was last seen alive. Sam managed to persuade him against the idea."

Folding my arms across my chest, I ask, "And what did he say to alter the chief's perspective?"

"That he was with Luke when he pulled the trigger, and that it was his men who helped bury the body down in the keys."

My throat goes dry at the idea of being sent away for life after everything I've already been through. "I'm surprised he's not in prison for acting as an accomplice."

Jake smirks. "He made a deal with Brett to avoid anything serious happening to himself."

I bite my lower lip. "Wallace Shaw."

He nods. "And the trip down here to get you out. Sam knew what might happen to him, given Dean's demeanor. He took the chance to save you." Moving closer, he nudges me with his elbow. "At least say good-bye to Sam."

I begrudgingly agree.

Exiting the room, we make a right and head down the hall, passing an empty nurses' station before coming to a bank of elevators. He presses the call button, and we wait just a few seconds before one of the doors open. As we ascend the two floors, I practice in my head what I'm going to say, since I honestly don't know how I'll react when seeing him. We step out onto a quiet floor, much like the one we just left, and I follow Jake down the brightly lit hallway nearly to the very end. He pushes open the door on our left, then gestures for me to enter.

"I'll wait out here."

The room is similar to mine, but with a single bed. The drapes for the windows are closed and the lights are currently off, so I leave them that way. Sam's eyes are shut, and the machines he's hooked up to beat in rhythm with his heart. There are various tubes and wires poking out from under the thin blanket covering his battered body. His left arm is in a sling, laying delicately over his chest. His left leg is in a cast, which is being held by a pully system attached to cables in the ceiling, allowing the limb to be elevated while it heals. The bruising on his face is dark making his soft skin appear fragile. Stubble covers his jaw, and his champagne-colored hair sticks up in places. I step quietly toward the window, placing a bit of distance between the two of us, dreading the encounter, and decide that if he doesn't wake within the next few minutes, I'm leaving.

Time ticks by slowly, and I'm about to head for the door when Sam moans softly, his eyes slow to open. Seeing me, he tries to smile, but it's pained.

"Hey, beautiful," he grumbles, his voice slightly slurred from the copious amounts of medication I'm sure he's on.

Wrapping my arms around myself, I move toward the bed. "Hi, Sam. I came to say good-bye."

"Jake told me you were being discharged today. Where will you be staying?"

I move a bit closer, but still keep my arms tight around me. "I won't be. Special Agent Ellis is waiting down in the lobby to take me home."

"When I'm done in here, I'll have Jake come get you and we'll spend a few months at Wolf Bay. Just the two of us."

I bite my lip and shake my head. "No, Sam."

He must sense my tone since his joyful expression falls. "I'm sorry, Liv. I really am." For once I hear genuine remorse in his voice, and it shatters me. "Do you think you'll ever forgive me for what happened? That we can put this nightmare behind us and move on together?"

As much as I want to rant, yell, and scream at him for stepping into my life and wrecking it even further, and that I never want to see him again, I can't bring myself to do it. "Brett is waiting for me." I abruptly turn and hurry for the door.

"Olivia, I meant it before. I love you."

My hand rests on the doorknob for just a brief moment, then I fling the door open and step out into the hall, letting his words linger behind me. Jake is leaning against the wall, but I ignore him and race for the elevator, rapidly pressing the button in the hopes that it'll arrive faster. I need to get out of here before I do or say something stupid, even regrettable. When I reach the first floor, there are only a few staff members milling about the small lobby. Brett is standing by one of the picture windows overlooking the sparse parking lot out front.

"You left some personal affects in your room," he says, once I reach him.

He shoves his hand into the pocket of his suit coat, removing a cloth bag cinched closed, and gives it to me. I open it, sort through the contents, then hand it back to him.

"This is Siem's. She loaned it to me for the party."

He puts the bag back into his pocket, then raises an eyebrow. "Even the engagement and wedding rings?"

Turning my gaze toward the sunshine cascading in through the windows, I reply, "I don't give a damn what you do with those. Can we leave now?"

Placing a hand on my back, he escorts me outside to an awaiting car that's parked in a spot several feet from the main entrance. We climb into the back, and the driver places the vehicle into gear. Brett reaches for a manila envelope that's sitting on the front passenger seat, and hands it to me. Inside are a temporary visa, travel documents, and a plane ticket.

"Since Dean flew you down here, the Navital government agreed to issue you a voucher so you can return to Leyon without issue. The visa is so you can get back into the country. Our flight leaves in roughly two hours. We should get home just in time for dinner. Of course, Chief Daven wants to speak with you right after we land, so a CSB detective is supposed to meet us at the airport."

I shove the papers into the envelope, then turn my attention to the scenery passing us, which consists of several military installations and a guard post, all surrounded by jungle. After passing through the gate, we head for a highway that winds north along the rocky shoreline for the coast. Taking an exit ramp nearly a half-hour later, we go through a security checkpoint, then are allowed to proceed to the departure terminal. Once the car has stopped, Brett gets out and retrieves his bag from the trunk while I clutch onto the manila envelope, fearing I might drop it and be trapped here forever.

It takes longer than expected to reach the gate because of all the supervisors that need to review the papers that Colonel Bolivar put together for me. Brett doesn't even bother checking his luggage, and simply stores it in one of the overhead compartments when we finally board the plane. The cabin is a little more than half full, and as the flight attendants are going over their emergency procedures, I close my eyes and zone out.

Brett rouses me just as we're pulling up to the gate for the airport in Asmor. It's even more of a hassle getting through immigration and customs because I no longer have a microchip embedded under the skin of my left wrist. I'm about to blurt out Frank's name when I catch myself, momentarily forgetting he's no longer here. It takes all of my strength not to burst into tears right there in the middle of the concourse. By the time we exit the building, the sun has started to set. Brett phoned CSB right after we landed, informing Chief Daven of our arrival. The horribly dented silver sedan that pulls in front of us is one I recognize immediately.

"Hey, Liv," Stephen says after shutting the car door and making his way around to the other side. He pulls me into a tight embrace, tears desperately pushing their way to the surface. After releasing me, he shakes Brett's hand. "The chief is waiting for us." Opening the front passenger door, Stephen gestures for me to get inside while Brett slides into the back once his suitcase is stored in the trunk.

From the airport, Stephen drives onto the outer expressway, then over one of the bridges spanning the Brimher River and into Nok Sector, exiting at Chestnut, which takes us past Verdigris, a sign plastered across both doors indicating the club is closed for renovation. A couple of blocks later we turn right onto Lange, taking that all the way into Hunnat Sector. Stephen pulls into the employee section of the parking garage and finds a spot on the first level. Normally spaces are hard to come by on this floor, but since it's technically after office hours, the majority of detectives, supervisors, and support staff have gone home for the day. Brett leaves his suitcase in the trunk, and the three of us hurry across the street.

The security normally posted at all entrances has gone home for the night, so Stephen needs to use the biometrics reader to enter the building, as well as get us past the reception desks and in front of the elevator core. When the doors open, he selects the top floor, and we ascend. Stepping out we go straight, bypassing Chief Daven's personal secretary's empty desk. Since the door is closed, Stephen knocks then waits for us to be summoned before opening it. Chief Daven sits behind his desk, the coat for his suit tossed onto a chair in the corner of the room, the long sleeves of his dark blue dress shirt rolled up to his elbows. His plump face is expressionless, adding to the tension gradually enveloping the room. His thick hands are clasped together on top of the manila folder in front of him, and I recognize it as the one I shoved the photos of Melia into months ago.

"Have a seat," he says, his thick voice booming while he gestures to the two office chairs in front of him.

Stephen and I each take a seat, while Brett stands off to the side, arms folded over his chest like a father ready to scold his child. I involuntarily shudder as the chief continues to bore his gaze into me, a lump forming in my throat.

He clenches his jaw before speaking. "How are you feeling?"

"Exhausted." *Please don't bring up Lane or Sam.*

"Did you know it was Dean who was responsible for the Red Rover murders?" he asks, a bit of accusation in his tone.

"Are you fucking serious?" I retort, stunned, my eyes widening in shock. "Of course not. How the hell would I have? I thought he was dead like everyone else."

"I told you, Chief, Olivia is a victim in all of this," Stephen interjects.

The older man holds up his hand, silencing the other detective. "Then how did Dean know you were alive?"

I finally manage to swallow the lump in my throat by clearing it. "Taylor Strum, Lloyd's assistant, told him. Apparently, she was informing Dean about my whereabouts, starting from the moment he went underground to work for the cartel, in exchange for keeping her sister out of the hands of some of Siem's buyers. Little good it did her."

The chief looks at me, baffled.

"It's true," Brett states, resting the bulk of his weight against one of the dark gray, upholstered club chairs that sit off to the side. "She confessed to it when her and the other girls were being transported to the Navital military hospital. Colonel Bolivar has his men searching for the girls we've been able to identify as having been kidnapped by Siem's recruiters. It's going to take a great deal of time, but he's confident."

"Lloyd will need to hire a new assistant," the chief says, rubbing his forehead. "How about where you and Matt were staying?"

My heart grows heavy at the sound of his name, and I start to tremble. "Director Cruz told Dean where to find us. Matt had mentioned the cabin in passing a long time ago, so the director took a chance that's where we were."

Stephen reaches over and covers my hand with his as it shakes in my lap. A move Frank would've done, which nearly pushes me over the edge.

"Can I have some water?" I ask, the quivering in my voice now obvious to everyone.

Brett exits the office, returning a few minutes later with water for all of us. I sip mine, then grasp the paper cup between my hands, trying desperately not to crush it.

An uneasy silence settles over the room, causing me to grow increasingly more anxious, so I break it. "When did you figure it out?"

Leaning back in his chair, the chief rests the ankle of one leg across the knee for the other, then folds his hands in his lap. "It took a few days for the information Frank had requested from Tigress Casino and those who had attended Dallas' party to arrive. Collins worked overtime to go through all of the security footage, photos, and interview notes. She phoned me early in the morning to tell me Dean was alive, since he was spotted on both the surveillance tapes and random shots of the party. It was the same day he came to the cabin to kidnap you. Since the satellite phone was still on after I heard you scream out his name, Hayden spent several hours searching for its signal. Brett called the CSB headquarters in Eris, but by the time they reached the location you were already gone."

I finish the water, placing the cup onto the desk. "What happens now?"

"A disciplinary hearing is scheduled to take place next week to determine your career," the chief replies coldly.

I glance between him and Stephen. "What for?"

"Releasing spyware into the Hub's systems," Brett answers, his tone icy as well.

"If I hadn't, you'd have lost everything regarding TITAN Industries and its holdings."

"While nearly costing two men their jobs." The chief's face turns crimson with anger. "You put the entire network in jeopardy, Detective Darrow. Be grateful I'm not firing you right now." He picks up the manila envelope and tosses it to me. "Hayden managed to salvage the memory from your cellphone, which was badly burned in the fire. He put it all into a new one for you. Stephen, take Olivia to your office, then drive her home and return here since we have a lot more items to discuss."

I glare at my counterpart. "Your office?"

"Don't make things worse," he mumbles, standing.

Brett moves to take my seat as we head for the door, closing it behind us. Once in the elevator, Stephen presses the button for the seventh floor.

"Was Frank's body even cold yet when you were promoted?" I growl, rage roiling just below the surface.

"That's not fair, Olivia," he responds, sorrow in his voice. "Nothing ever slows down here. Especially when we lose an officer. We're not given the luxury of grieving. You know that better than anyone."

The elevator stops and the doors open. There are a few supervisors for the other departments milling around, each giving us hesitant stares as we traverse the hallway toward Frank's office. Stephen flips on the lights when he enters. The furnishings are still the same, but the décor is different, and Frank's presence is missing. I linger in the doorway, hesitant to cross the threshold and officially acknowledge the change.

"That's for you." Passing by the couch that rests against the wall on the right, he points to a box filled with Frank's personal affects. "I assume you have keys to his house."

"It seems becoming a supervisor has turned you into a dick," I retort.

Stepping to the other side of his desk, he opens the top drawer and removes a stack of papers. "Don't bust my balls over this. It hasn't been easy for me."

"You?" I shout, finally moving inside of the stuffy room. "Frank was everything to me. He was the only family I had left." As I make my way toward him, Stephen tightens his jaw. "You didn't hear him gasping for his last breath, or see the terror on his face when he died, knowing there wasn't a damn way to stop it." Rivers of tears pour out of my eyes. "You don't have the raw, gnawing guilt that his death is all of your fault."

Setting the papers down on the desk, Stephen comes over and wraps his arms around me. "There's no way this could've been prevented, Olivia. Dean orchestrated all of it. If he hadn't lured you to the house, then he would've found another way to get at Frank. He was the next one on the hit list."

I pull away. "What are you talking about?"

He reaches for the stack of papers, pulls them over, then has me sit in one of the guest chairs while he takes the other. "These are copies of Frank's notes on the Red Rover case. Chief Daven has the originals." He hands the pile to me, and I carefully flip through it. "He was close to discovering who was stealing the money … the person Dean had conned into embezzling it for him."

"He told Siem he didn't know who was responsible," I mutter, still rifling through the information, my vision blurring from the tears that remain.

After taking back the papers, Stephen shuffles them until he comes across one that's a photocopy of the picture depicting Melia as a child on the swings, as well as the set of numbers written on the back. "Recognize this?" he asks, holding the image up.

"Yes. I found it in my sister's album, which is why I stuck it in the manila envelope, along with lots of other photos. I thought it might be important, but I don't know who's handwriting that is."

Lowering his hand, he puts the page back into the pile. "The problem is this isn't your photo. Frank found it while illegally searching Dallas' home just outside of Prescott. Because of that, we can't use it to implicate the rapper in either the theft or the murders."

I furrow my brow. "You really think Dallas is involved?"

"He had knowledge of all the players. Even knew Dean was alive and didn't tell anyone. Especially at your trial. His connection to Luke, and the cartel through him, gave Dallas the means to create his own legacy."

"And since the picture I found was with Melia's things, there's no way to connect him using that either."

Stephen nods. "Frank was killed right after that. But, again, we don't have any real evidence to implicate Dallas. We've tried interviewing him. However, he's lawyered up and we can't get within ten feet of him without being slapped with a harassment notice."

I tap on the papers. "Do you know where those numbers go?"

"Hayden tracked it to an offshore bank down in Ceriuse where they're known to cater to those who wish to hide their wealth and remain anonymous. Everything was handled electronically, so there isn't a paper trail to follow. Their privacy laws also restrict us from requesting details about the account holder and if, or when, another transaction will be made. For now, that part of the case hangs in the air."

"There shouldn't be any more deposits, since Aidan closed the account being hacked." I shake my head in frustration. "That still doesn't explain how Frank was supposedly the next one to be targeted."

"Because he was the only CSB officer left who was actively working the case."

I scrunch up my face in confusion. "What about Brett?"

"Even though he's been hunting down the cartel for years, he didn't officially get brought in until Frank's death. And that was after reviewing your notes and the connections you were making. The chief knew he needed help sorting out the finer details, which is where Brett comes in." He places a hand on my arm. "We should get you home."

I stand and go to retrieve the box from the couch, setting the manila envelope inside, while Stephen stores the papers into a file cabinet by the back window, then we retreat to the elevator core and head down. As we drive toward Crer Sector and eventually reach the outer highway, I blankly stare out of the window feeling numb and alone. I force myself to speak to prevent shutting down even further.

"Did you get the psych profile done for our potential serial killer?"

Stephen smiles. "We'll have that discussion once you're back at work."

"What about the person threatening club owners?"

He glances at me briefly. "It was just some lowlife using the arsons as an excuse to make a name for himself. He's now in the detention center until his extortion trial."

We exit onto the section of highway that takes us to the bridge for Waterside. Since Stephen isn't a resident, he has to stop at the visitor's gate, then show his badge in order to proceed. I wish the marina was just as secure, but anyone with a boat can easily dock and at one of the many piers. There aren't any guards stationed there, which is how Dean managed to sneak onto the island more than once.

"Everyone thinks I'm dead," I comment after the gate is raised and we're permitted to proceed.

"I wouldn't worry too much about it, Liv. The chief will put a press brief together."

Halfway across the bridge, he asks, "When do you think you'll head over to Frank's?"

"I'm not sure yet. Why?"

"It's something you shouldn't do alone, and I know how overwhelming sorting through someone's life can be. I had to do it for my mom when my older brother refused to help, and my dad was already in a nursing home."

"This isn't the first person I've lost, Stephen," I state bitterly.

"I'm aware of that." He lets out a long sigh. "If you want some help, I'll be there."

We remain silent for the rest of the ride. He offers to walk me inside when we reach my house, but I decline, claim the box from the backseat, and use the keypad for the garage to enter. The second I open the door from the garage into the hallway that connects to the laundry room, family room, and spare bedroom, I start to feel anxious. The air is stale and stifling, but it's too late in the day to open a few of the windows, so it'll have to wait until tomorrow. Moving into the family room, I turn on a few lights and spot the guns I'd placed around the wide space. Another reminder about the events leading up to Frank's death.

Setting the box onto the coffee table, I make a beeline for the wet bar and ransack all of the small bottles of rum I have stored. Plopping down on the couch, I crack each one open, downing their contents as quickly as possible, hoping to numb the pain and deep sorrow rising to the surface. I should call Joe and let him know I'm home, but for the moment I want to forget about the world and slip away into nothingness.

Sixteen

Something shakes me, so I blindly bat at it, hoping whatever it is will stop.

"Wake up, Liv," a soothing voice calls to me through the fog I find myself in, reluctant to leave.

Opening my tired eyes, I spot Joe and Tanner standing over me, worried expressions on both of their faces. I mumble for them to go away, then roll onto my other side, placing my back toward them and facing the inner cushions for the couch.

"Come on, darling, you need to get up and eat," Tanner coos like a mother hen.

"Just leave me alone."

"You know we can't do that. Frank wouldn't want you wallowing like this."

Fuck. And so it starts. The guilt-tripping.

"How did you know I was home?" I ask groggily, the world around me spinning as I attempt to sit up, holding my head in my hands.

Joe sits on the couch next to me now that there's room. "Stephen called us last night. We figured you'd be exhausted, so we waited until today to come by. Seems like we should've been here when you arrived." He gestures toward the empty bottles scattered across the carpet. "Do you have any more stashed away?"

"God I hope so." My legs wobble while I try to stand, causing me to fall back down onto the plump cushions. "What time is it?"

"A little after one," Tanner answers, collecting the bottles and taking them into the kitchen where he drops them into the recycling bin.

"Go shower and put on some fresh clothes. We're taking you out." Joe pats my knee.

"I'd rather stay here." Curling into a ball, I shove myself into the corner of the couch, hoping to disappear into its dark gray material.

Joe scowls. "Don't make me drag you into the bathroom."

"Sweetheart, why don't you head to the club?" Tanner suggests. "I'll stay with Olivia and bring her along in a bit."

After a brief moment of hesitation, Joe exits through the garage since that's where they must have come in.

Maybe I should change the code on the door and the alarm system to avoid any more unwanted intrusions.

Tanner sits on the couch perpendicular to mine, pulls the box with Frank's stuff close to him, then starts rummaging through its contents, extracting picture frame after picture frame.

"When do you want to visit his house?" the older man asks, placing the items onto the coffee table.

Abruptly standing, I snatch everything away from him and shove it all back into the box. "Never."

"Olivia, you need to come to terms with this."

"Why?" I practically shout. "So everyone else can move on and not be constantly reminded that I'm the reason the man I looked up to as a father is dead?"

"None of this is your fault."

Wrapping my arms around myself, I begin to pace. "Yes it is. If I hadn't let that asshole back into my life none of this would've happened."

Tanner looks startled by my remark. "They caught the person who attacked you?"

I drop my head against my chest. "Not exactly. I put a bullet between the fucker's eyes."

Standing, he places his hands on my arms to stop my movement. "Who was it?"

Tears once again streaming down my face, I reply, "Dean."

"What?" he exclaims.

Leaning against him, my body shivering, I break down and tell Tanner everything that happened. He lovingly strokes my back and holds onto me tightly.

"I'm so sorry, honey." He rocks me in his arms while I bawl.

When I am able to settle down, I step away and head toward the wet bar. "I need a drink."

"No, you don't." Tanner takes my hand, halting me for the moment. "I'm not supposed to tell you this, but Joe has a surprise waiting for you at the club. If you show up drunk, he'll be very disappointed, and I'll be in big trouble." A slight smile touches the corners of his thin lips. "You can drink there and will have plenty of rides home. Also, you still have your apartment above the club."

Rolling my eyes, I head for the bathroom, strip down, and step into the hot shower, scrubbing my skin practically raw in order to dissolve myself of the guilt eating away at my soul. After wrapping a towel around my hair, I don my comfy robe, then make my way into the walk-in closet and select a black, V-neck sweater, along with a pair of jeans from the shelving unit I had installed after Dean first died. Stepping into the bedroom, I close the door and open the dresser drawers removing a thong, bra, and socks. Once I'm clothed, I hang the towel and robe back in the bathroom, run a brush through my hair, and return to the family room where Tanner is waiting.

"Ready?" he asks, smiling devilishly. "My car is parked on the motor court. Joe and I drove here separately."

I briefly contemplate whether or not to bring the phone Hayden got for me, but it's more than likely in need of charging, and there isn't anyone I want to call. So before we leave, I open the manila envelope and tip it over, dumping out not only the phone into my palm, but also the necklace Matt gave me. The clasp is broken, along with part of the chain, from where Dean ripped it from my throat. I grow sullen at the memory, wishing it was me who had died and not Matt.

"Are you all right?" Tanner asks, placing an arm around my shoulder.

"I'll be fine." Taking the items, I go into the study and set the phone on the charger resting atop my desk, then slip the necklace into the front pocket of my jeans, wanting the reminder of everything I lost to a madman.

I return to the family room, and when we head into the garage, I notice Joe has left the door closest to the house open, probably in anticipation of Tanner working his magic and getting me to leave. The large sedan sits in front of the detached garage, so once it's unlocked, I get into the front passenger seat while Tanner climbs behind the wheel. I'm not much for riding shotgun—especially since Tanner drives so slowly—but if it'll allow me to drink, then I'm not going to complain.

When we arrive in Nok Sector, Tanner parks in the alley behind the club. There isn't a lot of room due to the dumpster nearly blocking a good portion of the asphalt strip, remnants of broken wood and drywall sticking out from the top. We enter through the back door, and the smell of fresh paint and plaster assault my nose. The first thing I notice is the door between the club floor and the rear hallway is missing, allowing for ease of access now that it's open. Passing through the doorway, I'm greeted by not only a new layout— minus most of the furnishings—but also my coworkers.

"Welcome home!" they shout in unison, holding up a hand-painted banner, standing behind a lengthy folding table topped with various trays of food and bottles from the bar, which is no longer there.

I glance at Tanner, who's next to me. "How?"

He chuckles. "When Stephen called last night to tell us you were home, Joe spent the entire evening informing everyone what had actually transpired. Alice, Chloe, and several others have been working nonstop to get this ready for you in the few hours that they had."

They each come up to me, offering their condolences for Frank while also expressing their relief that I'm alive. Chloe pours the drinks, handing me one, while Joe directs me to one of the remaining booths where blueprints for the redesigned club have been spread out over the table.

"The plan is," he begins with tremendous enthusiasm, "there will be a primary stage in the center of the main floor, and two stages at either end, each behind an oval-shaped bar. We've eliminated two of the pods to make room and the booths along this wall will remain since they're not in the way. The DJ will now be positioned in his own little niche in the floor in the middle of the main stage. Tables and chairs will be scattered around the rest of the area, and we've converted the apartments on the floor above to private lounges that can be rented. Those are being renovated this week." He pats my hand. "Don't worry, Liv. I'm not touching the apartments on the top floor, so yours will remain intact."

"Are you going with a color scheme?" I ask, noticing various swatches of not only fabric, but paint as well resting on the leather cushions of the booth.

"Yes." He beams with pride. "The entire club will be decorated in purple and gold. Each of the four lounges upstairs will be designated a jeweled tone. The girls have also decided to change the uniforms. They selected hip-hugger shorts that sit low around the waist with very little cuff material for the thighs, and a matching deep V-neck, sleeveless, halter top. Bartenders will be wearing gold, the waitresses purple, and the escorts—as well as those working the front counter—will be in white. As always, the strippers can wear whatever they want."

"We chose gold for the bartenders because we'll also be working the lounges, so it works as a neutral color with the jeweled tones," Alice says, sidling up to me, placing her arm around my waist. "God I missed you."

I hug her tightly. "I missed you, too. Don't be mad at Hayden for not telling you the truth. He couldn't."

She giggles. "I'm not." Taking my hand, she pulls me away from Joe and over to the other side of the room. "Guess what?" Her smile is so wide, it might swallow her face. "I'm pregnant."

My eyes widen in astonishment. "Seriously?"

"Hayden is so excited," she practically squeals. "Of course, neither his place nor mine is big enough to house three people. So, at the moment we're apartment hunting."

An idea slams into my head, one I never would've considered. "What if you rent Frank's house from me? It's a bit dated on the inside, but that's easily fixed. It has three bedrooms, a large living room, and a two-car garage."

She stares at me, awestruck. "Are you sure? We know how much Frank meant to you, and I wouldn't want to impose."

"Nonsense. It'll save me the hassle of putting it on the market. Also, the two of you can help me sort through the house in case there's anything you might want to keep."

Wrapping her arms around me, she holds me tight. "Thank you, Liv. I'm going to call Hayden." She darts for the rear hallway while extracting her cell phone from the back pocket of her tight fitting pants.

"That was awfully nice of you," Joe says, coming up to me.

I smile a bit. "I swear I heard Frank's voice shouting in my head to make the offer."

"I have no doubt that you did. Come, let's enjoy the party."

I return to the others, eating until I'm stuffed and drinking until I nearly topple over. For once, Joe doesn't give me any grief about it. In addition to all of the interior changes happening for the club, I also learn that Chloe has been promoted to assistant manager, which is great relief for Tanner since it means Joe will finally be able to take a day or two off. I have no clue about what time it is when I'm poured into the front of Tanner's vehicle. When we're back at my house, he makes sure I'm tucked in bed before leaving.

Monday morning is when I decide to venture away from the house alone. Before getting onto the bridge for the mainland, I stop at a flower shop and purchase a small bouquet of red carnations. My heart thumbs loudly in my chest when I reach the outer highway and head east toward the service road that'll take me to Holy Crest Cemetery, which is out near the power and recycling plants.

Parkholm, along with Wheatland and Lincolnway Cemeteries, are west of the state. Whereas Holy Crest, St. Margaret's, and Assumption are on the east side. The latter being just a few miles from Munwood Point, a popular party beach for young adults.

I haven't been this way since I was a teenager, going to a few bonfires at the MP when it was well past my curfew. Memories I've shoved deep down inside, hoping to never relive again, edge their way to the surface, but I'm able to hold them at bay.

After passing through the gates, I stop at the guard house to get directions to Frank's plot. Tanner and Joe both offered to accompany me, but I feel this needs to be done alone.

The older man hands me a map, then marks the various, winding roads to reach his section. I thank him, get back into the car, and slowly make my way. Tears well in my eyes, momentarily blinding me when I get closer to the upturned soil indicating his placement. After parking alongside the wide road, I turn off the engine and sit, terrified to move any farther, praying that this is all still a dream. I take a deep breath and let it out slowly, then snatch the flowers off of the passenger seat, and exit.

It's a surprisingly warm day for the end of March. Not a cloud clings to the sky. I choke on my sobs, my body trembling with each hesitant step until I'm standing at the foot of the grave.

"You shouldn't be here," I say softly. "I … I keep hoping that you'll call, or knock on my door. That I'll wake up from this nightmare." Wiping the tears from my face, I can't help but shed more. "It wasn't fair, Frank, for Dean to take you away from me like that. I should never have gotten involved with him in the first place, but it doesn't change what's already been done. I blame myself for all of it, and after this week I might not even be employed at CSB. And you're not here to make things right, cheer me up, or even yell at me for getting drunk when I know I shouldn't. Before you ask, I'm seeing Bev tomorrow," I comment as if anticipating a question from beyond the grave. "She called this morning when the story broke about me being released from protective custody. Or whatever bullshit the chief cooked up. I refuse to read about it, since it doesn't erase the truth of what happened to either of us."

Setting the flowers onto the dirt, a great heaviness falls upon me, knowing that my life has been permanently, and forever, altered. "You'll always be the father that I wish I had. When I was younger there were so many times I wanted to go home with you. To live in your house, and not the alcoholic one I wound up in. I'd pray that one day you'd say, 'Olivia, you're coming to live with me.' Only it didn't happen. I always wanted to ask you why, but never got the chance. Sometimes I think you were afraid to take on the responsibility, considering the hours you worked, and that there would be no one at home to take care of me during those times."

I take a step back and shove my hands into the pocket of my jeans. "You should know that I killed Dean. Placed a striker between his eyes. Too bad I didn't do it sooner. We could've avoided this whole mess." Staring at the ground, I can't help but want to flee. "I'm heading over to the house now, but I'll come visit. I promise."

Taking a last look at the flowers, I turn and retreat to the car. Once on the highway, I exit at Clover, turn left onto Tremont, then quickly go right back onto Clover. A six-foot high, chain link fence surrounds the remains of my home, which is nothing more than plywood covering up the tremendous gaps in the walls and where the windows used to be. Parking across the street, I get out and make my way over to the ruins. The roof is now inside of the blackened structure. Debris coats the ground, bits of insulation stick out from the lawn that's growing nothing but weeds, and there's still a strong odor of burnt plastic clinging to the air.

I have to make a decision on what to do with the property, besides razing the charred husk. I'm hoping the municipality which governs Range Sector will give me a fair amount of time, but I highly doubt it, considering it's already been two weeks, almost going on three since the fire. It would probably be best to sell the property. I don't relish the idea of living where Frank died. Though I'm not thrilled with staying on Waterside, it's more than likely the best option.

Getting back into the car, I make my way over to Frank's house, which is on Ridge, straight across the other side of the sector. After pulling into his driveway, I park, shut off the engine, then remove the keys from the glove compartment. My hands shake while trying to unlock the front door. The air is stuffy once I'm inside, so I go around both the kitchen and dining room, opening windows to vent the place. Everything is exactly how it was the last time I stepped foot in here. Newspapers cover the coffee table, and a half-filled glass of water sits on the end table beside Frank's favorite hideous brown recliner. Magazines lay tossed onto the floor, an empty tissue box sits precariously on the armrest of the couch, and several blankets are bunched into a pile in the corner of the room.

On the bookshelves flanking the television are picture frames containing photos of me when I graduated from both high school, then the academy, when I was promoted to detective, and the day Dean and I were married. Considering how much he hated my husband I'm surprised Frank took the time to frame the image. But, then again, he did walk me down the aisle in the courtroom where Dean and I exchanged vows.

Next to those are pictures of him and Jane looking extremely happy together. I haven't summoned up enough nerve to call, or even pay her a visit. I can't imagine how hard this has been for her. Making my way toward the kitchen, I hesitate in opening the fridge, afraid of what spoiled food I might find in there. Something clipped to the door catches my attention. It's a notecard with a phone number written in black marker across the crinkled white paper, Jane's name just underneath. It's not what's written that causes my stomach to sour, but the handwriting associated with it.

I reach into my back pocket, extract my cell phone, and call Brett. "How soon can you get over to 104 Highland in Range Sector?" I ask the moment he answers.

"I can have Stephen drive me since I'm not familiar with the area. Why?"

"I know who stole the money. Have him bring the photo of Melia on the swings. The one with the account number written on the back." Before he can ask questions, I hang up, then immediately call the Hub to see if Jane is at work.

"Ms. Crawford tendered her resignation this morning," the receptionist advises.

"Thank you." I bolt for the door, making sure to lock it prior to getting into the car, then tear down several side streets until I get to Highland.

Parking a few doors down, I wait for Stephen to pull up front, then exit the car. He looks annoyed when I approach the two of them.

"Give me the picture," I demand a little too forcefully.

After reaching into the inner pocket of his suit coat, Stephen extracts the photo and hands it to me. "Mind explaining."

"You'll figure it out in a few minutes."

I rapidly climb the stairs to the front porch, and ring the doorbell while the other two hover behind me. She doesn't answer right away, causing me to wonder if we've missed our opportunity. The bolt on the door gives, then opens slowly. The pair of eyes peering out widen, as does the door.

"Oh my God!" Jane exclaims, tears welling in her eyes. "It's true! You're alive." She pulls me into a firm embrace. "I saw it in the newspaper this morning, but couldn't quite believe it."

"Can we come in?" I ask when she finally lets go.

"Yes, of course." She steps off to the side, allowing us entry.

Moving away from the foyer, around the stairs that led down to the basement, and into the living room, I spot an assortment of boxes stacked against the far wall. A roll of bubble wrap sits waiting to be used.

"Going somewhere?" The anger in my voice rattles her.

"No," she replies timidly, closing the door behind Brett. "That's to pack up Frank's house. I just haven't found the time to get over there."

"Ms. Crawford, would you mind having a seat?" Brett's southern drawl seems to relax her a bit, so she takes a position on the couch underneath the front windows.

I sit opposite—afraid that if I'm too close I might lash out and punch her. It would probably make me feel better. Stephen sits beside me, while Brett wanders about the room with his hands clasped behind his back.

"Recognize this?" I ask, holding up the photo of Melia, the side with the swings showing.

Her face softens at the memory. "Of course I do. Your sister was three when I took that picture. It was one of the few times where I was able to get her to smile."

Flipping the image over, I point to the numbers. "What about this?"

Her pleasant demeanor suddenly hardens. "I don't know what those are."

Tossing the photo onto the coffee table between us, I say, "Sure you do. It's for the bank account where you funneled laundered money into. Money that you stole from the Vilks Cartel."

"Wh-What? That's … that's nonsense," she stutters, growing increasingly paler by the second. "I don't know what the hell you're talking about. Hey, where are you going?"

Brett slips into the kitchen, ignoring her inquiry.

"Agent Ellis is just having a quick look around," Stephen answers.

"H-He can't do that without a warrant."

"No, he's not permitted to rifle through your things," I say, correcting her. "If it's out in plain sight, then it's fair game."

Clutching her fingers together, she fidgets nervously. "I have nothing to hide."

"Why did you quit your job this morning?" I ask, leaning forward, resting my arms on top of my thighs.

"Because I was offered a new one out of state."

Stephen reaches into his coat pocket, extracts a small notebook and pen, just like Frank used to carry, and flips to a clean page. "Which company?"

"I don't see how that's relevant to you."

"Here, found something," Brett says, returning carrying a wall calendar in his hands.

He sets it on the coffee table next to the photo. Written across the top next to the current month is a series of numbers. Different than the ones on the back of the picture, but in the same handwriting and format. Using his phone, Stephen snaps a photo, then sends it to Hayden for him to research.

"Whose bank account is this?" the detective asks, tapping the calendar.

"Mine," Jane answers defiantly. "I just opened it and they haven't sent me any of the paperwork, so I wrote it down to remember."

"Why do you need one that's overseas?" I counter, rage coursing through my veins.

"I don't, and it's not."

Picking up the calendar, Stephen moves to sit beside Jane, then points to the first series of digits. "This right here, indicates the country, which just happens to be Ceriuse." Reaching for the photo of Melia, he indicates the same sequence of numbers. "This also means Ceriuse. They're known for the lax banking guidelines and strict privacy laws."

I glare at the nervous woman, using all of my anger to ask, "How did Dean convince you to steal the money?"

"He … I …" Her shoulders slump forward, and she starts to sob. "He told me it was Luke's, and that if I helped funnel it to an offshore account, he'd split the profits with me." The cries quickly turn to screams. "They owed me!" she raves. "Did you see what those bastards did to my daughter? What that rat shit father put his own child through?" She narrows her gaze at me. "Don't sit there, Olivia, and condone my actions when you know damn well they were justified."

"How long had you been pilfering the money?" Brett asks before I can open my mouth, saving me from getting into a shouting match with someone I considered a mother to me.

"I'm sure you have the printouts that Melia stole. God knows I couldn't find them after rummaging through her room. Maybe a few weeks after she was killed."

"Then why keep draining the funds when both Dean, and then eventually Luke, died?"

I ball my hands into fists. "Because she knew my husband wasn't dead. What did he threaten you with to keep working for him?"

Her body shakes as she starts crying again. "He was going to kill Frank if I didn't help."

"Why didn't you say anything?" I demand, my wrath exploding. "He'd still be alive if you'd just admitted to what was going on!"

Cradling her head in her hands, she mumbles, "I'm sorry."

Brett removes a set of handcuffs from the holster around his waist, while I head for the door, Stephen close on my heels.

"Where are you going?" he asks, stopping me before I can descend the front steps.

"Home."

"Olivia, don't—"

"Leave me alone!" I shout, cutting him off.

I practically trip over my feet because of the rush I'm in to get away from Jane. When I'm back on Waterside, the first stop I make is to the closest liquor store where I purchase several bottles of the most expensive rum they have in stock. The clerk gives me looks while checking me out, but I ignore him, snatch my purchases after paying for them, and head home.

With the car safely secured in the garage, every door locked, and the alarm system turned on, I sit on the couch in the family room, crack open a bottle, and drink myself into oblivion.

The doorbell rouses me from the stupor I wish to remain in. Forcing myself to stand, the world around me spins and I have to wait a few seconds for it to stop before I can make it to the front door. I struggle with inputting the code on the tiny panel in the foyer, then have difficulty with the locks. When I finally get the damn thing open, the scowl on Bev's face burns my soul. Her long, straight brown hair is braided down her back, she's lost some weight since the last time I saw her, and her eyes appear tired. She resembles the hell that I feel.

"You missed your appointment," she says, fuming.

My eyes try to focus, but it becomes nearly impossible due to the brightness of the sun outside. "What time is it?"

"It's more like what day is it." Brushing past me, briefcase in hand, she heads straight for the family room, leaving me to close the heavy door.

"Can we do this another time?" I moan, reclaiming my seat on the couch.

"No." She drops the case onto the hardwood coffee table, causing a loud thud that radiates through my ears and vibrates my teeth. After picking up the bottles of rum, only one of which is empty, she goes into the kitchen and proceeds to pour the luscious liquid down the drain.

"What are you doing?" I utter, bewildered by her actions.

"Pulling you out of the gutter you seem to be determined to stay in." Returning to the family room, she sits on the couch next to mine. "Do you know how many people have been trying to get a hold of you?"

I reach into the back pocket of my jeans, take out my cell phone, and toss it across the room where it lands with a slight thud against the carpet. "I shut it off."

"And changed the codes for both your alarm system and the garage. Joe and Tanner have been worried sick. You weren't answering the door for them, so they called me. I'm sure the only reason you got up this time is because you're starting to become sober." Her rapid breathing grows steadily on my nerves. "Do you know what Frank would say if he saw you like this?"

"Goddamn it!" I kick the coffee table, nearly knocking it over, in addition to hurting my foot. "Don't say that name!"

"Olivia," she says a little more calmly, "I know you're hurting, but this isn't the way to deal with it."

"You have no idea the pain and torment I've suffered," I say through clenched teeth.

Crossing her legs, she folds her hands into her lap. "Actually, I do."

I stare at her, perplexed.

She smiles briefly, then grows sullen. Her throat quivers, and it's clear she's struggling to speak. "When I was eighteen, I, uh, married a man I thought would love me forever. He was quite a bit older than I, my parents hated him and were completely against the marriage, but I went through with it anyway. Being young, I thought that I knew everything, that my parents were mistaken in their judgement about Al, that if they really tried to get to know him, they'd love him as much as I did."

Tears touch the corners of her already damp eyes. "We had an apartment in Berrin Sector, Al worked at one of the manufacturing plants in Crer, and I stayed home playing the happy housewife. Most evenings I spent alone, wondering where my husband was since the factory always let out at five. He'd stumble in around midnight, drunk off his ass, and looking to get lucky. I mean, that's what a wife is for. Right? At least, that's what he always told me."

She takes a deep breath, allowing it to escape her lips slowly, then lowers her head. "Anyway, one time I fought off his advances because they kept becoming more and more aggressive over the weeks, and wound up with a black eye. The abuse escalated quickly after that. I left him and went back to live with my parents." Her entire body starts to shake. "One night, while we were all asleep, Al broke into the house and shot both of my parents to death. He then came after me, but I hid. Neighbors called the police, and when they arrived gunfire was exchanged, and Al was killed. After a few weeks I started drinking to numb the guilt since I believed their deaths were my fault." Lifting her gaze to meet mine, she asks, "Do you know who helped me find my way out of that darkness?"

I choke up, tears streaming down my face. "Frank," I whisper, unable to speak any louder.

She nods. "He was the detective in charge of the case. I began seeing a counselor, discovered I enjoyed it, and became one."

I stare thoughtfully at her. "Tanner told you, didn't he?"

"Yes. He hadn't mentioned anything to Joe yet, but the three of us talked about what would help get you through this particularly rough moment in your life. I even spoke with Detective Jeffries, who's also concerned about your wellbeing."

"Great. Now I'm definitely out of a job."

"No, but there are conditions in order for you to keep it."

"Such as?"

"For the next month you see me twice a week, and starting tonight you attend AA meetings."

"Are you serious? I don't need to go to AA when I can handle this myself."

"Olivia, those are the stipulations. Be grateful Joe talked me out of having you quit bartending at Verdigris."

Leaning forward, I rest my face in my hands. "Fuck!"

"To ensure you go, Stephen has agreed to be your sponsor, so he'll be driving you to Trinity Hope Church in Range Sector where the meetings are held."

"Isn't that across from CSB station three? I know officers there. They'll recognize Stephen's car. Is there another location?" I nearly beg.

"Not during Wednesdays."

I scrunch up my face in disbelief. "It's Wednesday?"

"Yes. You've been passed out drunk for two days, which is why you need to start going tonight."

"Fine," I grouse. "What time?"

"The meetings start at seven, so he'll be here around six." Standing, she brushes the crinkles from her gray, tweed suit. "Now before I leave, I'm going to search your house to make sure you're not hiding any alcohol."

Bev methodically opens every drawer, every cabinet, even goes through the linen closet, my walk-in closet, and checks underneath the mattress. The only thing she finds are the tiny bottles in the wet bar, which she promptly dumps down the drain.

"Shower, change, and eat. Stephen should be along shortly."

After she collects her briefcase, I walk her to the door, lock it after she leaves, then head into the bathroom. I toss my dirty clothes into the hamper, then put on clean underwear, black leggings, and a heather gray sweatshirt. I'm almost done eating my peanut butter and jelly sandwich when Stephen rings the doorbell.

"Ready?" he asks when I answer.

"I just need to put some shoes on and grab my phone."

He lingers in the foyer while I go into the bedroom, then search for the phone buried somewhere in the plush carpeting. Snatching my purse from the study, I set the alarm, then lock the door. Neither of us says anything during the awkward drive. He pulls into the gravel parking lot, and we wait for the doors to open since we're a little early.

"What happened with the disciplinary hearing?" I ask as small drops of rain start to hit the windshield.

"One month probation, but you still get to work. Just not alone during that time."

I grumble. "Who's going to babysit me since there are currently only three homicide detectives?"

"Bryson Reynolds is switching over to our department, so you'll be partnered with him."

"That I can handle. Will you be hiring anymore?"

Stephen rests his arm against the door. "A couple of officers have applied for several positions I'm opening up, so we'll see how their tests and training go."

Additional cars stream in while an older man trots from the house next door, over to the front entrance, unlocking it.

We exit the vehicle and try our best to dodge the drops that have gotten thicker in the few minutes we've been waiting. Once inside, the interior wreaks of incense, nearly choking the air. A sign taped to the wood-paneled wall indicates the meeting is being held down in the basement. The stairs are wide and narrow, and Stephen has to duck so not to hit his head on the ceiling when we're close to the bottom. Berber carpet covers the floor, while the paneling from upstairs continues throughout the entire hallway. A wide door stands propped open on our left, and I dread going inside.

At least a dozen folding chairs are grouped around a circle, with more stacked against the back wall. Stephen takes one of the folded ones and opens it away from the main group where it appears other sponsors are sitting. Half the circle is filled, so I try to claim the farthest empty seat. A few more people trickle in, and I'm surprised at the diversity. Young and old, men and women, black and white, three-piece suits and oil-stained overalls. The same man who unlocked the door sits next to me. His face is severely wrinkled, the hair on his head has migrated to his ears, and the flannel shirt he's wearing is two-sizes too big.

"Thank you all for coming," he says cheerfully. "I'm sorry about the rain, but what are you going to do?"

This elicits a chuckle from a few.

He glances at every face as is memorizing them. "I see we've gathered a few newcomers. Welcome. Please introduce yourself." He points to me to start. Noticing my hesitation, he prods a bit. "Just your first name and why you're here. It's really simple."

Staring at Stephen, I watch as he nods his head, so I take a deep breath and pray I can make this work.

"My name is Olivia, and … I'm an alcoholic."